Once A Gentleman

Other **AVON ROMANCES**

Coming Soon

And Don't Miss These
ROMANTIC TREASURES
from Avon Books

CANDICE HERN

Once A Gentleman

AVON BOOKS
An Imprint of HarperCollinsPublishers

AVON BOOKS
An Imprint of HarperCollins*Publishers*
10 East 53rd Street
New York, New York 10022-5299

Copyright © 2004 by Candice Hern
ISBN: 0-7394-4225-2

Printed in the U.S.A.

Dedicated to Sherrie Holmes,
for inspiring certain aspects
of Pru's character.

Sherrie knows what I mean.
The rest of you will have to guess.

Chapter 1

April 1802

"I might have known I'd find you here."

Prudence Armitage looked up at the sound of the familiar voice. The warm smile that greeted her set off the tiniest fluttering in her breast, involuntary and inevitable. She had known Nicholas Parrish over four years, and he could still make her weak in the knees with that smile. Fortunately, she was seated at the moment and in no danger of an embarrassing collapse.

She quickly removed her spectacles and tucked them into the pocket of her skirt.

"You've been working late almost every night," he said. "You ought to go home, Pru, before you wear yourself out. What are you working on?"

She cleared her throat. Shy at the best of times, she was sometimes painfully so with Nicholas. Especially when alone with him, and that had happened all too frequently the last few months. "I am editing Mary Hays's latest essay on illustrious women of history," she said. The essay was intended for the next issue of *The Ladies' Fashionable Cabinet*, a popular monthly magazine of which Pru was temporarily in charge.

"Now, that's a job I don't envy," Nicholas said, "editing all that flowery prose. Chopping it up, are you?"

Pru smiled. "Only a bit. Edwina warned me that Mary has become very sensitive lately about any changes to her work. Somehow, though, I need to shave off half a column. If not here, then somewhere else."

Nicholas strode into the room and came to stand beside the desk, studying the various articles, letters, and essays strewn about the surface. "Feel free to cut whatever you think necessary from Augusta's article. I promise not to be the least insulted." He flashed a grin, creating little fans of creases around his twinkling dark eyes.

Nicholas wrote historical essays and biographical sketches under the pen name Augusta Historica. But as far as Pru was concerned, his prose, like everything else about him, was near perfect, and she wouldn't dream of modifying it. "Your essay this month is brilliant. I would sooner cut Mary's than yours." She looked away, embarrassed that he might find her words obsequious.

"You put me to the blush, my girl. But I'm sure you'll find a way to make it all work. You always do. That's why Edwina put you in charge during her absence. You're the only one who could possibly keep all this together." He made a sweeping gesture incorporating the entire room that served as an office for *The Ladies' Fashionable Cabinet*. "But you know you can call upon me for any help you require. I hate to see you putting in such long hours."

"Edwina did as much."

"My sister has been obsessed with the magazine since she took over as editor five years ago. It was her life, until recently. But I think it is a very good sign that she allowed herself to take an extended wedding trip to France, don't you?"

"Oh, yes." Pru had feared her stubborn friend had locked up her heart forever. She had been thrilled when Edwina finally admitted she was in love with Anthony Morehouse and married him.

Nicholas hitched one hip onto the desk and half sat on the edge. The fabric of his knee breeches pulled tight against a long, well-muscled thigh. Pru tore her gaze away. She would die of embarrassment if he realized how easily his nearness could discompose her.

"I must say, I was glad she and Morehouse hared off to Paris the moment travel restrictions were lifted," he said. "I know she hated to be away from the *Cabinet* for so long, but she needed to break away, to have something more in her life. As do you, my girl."

He reached out and chucked her lightly on the chin. Lord, how she wished he would not do that.

"It's too many nights now," he said, "I have seen the candles burning late down here."

Prudence wondered if he might be concerned with the number of candles she burned to the ends each week. The magazine's offices, such as they were, happened to be located on the ground floor of the town house Nicholas had long shared with his sister. Candles were a minor expense, but she was aware of his circumstances. She ought to have been more considerate. Starting tomorrow, she would bring her own candles.

"I am sorry to be staying so late again," she said, "but I so want to do a good job while Edwina's away. I don't want her to feel she must worry about anything when she should be enjoying herself. Thankfully, she is well organized—"

"To a fault."

"—and so it is easy enough to see what must be done each month. I will try to leave within an hour, and then you may have the house to yourself."

Prudence had often worked late with Edwina, but never as late as she had done since being left in charge. She wondered if her presence in his house was awkward for Nicholas. Though it pained her to consider it, what if he wanted to bring someone—a woman—home with him at night? As a gently bred spinster long on the shelf, she was not supposed to be aware of such things, but she had five brothers and was not a complete fool. As far as Nicholas was concerned, however, she would rather not know about that aspect of his life.

"Don't leave on my account," he said. "I am on my way out for the evening."

She had assumed as much from his dress. He wore satin knee breeches and stockings, and his shirt was frilled and pleated. No matter what he wore, he was one of the handsomest men she'd ever known—dark, almost black hair and eyes; even, white teeth so often on display in a roguish smile; a tall, slender frame that moved with feline grace. She'd foolishly fallen in love with Nicholas the first time she'd laid eyes on him. And like a schoolgirl of seventeen instead of a spinster of seven-and-twenty, she continued to harbor a ridiculous infatuation for him.

Ridiculous because Prudence was not exactly the sort of woman to attract a man like Nicholas Parrish. If they had not worked closely together for so many years, he would never have given her a second glance. Or a first, for that matter. She was small and colorless next to his dark beauty. Like a little gray pony beside a sleek, black stallion. A more mismatched pair could scarcely be imagined.

"And I'll tell you what, Pru." He leaned toward her and gave a conspiratorial wink. "I'm planning on making a full night of it. Good food, good wine, good play, and maybe, just maybe . . . a good bit of carousing. Oh, dear. You're blushing. I shouldn't say such things to a respectable lady, I know." He straightened and shook out his coat-tails. "But you're a good friend and a good sport, Pru. I know you don't mind."

"No, I don't mind," she lied. She was quite accustomed to his treating her like a sister. Or one of his male cronies. That did not mean she liked it. But it wasn't his fault. Prudence was accustomed to men forgetting she was female. She lived in a house full of men who forgot all the time.

"Well, I'm off then," Nicholas said. "You'll be all right by yourself?"

"Yes, of course."

"Are you certain you wouldn't like to finish up and allow me to escort you home?"

"No, thank you, Nicholas. I do want to continue editing this essay, if you don't mind. And it's always easy to find a hackney near the square, no matter what hour."

"Then I shall leave you to your edits. But don't work too late, my girl. You are looking tired, a bit haggard."

With a flash of white teeth and dark eyes, he was gone.

Prudence dropped her head to rest on her arms. She looked haggard, did she? How mortifying for him to notice. She did not look pretty under the best of circumstances. She must look a fright at the moment, even without her spectacles.

But she *was* tired. She'd been working long and hard on the magazine. It frankly astonished her how much Edwina had done to keep it running smoothly. But Prudence was determined to prove her friend's trust was not misplaced. Her work on *The Ladies' Fashionable Cabinet* was just about the only thing Prudence was truly proud of in her life. She was not blessed with a great deal of self-confidence. She was small and plain and shy—a spinster with no prospects. But the trust of Edwina, Nicholas, and the others at the *Cabinet* stirred a quiet sort of pride within her in a way that nothing else had ever done. She had a keen desire to live up to their faith in her. She was determined to do a good job, an outstanding job, as acting editor-in-chief.

Prudence had first become involved with the *Cabinet* by occasionally submitting articles. She had been impressed by the quality of the writing in the magazine, and also by its very subtle republican outlook, especially in its attitude toward women. Prudence had discovered the writings of Mary Wollstonecraft as a young girl, and strongly supported her philosophies regarding the role of women, the need for women to take charge of their own lives, to take responsibility for their destinies. When she recognized a hint of those philosophies in a magazine she had once considered no more than frivolous entertainment, she was intrigued.

Her articles were always accepted, and Edwina eventually solicited more from her. Finally, Edwina invited her to come on board in a more formal role as assistant editor, which Prudence had done with great pleasure. She had taken on some of the business aspects of publication and thought she knew all there was to know about publishing a monthly magazine. But she was fast discovering how little she really knew of all that Edwina had done to keep the business running smoothly, especially since their circulation numbers had more than doubled during the past six months.

It was invigorating, though, to actually be in charge. She felt important, valuable. It was a heady experience.

The only drawback was that the offices were in Nicholas's house. It had been Edwina's decision to convert the library into a business office and the dining room into a workroom. Pru had always thought of the town house on Golden Square as Edwina's house. She had never considered that one day her friend might not be there. With Edwina gone, Pru found it somewhat awkward to work alone in the home of a single gentleman—a gentleman whose smile could turn her knees to jelly.

It was less awkward when Flora Gallagher, the fashion editor, was about. Or even the Crimson Ladies, the street prostitutes Flora had hired for hand-coloring the fashion plates and other engravings in each month's issue. The noise and bustle of their company made for a much more comfortable atmosphere than when Pru was alone in the house with Nicholas.

Any discomfort in this very unconventional household, however, seemed to be hers alone. Nicholas had never indicated any degree of awkwardness. Most likely, he never even noticed her.

No, that was unkind. He was not like her brothers. He was always a gentleman and treated her as a good friend. It was only her own idiotic calf love that brought any awkwardness into the situation. And since she'd never admitted it to a single soul, all the discomfort would remain a private trial.

She was a fool. Instead of squirming within a hopeless and quite childish infatuation, she ought to accept the genuine friendship Nicholas offered and be happy for it. She would have to be the last woman on earth before she could expect anything more from him. If then.

She was overcome by a tremendous yawn that reminded her she had lots of work yet to do. There was no time to spin fantasies a woman of her age had no business spinning. She stretched her arms to the ceiling and out to her sides, working out the kinks in her back and shoulders. Then she replaced her spectacles, bent once again to Mary Hays's essay, and forced all thoughts of Nicholas out of her mind.

The pounding woke him instantly. Nick had only just dropped off to sleep, having come in quite late—or early, depending on how one looked at it—after a rather boisterous evening with friends. But Lucy, the part-time housemaid, would not be in until the afternoon, and since he had no other servants, it was up to Nick to deal with whoever was pounding on his front door.

He rolled out of bed, reached for the breeches he'd flung on a chair, and tugged them on. He grabbed a shirt and pulled it over his head as he bounded down the stairs. The hall clock showed it to be not yet seven. Who the devil was making such a racket at this ungodly hour?

Nick opened the door to find a middle-aged gentleman of above average height, broad shoulders, and graying blond hair scowling at him. Several taller, broader, blonder younger men stood behind him wearing matching scowls.

What the hell? It looked for all the world like the Viking hordes had landed on his doorstep.

"Nicholas Parrish?" the older man asked.

"Ye—"

Before he could complete the syllable, the man's fist connected with Nick's jaw with enough force to send him stumbling back into the hallway. He remained upright only by grabbing hold of the hall table, which he almost managed to overturn.

"Bastard!" the man shouted as he moved toward Nick.

Nick raised his fists, planted his bare feet wide, and bent his knees in an instinctive posture of defense. He wasn't letting this maniac take one step closer. "Who the hell are *you*?"

"The father of the woman you defiled last night, that's who."

Nick was abashed but maintained his stance. "What?"

"Don't play dumb with me, you black-hearted cur. You know exactly what I mean."

"Forgive me, sir, but I do not." He took a step

forward. "And I think you had better leave before I feel obliged to return that blow."

"I'm not moving until I have satisfaction."

The man's younger cohorts joined in as they pressed themselves farther into the hallway.

"That's right. Satisfaction"

"Let's beat the fellow senseless."

"Darken his daylights."

"Show him what's what."

"He won't get away with this."

"The dirty scoundrel."

"The blackguard."

Nick's mind whirled with confusion and a niggling of alarm. These large fellows meant business, yet he had no idea what they were talking about. It did not matter. He was not going to be bullied by a pack of strangers.

"You had better explain yourself, sir," he said, addressing himself to the older man, "unless you are prepared stain to my doorway with your blood. I don't care how many lackeys you've brought with you."

"There's nothing to explain," the man said. "It's clear as daylight what's happened here. Just look at you."

Nick kept his fists raised but glanced down at his loose shirt and bare toes. "How the hell do you expect me to look? You got me out of bed, for God's sake. And for what? To be planted a facer by some mad-as-a-Bedlamite stranger."

The man growled and lunged, but was held back by one of the younger men. "Easy, Papa," the

Viking said. "It pains me to say it, but perhaps we should hear him out first."

"Nothing easy about it, Roddy. This cad has trifled with your sister and he shall not get away with it."

"Trifled with *who*?" Nick shook his head in confusion. "Listen here, I think there's been some mistake. You have the wrong house and the wrong man." He began to ease the group of them back toward the door. "Leave now and we'll call it an honest mistake. Painful"—he rubbed his jaw—"but honest. I bid you good day."

He tried to encourage them out the door, but the solid wall of five large, irate gentlemen was not to be moved.

"You admit you are Nicholas Parrish," the leader said, "the debaucher who took advantage of my daughter last night. And by God, sirrah, you will pay."

"Took advantage . . . ?"

And suddenly the whole business became perfectly clear. Nick's somewhat rowdy evening had included an hour or so in the bed of a very willing young actress from Drury Lane. Was she trying to set him up, to extort money or marriage from him? A cold, vicious anger cut through him like a knife. She would not get away with it, the little trollop.

"Go to hell," he said and pressed forward, forcing the man and his minions back toward the doorway. "And take that hussy of a daughter with you. I'll be damned if I'm tricked into a trumped-up leg-shackle with a girl who's no better than a lightskirt." And probably no relation at all to this hired gang of thugs.

The older man, obviously an actor in his own right, turned purple in a pretense of rage. "How dare you speak that way about my daughter!"

The younger men—more actors? a whole troupe of actors?—exploded in an outburst of shouts and curses. Their "father" rushed at Nick and grabbed him by the collar. The others surrounded him, pressing against him, trapping him in his own hallway. Nick tried to wrench away from the leader's grip on his collar, but the tenacious fellow clung like a leech. The man spoke through bared teeth, playing his part with melodramatic relish.

"It cuts me to the quick to think of my girl with such a bounder. Where is she? What have you done with her?"

Nick sneered. "I left her in a pile of rumpled sheets some hours ago. And if you expect me to believe I'm the first to plow that field, then you're a bigger fool than I am."

The man growled and pulled back his fist in preparation for another blow, but Nick caught his arm and held tight. The others grabbed Nick by the shoulders, but he held firm to the leader.

"You've picked the wrong pigeon to pluck," Nick said. "If your girl thought she'd landed a plump one, I am afraid I must disabuse you of that notion. You won't get a sou more from me than I left on the bedstead."

The older man uttered a sort of howl and the

younger men descended upon Nick in earnest, eyes blazing with fury. His hold on the leader was lost, and both arms were pinned behind his back. It was all he could do to stand upright.

"I should kill you right now," one of them said.

"For what?" Nick asked, full of righteous bravado despite being seriously outnumbered. "Not falling for your game? For speaking the truth about your so-called sister? Get out of my house. All of you." Using every ounce of strength at his disposal, he wrenched his arms free and shoved two of the assailants aside. "*Now.*"

The older man held his ground and refused to budge an inch. "This is no game," he said in an ominous tone. "You will do right by my girl or face the consequences."

"Do right by her? If you are suggesting a marriage, then you may be assured it will be over my dead body."

"That can be arranged. But the girl will be left a widow, not a hopeless ruin."

"That one was ruined long ago," Nick said. "And frequently, I should guess."

"Kill him, Roddy."

"No, let me do it."

"We'll take turns."

"Not yet, boys. We need him for the wedding." The leader had grown so red in the face he looked near apoplexy. He was shaking with feigned anger. It was a performance worthy of the legendary Garrick. "You will give her your name, Parrish, and then I'll let her brothers do with you what they will. And I hope never to lay eyes upon you again."

Nick shoved the man in the chest, sending him back into the doorway. "Your threats grow tedious, sir. I would not marry your wretched daughter if you put a gun to my head."

The man looked over Nick's shoulder. He drew in a sharp breath, and his eyes widened.

Nick turned and saw Prudence coming down the hallway.

Prudence?

Her hair had fallen down on one side and spilled in a mass of tousled reddish-gold curls over her shoulder. The bodice of her dress hung slightly askew. Her eyes looked drowsy with sleep even as they widened with apprehension.

"Papa?"

Chapter 2

Pru closed her eyes tight and rubbed them with the balls of her hands. Perhaps when she opened them again, she would not see what she thought she had seen. And maybe the words she thought Nicholas had spoken were only imagined. It had to be a dream.

"Prudence?"

It was her father's voice. She was not dreaming. She opened her eyes.

"Girl, what have you done?"

She stared at her father, who looked more furious than she'd ever seen him in her life. His blue eyes blazed, his face burned red with anger. She glanced over his shoulder to see four of her five brothers lined up behind him. All of them looked confused and angry, except for William, the youngest, who shuffled his feet in that nervous way of his and refused to meet her eyes.

And then there was Nicholas, who had stepped back and was pressed against the wall, stiff and unmoving. His mouth was set in a grim line, and the expression in his eyes had grown flat, unreadable. He was in a shocking state of undress. Her gaze briefly swept over his bare legs and the expanse of chest revealed beneath the open collar of his loose shirt. Heat flooded her cheeks, and she turned her eyes away to look at her father.

"Well?" he said. "What do you have to say for yourself?"

Pru knew exactly what he was thinking, why he had come storming across town at this hour. But what he was thinking was so ludicrous she could not suppress a smile. Could he really have imagined that she and *Nicholas* . . . ?

"I fell asleep," she said.

"You what?"

"I was working late, and I suppose I must have fallen asleep. I didn't wake up until I heard all the commotion here in the hall."

"You were working?"

"Yes."

"Then you did not spend the night in this scoundrel's bed?"

"Papa!" Her cheeks flushed with embarrassment. "Of course not."

Her glance darted toward Nicholas, who glared at her father as though outraged at such an unthinkable suggestion.

"You will oblige me, sir," her papa said, returning Nicholas's glare, "with an explanation for the despicable things you said about my Prudence."

Nicholas had said despicable things about her?

I would not marry your wretched daughter if you put a gun to my head.

She tried to catch his eye, but he looked away. What else had he said? Her stomach turned over to think that he had maligned her in some way. She had thought they were friends.

Nicholas cleared his throat. "I, um, wasn't speaking of Prudence."

"Then who?" Her father's voice was sharp with anger.

"Someone else. I did not know Prudence was here, I swear it."

Her father turned his furious gaze upon her. "You stayed late working on that idiotic magazine?"

Her gaze darted to Nicholas. She didn't understand. He had said despicable things about someone else? She furrowed her brow in confusion.

"I'm talking to you, girl!"

She tore her eyes from Nicholas and looked at her father. "Yes, I worked late and fell asleep at my desk. But—"

"Had it perhaps slipped your mind that you were expected elsewhere last evening?"

Pru gave a little gasp and covered her mouth with her hand. Good heavens, she had completely forgotten. "Oh, dear."

"Ah, so you *do* remember. How good of you. Yes, your niece's breakfast is this morning, and Margaret expected you to stay with her last night so that you would be on hand to help. The whole damned family will be there, as you know. And apparently there are a thousand things your sister needed you to do that are not being done."

Yes, Margaret would be having fits. Her daughter, Arabella, had been brought to Town for her first Season. Before she was introduced to society, there were to be several family gatherings, the first of them an al fresco breakfast at Daine House, Margaret's London home. And Pru, of course, was expected to be there early to help "keep the servants in line." How could she have forgotten?

"Oh, Papa. I'm so sorry. I got so involved in my work, it slipped my mind. I'll just get my hat and pelisse and come home with you right now. I can quickly change and be at Daine House well before the guests arrive."

"Not so fast, girl. We still have *this* to sort out." He made a gesture encompassing the hallway.

"What?"

"You have spent the night under this man's roof."

Her cheeks flamed. She was thoroughly ashamed that Nicholas should have to be a part of this foolishness. How could her father do this to her? She wasn't a schoolgirl, for heaven's sake.

"No harm has been done, Papa. Nicholas did not even know I was here." Pru glanced at

Nicholas and gave him a shy, but hopefully encouraging, smile. Surely he knew she did not hold him responsible in any way for her own forgetfulness.

"That is of no consequence," her father said. "Your reputation has been compromised."

"Nonsense. Besides the lot of you, who will even know I was here?"

"The whole blasted family by now, if I know your sister."

"What are you talking about?"

"When you did not show up at Daine House last night, Margaret was furious. She sent everyone searching for you, and when you could not be found . . . well, you can imagine the ruckus."

Pru rolled her eyes. If they'd paid the least attention to her, they would have known where she was. She was forever reminding them all of her work on the magazine, but she was generally ignored.

"Finally," her father continued, "when your brother Willy dragged his tail home, from God knows where, at the crack of dawn, he suggested you might have spent the night here."

Nicholas groaned.

Pru looked at him. He had gone quite pale, and rubbed the back of his neck with a hand. She was feeling anything but pale as heat continued to flood her cheeks. She turned to her brother. "Willy! You didn't."

He had the good sense to look embarrassed. "I never meant it like that," Willy said. "I only mentioned that you sometimes worked late at Parrish's house, and if you had not come home, you were likely still there." He gave a little snort. "I ought to have known Margaret would have a fit of the vapors. She decided you'd been . . . Well, you know how she is."

"When your brother was so obliging," her papa said, "as to reveal that you had probably spent the night in the house of a single gentleman—"

"Margaret asked who he was—"

"—and that no other female was present—"

"Well, you told me, Pru, that your friend Edwina was on her wedding trip—"

"—your sister decided the worst had happened. And so now you're in the suds, girl. There's only one thing to be done." Her father glanced at Nicholas.

"No, Papa, there is nothing to be done," she said. "It was an innocent mistake. I will explain it all to Margaret."

"She has already taken to her couch in a flood of tears," her eldest brother Roderick said. He could not keep the hint of scorn from his voice. They had all experienced Margaret's dramatic collapses over the years. "Says you are trying to upstage her daughter's come-out Season."

"What nonsense."

Nicholas pushed away from the wall and came to stand beside Pru. "It is not nonsense. It is quite serious, Pru. Your reputation has been compromised, and it is all my fault."

She wondered if a person could actually die of mortification. "No, Nicholas," she said, her voice barely above a whisper, "it is not your fault."

"Oh, yes it is," her father said. "And I am glad to hear this *gentleman* admit it. You had no right, sir, to allow my daughter to remain alone under your roof."

"But Papa, I was only here downstairs in the magazine office, not—"

"It does not matter," Nicholas said. "Your father is right. I should not have allowed it. My only excuse is that I always considered you one of the family, Pru. I am deeply sorry."

"I'll bet you are," her father said.

Nicholas gave him a challenging look that was quite startling in its intensity.

"But you *will* marry Prudence," her father said.

Dear God. Her heart thumped so fast and high in her chest, she thought perhaps she really would die. But she could not allow this to happen. She could not. "No," she said in as firm a voice as she could muster. "No."

Her father grabbed her upper arm and swung her around to face him. "What do you mean, no?"

"No, you cannot make him marry me." She turned to Nicholas, though she could not bring herself to look him in the eye. "I will not have you forced into marriage with me. It's ridiculous."

"It is not ridiculous," her father said. "It is necessary."

"Papa, I am twenty-seven years old. I am nobody important. People will not talk about me. There is no need to force Nicholas into this situation. I will not agree to it."

"Your family will talk," her father said. "They are talking already. You *will* marry Parrish."

"No."

Nicholas moved to stand in front of her and took both her hands in his. Oh, how she wished he had not done that.

"Your father has a point, Pru. If there is any possibility of damaging your reputation—"

"I have no reputation." She gave a little laugh at the very idea. "I'm nobody, Nicholas. There is no reason in the world for you to have to throw away your life because I happened to fall asleep in your office."

"Pru—"

"Truly, Nicholas, there is nothing to worry about. My father is overreacting. It is very kind of you to accept responsibility, but it really is not necessary. I promise you there is no need to marry me."

Relief flickered in his eyes for the merest instant, but she saw it.

I would not marry your wretched daughter if you put a gun to my head.

Pru would rather die, then and there, than force Nicholas into a marriage he did not want. He might consider her a friend now, but how long would it be before he held her in contempt? Before he despised her? It would be preferable not to have him at all than to have him like that.

Though she loved him—*because* she loved him—she would not be able to bear it.

"Are you certain?" he asked.

"Quite certain."

A fleeting pressure of his hands expressed his gratitude. Her heart contracted with a tiny stab of pain at the knowledge of his relief, but she forced a smile. She had done the right thing.

Nicholas released her hands and turned to her father. "Mr. Armitage, I have—"

He was cut short by a cacophony of huffing, snorting, and choking from her brothers. Good Lord. She'd forgotten he didn't know.

Of course he didn't know. She'd quite deliberately avoided any specific discussion of her family. Both Edwina and Nicholas were republicans at heart, had even gone to France in support of the Revolution. Pru had not known how they would feel about her if they knew her background. And she had *so* wanted them to accept her.

Pru began to feel as if the floor sank beneath her feet. If only it would open up and swallow her whole, she might be put out of this misery.

"He is Lord Henry to you, sir," Roderick said with every ounce of arrogance he possessed, which was a great deal.

Nicholas blanched. "*Lord* Henry?" He glanced at Pru and raised his brows in question.

This was going to change everything. She could tell by the look on Nicholas's face.

Damnation. There was nothing for it, though, but to tell him the truth. She took a deep breath.

"You have not been properly introduced. Papa, this is Mr. Nicholas Parrish. Nicholas, this is my father, Lord Henry Armitage."

Nicholas's mouth had turned grim once again, but he nodded and said, "My lord."

"And these are my brothers—Roderick, Daniel, Charles, and William."

Nicholas nodded warily at each.

"Not to worry," William said cheerfully. "We're only Misters, not Lords. Not even Honorables."

Daniel punched him in the arm and told him to shut up.

Nicholas ignored them and spoke directly to her father. "I must beg your pardon again, my lord. I had no idea Prudence was from a noble family. May I be so bold as to ask—"

"My father was the Duke of Norwich," her papa said, his chest puffed out and his voice dripping with aristocratic pride, "and my brother is the current duke."

Nicholas closed his eyes briefly. His mouth twisted into a grimace, and he looked as though he might be ill. "Prudence is the granddaughter of the Duke of Norwich?"

"She is indeed."

"And niece to the current duke?"

"That, too. You see the problem?"

Nicholas nodded. "Lord Henry, may I humbly request the hand of your daughter in marriage?"

Oh God oh God oh God. Pru's stomach seized up in knots and she closed her eyes tight. This wasn't happening. This could not be happening.

"No!" Pru grasped her father's arm. "No, Papa. Please!"

"Not only do I agree to the marriage, sir," her papa said, ignoring her pleas, "I insist upon it. And you, girl, will do as you're told. I will not have your odd behavior tattled around the family. Especially now, when everyone is gathering for Arabella's Season. You *will* marry. Quietly, and before the day is over. Then we may get on more peacefully with this come-out business."

She simply could not believe what was happening. There she stood, with her clothes in disarray and her hair falling down. And there he stood, the man she loved, half dressed, feet bare, hair tousled, a dark stubble marking his chin and jaw, looking more gloriously male than she'd ever seen him. And he had just asked permission to marry her.

It was not exactly the stuff of dreams. In fact, it had all the makings of a nightmare.

For the first time in her life, Pru thought she might actually swoon. Her knees felt wobbly, her head spun, and she could barely breathe. Someone took her hand.

"I will not allow your name to be sullied in any way, Pru," Nicholas said, "especially among your family."

"B-but I heard what you said before. About how you wouldn't marry me even if a gun was held to your h-head. There is no gun, Nicholas."

"That is easily remedied," her brother Roderick said.

Nicholas tugged on her hands, and she forced herself to look up at him. He wore a chagrined expression, and she could swear he was blushing. "I wasn't speaking of you, Pru."

"Then who—"

"It doesn't matter. I did not know this gentleman was your father. I thought he was . . . someone else."

"But—"

"And now that I know who he is, and who *you* are, it is clear what must be done. I have been careless of your reputation in allowing you to work here alone. I am ashamed to say it never occurred to me how it might look to others. But the damage is done. I am sorry, Pru, for bringing this on, but we must marry. There is no other choice."

No other choice. Because he was a gentleman and she was the granddaughter of a duke.

Unfair! There had to be other choices.

A bolt of lightning could strike the very spot where she stood. She could curl up into a ball so tiny she would float away on the wind. She could succumb to heart failure and save everyone a great deal of trouble.

But none of those things was likely to happen. And so there was no other choice.

How was she to bear it?

The tears she'd been holding back could no longer be contained. They welled up and flowed down her cheeks, completing her humiliation.

"I'm so sorry, Nicholas. I'm so sorry."

* * *

"Good God, Nick. I cannot believe it."

Nick sat in Simon Westover's library, his head down, arms resting on his knees, and his hands hanging limply between them. He felt such a pressure on his stooped shoulders it was as though the world—his world, at least—had come crashing down on him. Somehow he'd managed to get himself to his friend's house. He assumed he had dressed properly, though he could not remember doing so. He could barely remember how he got there. In fact, the events of that morning were still so jumbled in his head, he was not sure if he was coming or going.

"Perhaps you will believe it," Nick said, "when you stand up with me for the vows. I need you with me, old man."

"Of course. It is just . . . Well, it's a bit of a shock. You've always been impulsive, but I never expected this."

"I assure you, the impulse was not mine."

"The situation was innocent. You might have resisted."

"I suspect if I had been so inclined, her father and brothers would have ripped me to pieces and left me a bleeding hulk on my own doorstep. And those brothers are not tiny like Pru. I swear they looked like of gang of Viking warriors."

"Egad. No wonder you capitulated."

"That was not it at all. Her honor was indeed compromised. I ought to have been more cautious since Edwina left. Dammit, there was not even a servant in the house. And I suppose I never thought of Pru as . . . I don't know . . . someone to be compromised. She was always just Pru."

"How did she handle it?"

Nick looked up. "It was perfectly dreadful. I felt so badly for her. She kept repeating over and over how sorry she was, the tears streaming down her face. She doesn't want to be stuck with me any more than I . . . Well, she isn't any happier than I am."

Simon blew out a breath through puffed cheeks, then ran a hand through his red hair. "I suppose it could be worse."

Nick snorted. "How?"

"Well, at least you and Pru are friends. You like each other. That's a better beginning than many marriages enjoy. Who's to say that friendship won't eventually grow into love?"

"This is not one of your romantic tales, Simon. I seriously doubt this story will end happily ever after like one of your serials in the *Cabinet*. This one has all the earmarks of a tragedy."

"Only if you make it so. There is no possibility that this marriage can be avoided?"

"None."

"Well. I know it is not what you wanted, but since you cannot escape it, you had better start thinking of how to make the best of it."

"I did not come here looking for advice from the Busybody." Simon's popular advice column in the *Cabinet* was known for its rose-colored outlook on life, and Nick wasn't feeling particularly rosy at the moment. "I came looking for a friend, for someone who will commiserate with me, listen to my woes, and allow me to wallow in a bit of self-pity."

"You only have a few hours before the wedding. You do not have time to wallow."

"Only a few hours." He could almost feel the noose tightening. "Enough time to make a run for it. I could bolt to the continent and avoid the whole wretched business."

"You would never do that."

Nick shook his head. "No, of course not. I couldn't do that to poor Pru. But that doesn't stop me from wishing I could."

"Exactly how much time do you have?"

"I'm not certain. Her father is to send around a note telling me when to meet them. He is seeing to the license, of course. His connections make it easier for him to obtain it than for a simple Mr. Parrish with no position, little money, and nothing to recommend him. He's probably on speaking terms with the Archbishop of Canterbury himself."

"That was certainly a surprise, was it not? Pru, the granddaughter of a duke." Simon shook his head as though he still could not believe it.

"Surprise is something of an understatement," Nick said. "I've known her for years, and she never once mentioned it."

"Did you ever ask about her family?"

"Well, no. I just assumed . . ." He hunched a shoulder.

"What?"

"That she was like us."

"Like us?"

"How can she pretend to support republican ideals when her grandfather was a duke?"

Simon bristled. "My father is a baronet, and so will I be one day. Yet I support the same philosophies as you."

"But a *duke*, Simon."

"Even so, I would not be so quick to question the sincerity of her views."

"Point taken. I'm all at sixes and sevens over this mess. Not thinking clearly." He brought his hands to his head and massaged his temples.

"Did her father speak with you about her dowry?"

Nick's head snapped up? "Her dowry?"

"You could be marrying an heiress, my friend."

"Oh, Lord, I hope not." They had not discussed any details, only to agree that a wedding would take place. Her father might have said something about talking with him later regarding settlements or some such thing, but Nick had been in no state to absorb seemingly irrelevant information when his life was crumbling into pieces.

But what if Pru was an heiress? His shoulders shook with an involuntary shudder. The idea unsettled him, almost frightened him. He had borne enough without adding that blow to his already battered spirit.

"I doubt she has much of anything," he said, more to himself than to Simon. "She seems to

have a boatload of siblings. And I have dropped
her off at her father's house on occasion. It's on
Brooke Street, but rather small and modest. I'm
guessing there isn't much in the way of a fortune
in that family, despite the ducal connection. Besides, I don't want Pru's money."

"You could use it. That warehouse up in Derby
can't sit empty forever."

"Of course I could use it. Especially after last
month's losses. I will miss the best opportunities
to outfit the factory if I don't move soon. But I
would never take her money. Good Lord, Simon,
the last thing I need is to be thought a fortune
hunter. It's bad enough that I'm marrying a
duke's granddaughter. Gad, how will I ever face
them at the Scottish Martyrs Club?" He threw his
head back and closed his eyes. The more he talked
about it, the worse the whole situation became.

"Damn and blast," he said. "Would it be terribly
craven, do you think, if I just put a gun to my
head?"

"Terribly."

"What the devil am I going to do?" He hauled
himself from the chair and began to pace the
room. "Marriage was not in my plans. I cannot afford a wife and family. Not yet. And even if I
could, Pru is the last—"

"Careful."

"Well, damn it all, she would not have been my
choice. You know that. She's about as different from
the type of women I prefer as she could possibly be.
Too quiet. Too shy. Too pale. Not exactly a beauty."

"Neither is she an antidote, Nick."

"No, of course not." He stopped pacing and looked at Simon. "But don't you think she is just a bit . . . mousy?"

"You are speaking of your bride-to-be, my friend. I suspect you would level any other man who said such a thing about her."

"I would do so even if we were not to be married. I speak bluntly to you only because I know you will not repeat it. You must understand how I feel. She is to be my *wife*, for God's sake. We will be . . . But I don't . . . Oh, God, what if I can't . . ."

"You underestimate yourself. And Pru. Give it time."

Nick raked agitated fingers through his hair. Every aspect of this wretched business was distasteful to him. "Pru is a sweet woman, but not . . . not what I had in mind for a future wife. She is not the type of woman I pictured holding in my arms at night. Dash it all, I feel like . . ."

"Like what?"

"Like I've been cheated."

Simon glared at him. "You had better not let Pru know you feel that way."

"Dear God, no. No, of course not. Though I'm sure she feels the same." He groaned aloud. "What the devil am I going to do?"

"You are going to marry her and be happy for it."

Nick sputtered in disgust. "Happy?"

"If you will quit feeling sorry for yourself, then I have a feeling this marriage may just be the best thing that's ever happened to you."

"I seriously doubt it."

"I will remind you of those words in a year. Now, hadn't you better go home and get dressed for your wedding?"

A very short time later, Nick stood beside Prudence in one of the smaller chapels in St. George's and repeated the vows that made her his wife. He looked down at her to see a tear inching along her pale cheek and knew in that moment there could not be two more miserable people in all of London.

Chapter 3

Pru tied off the ribbon she had wrapped around the signet ring that would now serve as her wedding ring. It was miles too big, of course, and so she had pulled a ribbon from her hair and woven it around the bottom of the ring so it would fit securely on her smaller finger.

It also gave her something to do while she and Nicholas—her husband!—rode from the church to Daine House. Something besides talking, which Nicholas seemed disinclined to do. He appeared lost in his thoughts. It was just as well. She would likely embarrass herself if she attempted a normal conversation. She sometimes became tongue-tied when she was nervous, the words trapped in her throat, inching their way out in stammered fits and starts. And what could be more unsettling than her wedding day?

Her wedding night?

But she would not think about that just now. She would make herself crazy and would not be able to string three coherent words together.

"I'm sorry about the ring," Nicholas said, breaking the awkward silence that had hung heavy in the air since the moment the carriage door had closed on them. "I ought to have dashed out and bought one for you, but I honestly forgot."

Pru shrugged and fiddled nervously with the ring. "It's all right," she managed to say, and surprised herself when there was no hint of a tremor in her voice. She was certainly trembling inside, trying not to think of—

"No, it's not all right," he said. There was a note of strain in his voice.

He'd been the perfect gentleman since arriving at the church with Simon Westover, but Pru knew he must be near to bursting with anger over this wretched trap he'd been caught in, forced into a ramshackle marriage with a little dab of a woman who wouldn't catch his eye on her best day. But he had not complained at the injustice of it. He had not scowled or grown sullen or stormed about like a caged bear. He had repeated the vows in a clear voice and treated her with deference and extraordinary kindness throughout the brief ceremony.

She had been the one to cry. For ruining his life.

"I am sorry, Pru. I ought to have done better by

you. It's been a rather hectic morning, to say the least, and the business about the ring just slipped my mind."

"It doesn't matter," she said, her voice almost a whisper. She had long ago learned the trick of keeping her voice pitched very low in times of stress, making any timorousness less apparent. She made a concentrated effort to do so now. "The ring is—"

"But I'll make it up to you. I promise I'll get you a ring of your own so you don't have to wear that old signet of mine."

"No, this ring is fine. Truly." And it was. It had been on his own finger so long his warmth had seeped right into the gold. She liked the feel of it. She would much rather have something of his than some cold thing he bought that meant nothing.

"But Pru—"

"I like it, Nicholas. I would prefer to keep it." She looked up at him from beneath the brim of her bonnet. "If you don't mind, that is."

He narrowed his eyes and studied her. "Of course I don't mind. But if you're worried about the expense, I assure you—"

"I'd like to keep it. Please."

He gave a sigh. "All right, then. I just hope your family won't think less of me—or you—for not having a proper ring."

Lord, how was she to get through this? Nicholas was so proud. She didn't care that he wasn't rich. Neither was she. Just because her father was titled did not mean he had a fortune to go with it.

And yet Nicholas worried what her family would think of him—not for himself, but for what he could, or could not, do for her.

Dear Nicholas.

"About my family." She had better warn him now, before they reached her sister's house. "I'm very sorry you have to be tossed into their midst so soon. They can be rather . . . daunting."

He sent her a rueful glance. "So I have experienced. They are certainly a *large* company."

"I'm afraid so. I would not drag you along to this breakfast if Papa had not insisted. My sister, Margaret, has some silly notion that she absolutely cannot do without my assistance. Ridiculous, of course, since she has quite a competent household staff. But I will try not to be pulled away to help too often."

"Don't worry about me, Pru. I can make my way with any group. Even a gathering of the aristocratic Armitage family."

The sarcastic edge to his voice made her wince. She had agonized over how he would feel about her background. A republican to his fingertips, he must be fuming inside to be tied now to such a family as hers. Not that she was ashamed of them. She held many of the same beliefs as Nicholas, but she would never reject her family. It was just that they were exactly the type of people he despised. She hoped he would be able to bear with them just for this one afternoon.

"I promise not to hold forth on factory reform," he said, "or child labor laws or the Combination Acts, or to distribute Jacobin pamphlets. Or tell them the truth about that little magazine you're editing. I won't embarrass you, Pru."

She blushed that he had so nearly read her thoughts. "I know you won't."

"Besides, you did say it is only a small family gathering, did you not?"

Pru gave an involuntary little sputter of laughter. *Small family gathering?* "Oh, dear."

"What? Have I got it wrong? I thought your father said it was only the family, getting together to welcome your niece to her first Season in Town. I must tell you, Pru, it will take some getting used to, this blue-blooded family of yours." He reached up, unconsciously it seemed, and adjusted his collar points. "I confess I had worried that perhaps I would be faced with half of London's aristocracy this morning. Frankly, I am rather glad it will be only a small family affair."

"Oh, dear."

His brow furrowed. "Pru? What is it? What have I missed? It *is* just the family, right?"

She drew in a deep breath and let it out slowly. "Yes, it is just the family. But there is nothing small about it."

"Oh, I know that. I had a good, close look at your brothers, remember." A glimmer of amusement lit his eyes. "How does a tiny little thing like you come to have such hulking big siblings?"

She smiled at him, encouraged by that wry look. "You are stuck with the runt of the litter, I'm afraid. But I warn you, there are lots more of us. We are large in more ways than one."

He lifted his brows. "Really? How many more brothers do you have?"

"Oh, only one more brother. Gerald is a captain in the army, so you will not get to meet him yet. And Margaret is my only sister. Just seven of us. But I have quite a few cousins."

"Do you? And all of them large?" He chuckled softly. "Don't worry, Pru. I shall not be overwhelmed by a handful of cousins, no matter what strapping big fellows they are."

She brought a hand to her mouth to cover the smile she could not suppress. Poor Nicholas. "You do not understand," she said. "It is rather more than a handful. Did Papa not mention he was the youngest offspring of the old duke?"

"Yes, he did."

"The youngest of *twelve*."

"Twelve?"

"Yes. I have twenty-six aunts and uncles, counting those by marriage. Six on my mother's side, twenty on my father's side. There were twenty-two at one time, but his eldest sister and one of his brothers are deceased. And I have fifty-two first cousins."

Nicholas had gone quite still. He stared at her, his eyes huge, his mouth gaping. "Fifty-two cousins?"

"First cousins. Only eight on my mother's side, but forty-four on Papa's side. And almost all of them have spouses and children, so there are really several hundred of us altogether."

"My God."

"So you see, there is nothing remotely small

about an Armitage family gathering. Even when only half of us show up."

He continued to stare, as though the idea of such a family was completely beyond his comprehension. And then all at once, he burst out laughing. Loud and uninhibited, his laughter filled the air, bouncing off the carriage walls and shattering all vestiges of tension and awkwardness. In his glee, he grabbed her hand and squeezed it. Her heart did a little dance in her chest, and she joined in the laughter.

"What a paltry family you have married into, Pru," he said at last, and wiped a hand across his eyes. "I have only a single first cousin to my name."

"No! Only one cousin?"

"Only one." He grinned. "How pathetically inadequate we Parrishes must seem to you."

"Actually, a small family sounds rather nice. Sometimes all those cousins can be a tiresome lot."

"And they will all be at your sister's party this afternoon?"

"Not all of them. But a great many of them, I'm afraid."

He shook his head and clucked his tongue. "This is going to be even worse than I thought."

She sucked in a sharp breath at his words, quite before she realized she'd done so, and he turned to her.

"Oh, Pru, I didn't mean—"

"It's all right. I know how you m-must feel. This whole morning has been rather . . . unpredictable. I'm so s-sorry about . . . about everything."

He still held her hand, and he took it to his lips, making her want to swoon and sob at the same time.

"I am sorry, too, Pru. Sorry you were forced into this against your will. I know that marriage to me was probably the very last thing you dreamed of—"

Ha! If he only knew.

"—but we shall muddle through. We have always been friends. As Simon reminded me, that is more than many marriages have. We will get through this. Together. The blue blood and the reformer." He smiled. "But first, I have to meet all those cousins."

Several carriages lined all sides of the square when they came to a stop in front of a large neoclassical house of stone and brick. Nick was relived to find it was not overly grand or imposing, though it was several times larger than his own small row house on Golden Square. It was known as Daine House, Pru had told him, and her sister was married to Sir Felix Daine—a mere baronet, but obviously one with deep pockets.

"Oh, dear."

Nick turned to Pru, who was chewing on her lower lip. "I am beginning to dread those *oh, dears* of yours, Pru. What now?"

"It is just that so many of them have already arrived. Margaret will be displeased with me at best."

"You said she had a competent staff."

"Yes, but she still relies on me to take care of

some of the details. She does not like to worry about anything more than getting herself and Arabella dressed properly and being on hand to greet her guests."

"She leaves all the worrying to you, then?"

"I don't mind. It gives me something to do."

"Besides enjoying yourself."

She gave a little shrug. "I am not always . . . comfortable in social situations. I am not outgoing like the rest of them."

"And so you prefer to stay in the background."

"I suppose. But Margaret can be somewhat frantic at times like this, and someone needs to give direction to the servants."

"Well, it will have to be someone else today."

She looked at him quizzically.

"Today is your wedding day, Pru."

"But—"

A liveried footman opened the carriage door before Pru could protest. Nick jumped down and held out a hand for his bride.

His bride. If he'd ever thought about it at all, he would never have associated those words with a woman like Pru. Nick had always preferred his women with dark, even exotic looks. He was easily seduced by sensuous mouths and deep-set eyes and voluptuous curves. And he was partial to women with open, uninhibited sexuality. Pru could not have been more different if she tried.

He studied her as she stepped out of the carriage and glanced apprehensively toward the house. She was slender and small, the top of her head barely reaching his chin. Her hair, hidden beneath a plain white straw bonnet with pink ribbons, he knew to be thick and curly and of an indeterminate shade somewhere between blond and red. The face tilted up to him was heart-shaped, with round cheeks dipping down to a small chin. Her skin was clear but very pale, with a light dusting of freckles across the nose. She had a tiny pink rosebud of a mouth and small, white teeth. Her eyes were large and a very light shade of blue framed in pale lashes. Her eyebrows were rather nice, he decided. They were reddish blond and elegantly arched.

He had never considered it in all the years he'd known her, but he supposed she was not unattractive. Not exactly. She was such a shy little thing, though, that she drew little attention to herself, so that one never really noticed her.

Yet he was going to have to do more than notice her now that she was his wife. He wondered if he should bed her tonight and get it over with, or wait until she—and he—had become more accustomed to the idea.

Now, though, was not the time to think of consummating his marriage. He had a houseful of damned blue bloods to meet. And he had to be on his best behavior and stay away from politics. He resigned himself to smiling and speaking of nothing more consequential than the weather.

He stifled a sigh and placed Pru's arm on his as he led her to the door, where a stern-faced butler met them. His eyes softened when he saw Pru.

"Good afternoon, Miss Prudence," he said.

"Lady Daine will be glad to know you have arrived. And Lord Henry has just arrived as well." He stepped aside to allow them into the entry hall.

Pru's father and two of her brothers, William and Charles, had been the only members of her family to attend the brief wedding ceremony. Their carriage had been just ahead of the one carrying Nick and Pru, and they now stood at the other end of the hall. They turned and waited while Pru spoke to the butler.

"Thank you, Symonds," she said. "We shall make our own way outside. This is Mr. Parrish, by the way."

Hats and sticks and gloves were not relinquished, as the party was outdoors. Nick kept Pru's hand on his arm and they joined her father and brothers. Lord Henry drew them aside.

"There is no keeping a secret in this family," he said, "so I have no doubt most everyone knows there has been a wedding this morning. Much as I wish this could be celebration for you, my girl, I am afraid it would not be right to spoil Arabella's day."

"No, of course not, Papa."

"And in any case, the circumstances . . ." Lord Henry looked at them both and heaved a sigh. "This is not what I would have wished for you, Prudence. But Parrish has done the right thing. I am sure it will be for the best. Now, let us join the party. Oh, blast. Here is Margaret."

A tall, pretty, blond woman sailed into the hall like a ship of the line. She was fashionably dressed in white muslin and lace, her skirts billowing behind her as she launched toward them at impressive speed.

"Thank *God* you have finally come," she said, one hand punctuating the air in a little burst of outstretched fingers. She came to a halt in front of Pru, looming in her greater height, eyes blazing. It was an entrance worthy of Mrs. Siddons. "I have been at my *wits' end*." The hand, once again, etched the air with an expansive flourish of frustration.

"Hullo, Margaret," Pru said, unruffled by this impassioned onslaught. "I am sorry to be late."

"I do not know *what* has got into you," her sister said, "disappearing like that and worrying us all half to death last night. When you *knew* I needed you here." She slid a withering gaze in Nick's direction. "I suppose this is *him*."

Pru sent Nick an apologetic look. "This is Nicholas Parrish," she said. "My . . . husband."

She seemed almost to choke on the word. Hearing it said aloud like that was no less unsettling to Nick.

"Nicholas, may I present my sister Margaret, Lady Daine."

She looked as though she expected him to offer an elegant leg and bow deeply. But Nick would be damned before he would kowtow to the aristocracy. He reached out a hand. "Lady Daine. I am pleased to meet Pru's sister."

Momentarily flustered, she stared down at his hand as though the glove were soiled. Finally, she condescended to put her own hand in his. And just for the sheer pleasure of discomposing her, he brought her fingers to his lips.

She twitched a little in surprise, then glared at him and retrieved her hand. "Well. This is a beastly business, to be sure. But we shall carry on, somehow. Prudence, did you have nothing more becoming to wear? Oh, it is of no consequence. No one will notice. Now, come with me. I am not at all pleased with the way the footmen have arranged the—"

"I beg your pardon, Lady Daine," Nick said, and took hold of Pru's elbow as she made to follow her sister. "I am sure you have well-trained servants to manage things for you." Even as he spoke, a small parade of liveried footmen crossed the hall, each bearing a silver tray laden with dishes or glasses. "They appear to have matters well in hand. I am sure you can manage without Pru's help. I am a blushing bridegroom, you may recall, and should prefer to keep my bride by my side, if you please."

He could hardly believe he'd said such a thing—blushing bridegroom, indeed!—but the damned woman annoyed him, treating poor Pru like a servant.

Lady Daine was not amused. Wrenching her chilly gaze from Nick, she turned to Pru. "If anything goes wrong today, it will be all your fault, my girl. And I shall never forgive you for ruining dear Arabella's first appearance in town."

She spun on her heel and marched away.

"I say, Parrish, that was well done." Pru's youngest brother, William, wore a broad grin as he

watched his sister's stately exit. He clapped a
hand on Nick's shoulder and said, "Let's go face
the mob. I will help Pru introduce you around."

And so the five of them—Nick, Pru, Lord Henry,
William Armitage, and Charles Armitage—made
their way through an elegant drawing room where
the French doors were open to a large terrace. Nick
could see beyond it slightly to a formal garden below. It was surely ten times the size of the tiny patch
of garden behind the house on Golden Square. And
it was teeming with people. The din of a hundred
conversations wafted through the open doors.

Lord, this was not going to be easy. He hated this
sort of *ton* gathering. He looked down to find Pru
gazing at him apprehensively. Of course, she would
know how he felt. She had read every article and
pamphlet he'd written over the last four years. And
several times, he and Edwina and Pru had sat for
hours talking of politics and dreams of reform. She
would know how uncomfortable he would be in a
room full of privileged aristocrats. She claimed to
support the same republican principles as he did,
and yet these were her people, her family.

No wonder she had never revealed her background. He would never have trusted her again.
How he hated those highborn noblemen who
dabbled in reform because it seemed a modern,
sophisticated thing to do—until it affected them
personally. Is that what Pru had done? Found herself a cause to occupy her time, without any true
commitment?

"I am dreadfully sorry," she said, her voice barely above a whisper so that the others would not hear.

He wondered if his face had revealed his disdain and made an effort to school his features. More likely she was apologizing for the sheer numbers and not the politics of her relations. "You did warn me it was a large family," he said.

"That's not what I meant. I am sorry they are so . . ."

"Aristocratic? Wealthy? Privileged? Tory to a man, I suspect."

"Yes. All of that. I know how you must despise them."

He looked into her clear blue eyes and saw nothing of guile or deceit. He knew in that instant that her ideals were as true as his own, that she had never "played" at reform, but had been a true colleague. He only had to recall how tireless she had been in her work on the magazine, especially with Edwina gone.

It was this wretched forced marriage. There was a simmering anger deep down in his gut that he had kept in check all day, and the effort made him a bit crazy. He ought not to have doubted Pru. None of this was her fault.

"They are your family," he said. "Some of them may have different ideals than mine, but it does not matter. This is not a political meeting or public debate. It is a family affair, and I promise to exert myself to be charming."

She smiled and looked away, then, in a very low voice said, "That should not be difficult."

And so Nick steeled himself to face the noble Armitage family.

They stepped onto the terrace, where several dozen fashionably attired people mingled and talked loudly above the din of voices. Covered tables were scattered about, and some guests were seated at them, picking at small plates of dainty-looking morsels. A few guests looked Nick's way, but William led him and Pru down the steps to the garden below.

"Let's grab something to eat first," William said. "I declare I am starved to death. I do hope Margaret has laid out a good spread. She likes to call this a breakfast, even though it is afternoon. I sincerely hope it is more than tea and toast."

The garden was filled with more small tables, but most people were standing or strolling about the gravel paths. It was an elegant crowd. Beneath the top hats and bonnets and turbans, it seemed that almost everyone was fair-haired, like Pru's father and brothers. It was indeed a tall, big-boned, good-looking family. A gathering of Vikings. There was an occasional brunette and one or two redheads. Relatives by marriage, no doubt.

His own dark coloring—inherited from his Italian grandmother—made him feel like a blot of ink on a pristine sheet of parchment. No wonder heads turned his way when they entered the garden.

William filled a plate with food from the buffet

table, though neither Nick nor Pru was inclined to eat. She was probably as wound up inside as he was. He did convince her to take a glass of champagne when a footman passed with a tray of glasses. He took one as well, and clinked his glass to hers in a silent toast. She stared at him for a moment, a quizzical, uncertain look in her eye. Then she gave a small shrug and brought the glass to her lips.

"Come, Parrish," William said, carrying a plate with him. "Let me introduce you to my aunt Jane, Lady Gordon."

And so it began.

William led them to a tall, handsome woman who looked to be in her sixties, elegantly dressed in spotted muslin. "Hello, Willy," she said. "You are looking positively mischievous. And who is this gentleman?"

"May I introduce Nicholas Parrish, ma'am."

She offered her hand and peered at him through a quizzing glass held in the other. Nick took her hand but did not bring it to his lips. Not with a quizzing glass pointed at him.

"How do you do, Lady Gordon?" he said.

"I thought this was to be the family only, Willy. I will, however, forgive you bringing along your friend since he is such a handsome devil."

"He *is* family, Aunt Jane. He is married to Prudence."

Her brow furrowed. "To whom?"

William inched his sister forward, though she

had not been hiding in the background. She was standing right beside him. "To Prudence, Aunt."

Lady Gordon looked at Pru as though only just noticing her. "Prudence? Married?" Her eyebrows disappeared beneath the silvery-gold curls peeking from beneath a turban of twisted muslin, and her wide-eyed gaze moved back to Nick. "To this young man?"

"Yes, Aunt Jane," Pru said.

"My my my." Her gaze stayed on Nick, and her eyes twinkled. "Who would have dreamed such a thing? Well, you are welcome to the family, young man. I am giving a small rout next Thursday, the day after Arabella's come-out ball. You must promise to attend. You may bring along Prudence, of course."

"I'd be delighted," he said, lying through his teeth. He had hoped not to be forced into any more *ton* events. But he could hardly refuse. Even if she did manage to ignore Pru.

William took them around to several other grand personages—Lord and Lady Phillip Armitage, the Earl and Countess of Totteridge, Sir Thomas and Lady Vaughn, Lady Randolph Armitage—before he was called away and Prudence was left to the introductions on her own. Everyone they had met so far had reacted in much the same way when he was introduced as Pru's husband. It was as though none of them imagined she would ever find a husband—if they imagined anything about her at all. It was almost as though because of him—because he had married Pru—they noticed her for the first time.

What was wrong with these people? Pru was as well-bred, as highborn as the rest of them. She was intelligent and sweet-natured and attractive. How had she been so easily overlooked for so long? It was not as though she cowered in the shadows. Yes, she was shy, but she was not timid. She stood straight, looked everyone in the eye, and spoke clearly. Of course, she was not as loud as the others. It seemed that many of them had decided the best way to make their mark in this large company was to shout louder than anyone else. The noise was almost deafening.

No wonder Pru had tried to find interests for herself outside this mob. He could never imagine her voice raised.

He saw no women as tiny as Pru, and none with her unique reddish-blond coloring. And certainly none of them seemed shy. Not in this loud, gregarious, almost boisterous family. If not for similarities in the shape of her face and the hint of aquilinity in the nose—how had he failed to notice that aristocratic line?—he would never have guessed Pru belonged to this family.

She led him to meet the others. So many cousins and aunts and uncles—it made his head spin.

"Do not even try to keep us all straight," one of them said. Nick was fairly certain it was Lionel Armitage, son of Lord Arthur Armitage. "It is a lost cause. Even those of us born to the family have trouble remembering all the relationships. I have always thought we should all wear name badges at these events. Or colored armbands to identify us with one of the twelve children of the old duke."

"That would certainly help a newcomer," Nick said.

Pru was borne off by some of her female cousins. No doubt they wished to hear all the details of her sudden marriage. He wondered how much of the truth she would tell.

Lionel Armitage tugged him along to meet more cousins. Within moments, a group of tall, fair-haired men surrounded him, punching him in the shoulder and laughing loudly.

"Foot caught in the mousetrap, eh, old chap?"

"Bit of a sticky situation, I hear."

"Compromised beyond hope, they say."

"A pity you could not have compromised a beauty."

"Prudence, of all people."

"Deuced bad luck, that's what it is."

"She's a quiet little thing, though."

"Biddable."

"Won't complain if you lead your own life, I daresay."

"Still, it's a damned shame."

"Frightful predicament."

"Not exactly the sort of woman a man dreams of."

"Ha! A nightmare, more like."

"Plain little Prudence."

"Sad bit of dowd."

A sudden chorus of throat clearing told Nick that Pru was near. She was, in fact, just behind him. Damnation. How much had she heard? She was turning to walk away when Nick took her by the elbow and brought her close to his side.

"I am afraid you are under the wrong impression, gentlemen," he said. "As it happens, she is precisely the woman I have dreamed of. Prudence and I have been in love for some time now, have we not, my dear?"

Chapter 4

Pru was stunned into silence. How to respond to such a bouncer? But she had heard her cousins commiserating with Nicholas on his misfortune. He must have known she'd heard their barbs. It was not pleasant to hear oneself spoken of as a sad bit of dowd, even though she knew it to be true. And knew, too, how unfair it was that Nicholas was now stuck with her. That did not make it any easier to hear it spoken aloud and laughed about.

But he knew she had heard and tried to make amends. Dear Nicholas. She looked at him and smiled, unable to offer any coherent words of confirmation.

He pulled her closer. "We had planned to wait," he said, "but circumstances forced an early marriage. Your cousin, gentlemen, is a priceless little jewel. I suggest you remember that."

He turned and led her away from them. Never one for discretion, her cousin Rupert was clearly heard to say, in a typically loud voice, "Well, if that don't beat all."

She could not suppress a giggle. "Nicholas, what a whisker. How could you say such things with a straight face?"

"I could not bear them another moment." His voice bristled with anger. "They were downright insufferable."

"I daresay they were. But that surely was not reason enough to tell such a ridiculous lie. No one will believe it."

"Then we shall make them believe it. I do not care to have your hundreds of cousins feeling sorry for us."

Such consideration made her almost want to cry. "That is very kind of you, Nicholas, but truly not necessary. There are far too many other interesting people in the family for anyone to spend time feeling sorry for me."

"I suppose your female cousins wanted all the details. What did you tell them?"

"Not much. Everyone had heard of the rushed wedding, of course. That sort of news spreads like wildfire in this family. Most of them just wanted to know who you were, and how was it that someone like me had been able to entrap someone like you."

"Someone like me?"

"Someone so . . . handsome."

Her cousin Beatrice had stated quite boldly that she and Nicholas were horribly mismatched. Of course they were. No one knew that better than Pru. He was gorgeous; she was ordinary. He was charming and gregarious; she was shy and diffident. He was brilliant, with a mind that could tear apart a political argument with ease and formulate new and profound ideas with persuasive eloquence. And she was . . . average.

No, she was no proper match for Nicholas. He ought to have been embarrassed by her shortcomings. And yet he was willing to pretend a love match.

He gave a little growl of frustration. "Pru, I swear I do not understand how you have managed to live with these people all your life."

She shrugged and smiled. "I get along."

"By remaining invisible to them?"

"I suppose. But I don't mind, really. I am not like the rest of them, you know. I've never . . . fit in."

"I can see that. Well, everyone is noticing you today. Let us give them something to notice. Look at me like you love me, Pru."

He took her hand to his lips and kept it there longer than was proper, all the while gazing at her as though he wanted to devour her on the spot.

Lord, how she had longed for him to look at her like that. It was sheer heaven. Of course, it was mock desire. There was a hint of laughter in those dark eyes. But it was easy enough to pretend, if only for a moment, that it was real.

She wanted that moment to last foever.

"Keep looking at me, Pru," he said as he tucked her hand into the crook of his arm and laid his other hand upon it. "Let them think you're in love with me. That's it. Oh, very nice. You almost convince me, my dear. I do believe you might have had a career on the stage, Pru."

"So this is the handsome bridegroom."

Pru pulled her gaze from Nicholas's—just in time, too, before he realized she was not playacting—to find her cousin Eunice at her side. She was not looking at Pru, but was staring with open admiration at Nicholas. Eunice was very beautiful and terribly vain. Pru ought to have known she would seek out the newest handsome face in the crowd.

"Hello, Eunice. May I present Nicholas Parrish. My husband." She despised the hint of possessiveness she heard in those words. What was wrong with her? The warm, longing look Nicholas had just given her was not real. She must not forget that. "Nicholas, this is my cousin, Mrs. Shelbourne."

Eunice held out a hand, but Nicholas did not kiss the air above her fingers, as he had done so many times this afternoon, charming all the ladies. He simply took her hand and bowed over it. "Your servant, madam."

Eunice gave him a provocative smile and never took her eyes from him. "Goodness, Prudence, what a coup. Such an attractive husband you have snared."

Nicholas pulled Pru closer to his side and said, "If there was a snare, madam, I assure you I stepped into it willingly."

Eunice's eyes held more than a hint of mockery when she glanced briefly at Pru. "Indeed? Well, they always say it is the quiet ones who will surprise you, and you have certainly done that, Prudence. I trust we will be seeing more of you this Season, Mr. Parrish. Will you be at Arabella's come-out ball next week?"

"We are hoping for some time alone, are we not, my dear? But I am sure we will make an appearance now and then. I shall let my bride decide which invitations to accept."

"Well, she will certainly want to attend her niece's ball," Eunice said, "so I will hope for a dance, Mr. Parrish."

"May I interrupt?"

Pru's father had stepped up to join them. "Of course, Papa."

"May I take Parrish away for a short while? I promise not to keep him long."

"Of course, my lord," Nicholas said, and then turned to Pru. "I shall find you later, my dear." Once again, no doubt for the benefit of Eunice, he placed a fulsome kiss upon her hand. He shot her one more look of mock longing, then he and her father walked away together.

"I confess, you have astonished me, cousin," Eunice said. "What a splendid-looking man he is. If one is to be compromised, he is certainly the man one would choose to do it." She went on to chide Pru about trapping the poor man, as though it would have been less objectionable had it been any other woman, someone more equal to him in beauty.

Eunice had not been the first one to suggest Pru must have deliberately set up a compromising situation to trap Nicholas. Several of her female relations had implied as much. Her cousin Susan, Lady Lambrooke, had stated outright, in a loud, ringing voice, that there was no other possible way Prudence could have attracted such a man.

It ought to have been very lowering. However, in the deepest, most secret corner of her soul, Pru felt rather proud of herself for having the handsomest, most charming husband of any of her cousins.

"I sincerely hope you do not expect to keep him to yourself," Eunice said. "A man like that will not be content to sit quietly by the home fire each night, faithful as a hound. And I trust you will not be so foolish as to fall in love with him. That would be unwise, my girl. Ah, there is Roland. I must have a word with him."

Pru was left standing alone on the garden path, with Eunice's words jangling in her head. She had not yet had time to consider how this marriage would proceed. *Had* she expected Nicholas to be a faithful husband? Faithful to a wife he never wanted? She supposed that was indeed an impossible dream. She only hoped he would keep silent about any other women in his life. She did not wish to know about them.

And she prayed none of them was one of her numerous cousins. Almost every woman today below the age of ninety had cast eyes in his direction. Several had gazed with open admiration. Nicholas had been charming, but had not flirted back with any of them. Not that she knew of, at least. She wondered if he even realized the effect of his careless charm.

So, this was how it was to be. Married to a man she loved to distraction who did not love her, did not want her, and never would. Any woman still breathing would find him attractive, and so Pru would constantly have to endure the open interest of other women. And because just about any one of them would be more desirable than Pru, she would have to constantly wonder if he returned that interest. And keep silent about it if he did.

How was she to bear it?

Was she destined forever to compare herself to some unknown woman who might be his lover? And to wonder how miserably she measured up? Were there women already in his life to contend with?

Good heavens. It occurred to her that she knew very little of his personal life. What if he was in love with someone else? What if he had been courting someone in hopes of marriage?

"Aunt Prudence?"

Pru took a deep breath and forced aside all thoughts of how else she might have ruined Nicholas's life. She composed herself, looked up at her niece, and smiled. "Arabella. Did I tell you how pretty you look today? That shade of blue was a good choice after all. It is most becoming."

The girl gave a wave of casual dismissal and took Pru by the arm. "I am glad we have a moment alone, Aunt Prudence. I wanted to tell you how happy I am for you. Mr. Parrish is exceedingly handsome, is he not?"

"He is indeed."

Arabella sighed wistfully. "I hope I can find such a handsome husband. I do pray, though, I don't have to wait as long as you." She gave a little squeal and covered her mouth. "Oh, forgive me! That was badly stated. I just meant that I do not have your patience. I want to find my handsome hero *now*. All the cousins are frightfully jealous, you know. Have you really been in love forever? That's what Cousin Hugh said. Mr. Parrish told him that even though the timing of the marriage was forced, it was not unwelcome. I am so glad to know that you have made a love match at long last. But why have you never mentioned him before?"

Pru shrugged. She was reluctant to play along with the yarn Nicholas had spun, but neither did she want to contradict him in public. "It was a private matter, Arabella."

"And you have always been a very private person." Arabella smiled and patted Pru's arm. "Well, I, for one, am enormously pleased for you. I only wish you could have had a grand wedding and lots of parties. It does not seem right that there are no celebrations." Her eyes lit up with sudden excitement. "I have it! You can share my come-out ball. It can be in honor of your wedding as well."

An instant of sheer terror sent an involuntary shudder through Pru's body. "No, no, my dear. The ball is for you alone. It will be your very own special night, after your presentation to the queen in the afternoon. Besides, I do not want to make a public fuss over this marriage. I am much too old for that. And considering the circumstances, it would not be appropriate."

"Oh, pooh. What do the circumstances matter if it is a love match?"

"Please, Arabella, let me do this in my own way. Besides, even if I was willing—which I am not— your mother would never agree to sharing your ball with me."

Her niece giggled. "She would not, would she? Well, at least you must come and dance with Mr. Parrish. You may pretend it is your ball, even if nothing is said of it."

A pretend ball. A pretend love match. What other fictions lay ahead in this new make-believe world she'd entered this morning? And how long could she pretend that she was not miserable?

Nick followed Lord Henry into the house. He supposed they were about to have a man-to-man talk about Pru. There had been no time to do so before now. Lord Henry had spent the morning arranging for the special license and use of the church. But the moment for plain speaking had come, and Nick was not looking forward to facing the man who earlier had punched him in the nose.

Lord Henry led the way through the drawing room and down the stairs to a library. After indicating that Nick should be seated, he closed the door and took a seat behind the desk.

"Daine has given us permission to use his study," he said. "He has assured me we will not be disturbed." He placed his elbows on the desk, leaned forward, and steepled his fingers. He looked at Nick for a long while before speaking again.

"I understand you are claiming this is a love match."

Good Lord, is that all the man wanted to discuss? Surely he did not object to that little bit of prevarication?

It had been a thoroughly impulsive response to those overgrown loutish cousins. Their insulting references to Pru had not only angered him, but had triggered a wave of protectiveness that had swept over him with astonishing strength. Perhaps it was because Pru had spent so much time in Edwina's company that he'd begun to think of her as a sister. He would certainly never have allowed anyone to speak of Edwina in that offensive manner.

"I confess I did not like the way some of your relations were treating Pru," he said, "as though she were some sort of unsightly toad unworthy of happiness. It made me angry, and I said what I said in order to put an end to their jibes."

Lord Henry stared at him through narrowed eyes—clear blue like those of his daughter. "You surprise me, Parrish. Considering how things began this morning, I had not expected such . . . thoughtfulness. I assumed you would be so angry, you would remain stiff and silent throughout the day, but you have handled yourself well. We are not an easy family to foist upon anyone, especially on such short notice. I appreciate your consideration of Prudence."

"She is my friend, Lord Henry, and not deserving of the cruel words being thrown about by her cousins. It is true that I am angry about this whole situation. For myself and for Pru. But what's done is done. And I have no intention of allowing your family to make this any more difficult for Pru than it is already." Or for himself, either, by God.

Lord Henry's eyes widened slightly. "Well, then. I commend you, sir, on your sense of honor. You are a true gentleman. It appears my daughter has made a good match, after all."

Had she? Nick doubted it. The marriage had been against her will as much as his.

"We will make the best of it, my lord."

"By Jove, I believe you will." The ghost of a smile crossed his face, and vanished. "Now, I am afraid we must discuss more practical matters. Prudence's dowry."

Nick stifled a groan. He'd been dreading this discussion.

"You know by now that ours is quite a large family."

"Indeed."

"It is true, my father was a duke. But as the youngest of twelve, I fear there was very little in the way of a fortune left by the time I came along. I am not a rich man, Parrish."

Nick breathed a sigh of relief. Thank God, he would not be saddled with an heiress.

"And I have seven children of my own," Lord Henry continued. "So I am afraid I have very little for Prudence. I set up an annuity for her some years ago. It only gives her about a hundred a year. And I am unable to provide a dowry for her of much more than that. To speak quite bluntly, I never thought she'd need one."

Lord, even her own father did not value her. "She does not need one," Nick said, unable to control the edge of anger in his voice. On this matter, though, he intended to remain firm. "I certainly had not expected a dowry at all, considering the circumstances. I did not stage this morning's events in order to get my hands on Pru's money. I will not touch her annuity, of course. And I will accept no dowry, my lord."

Lord Henry's brows rose sharply and his eyes grew wide with astonishment. "Why the devil not? I do not believe you are a man of great fortune. Take what you can get, Parrish."

"No, my lord. She is not some property to be sold. It is true, I have no great fortune of my own. But I have a comfortable house and some savings, along with several investments from which I expect high returns."

"Such as?"

"Some shipping ventures. Re-exports of West Indian cotton and sugar to Europe. Some imports from France, since the treaty. Shares in a few copper mines and canal projects. And one or two new industrial patents."

Lord Henry frowned. "Risky business, all of it. More speculation than investment, I'd say."

"But with the potential for significant returns." In fact, he was hoping for some good news in the next weeks and already had plans for the anticipated profits. At least he had, until this morning.

"Have you had success with such ventures in the past?"

Nick shifted his weight nervously. "I, um, I've had a recent patch of bad luck, as it happens. The February storms and all. But I am much more confident of my current interests."

Lord Henry studied him thoughtfully. "And the house on Golden Square—it is yours?"

"Well, not exactly." This conversation was becoming decidedly awkward. "It belongs to my father. But he almost never comes to Town and has made it available for me and my sister these last eight or ten years. Now that Edwina has married, Father will have no objection to Pru and me making it our permanent home. And I have some income from writing as well. Not much, but it is enough. We shall be fine, my lord, I promise you.

And Pru will have her annuity to spend as she pleases."

"She will have more than that."

"I beg your pardon, my lord, but I thought I made it clear that I will accept no dowry for Pru."

"I'm not talking about a dowry. I think you're a damned fool to turn it down, but it does not signify. Pru has her inheritance, after all."

A tiny knot began to seize up in Nick's stomach. "What inheritance?"

"Did she never mention it? Well, she always was a quiet little thing. My sister Elizabeth left her a small inheritance a year ago."

"Oh?" A new knot joined the other, low in his belly.

"Yes, Elizabeth was always a bit eccentric. She was the firstborn of us twelve. She married the Marquess of Worthing when I was still in skirts, so we were never close. When she died last year, there was a clause in her will leaving a tidy little sum to Prudence. She wanted the youngest offspring of the duke's youngest offspring to be provided for. Something about not getting lost in the crowd. I am sure Elizabeth thought it a great joke."

Nick's throat had gone quite dry, but he forced himself to ask the question hanging unanswered in the air between them. "And how big was this inheritance?"

"Only a few thousand guineas, as I recall."

Good God. And the man spoke as if it were pin

money. Nick began to feel sick as a whole series of knots twisted and coiled inside his gut. "A few thousand guineas."

"It is likely a bit more now. I know Prudence has put some of it into the five-percents. She may have made other investments as well. None as risky as yours, if I know my daughter. She manages it on her own, so I cannot be sure. But it is her money, and she brings it to the marriage with her, so it is legally yours now. I thought you should know."

"I won't touch it."

Lord Henry heaved an exasperated sigh. "That is between you and Prudence. But I will say this much, Parrish. My daughter is fortunate to have enough money to live very comfortably. At least as comfortably as she has lived under my roof. And by God, I will not sit quietly and watch her living like a pauper if your investments fail, just because you are too proud to spend her money."

"She may do as she wishes with her money. I will not stop her from spending it any way she pleases."

"Including household expenses?"

Nick bristled. Lord Henry certainly aimed his darts well. "It is my house, my lord. There is no need for her to spend money for its maintenance."

"What about servants? You answered your own door this morning. Do you keep no servants?"

Nick squirmed in his chair. "There is a maid who works half days, and a cook who comes in the mornings to prepare the day's meals."

"And what if Prudence wanted a personal maid? Would you allow her to spend her own money to obtain one?"

"I have enough to increase the staff as needed. If Pru wants a lady's maid, I shall see that she has one."

"And what of clothes? There will be a great many balls and routs and such this season. Because of Arabella's come-out, Prudence will be expected to attend several of them, at least. Will you allow her to buy her own clothes?"

Damn the man! Nick's hands had balled into fists, and he had to remind himself that it was his father-in-law who sat behind that desk, and it would be unwise to reach across and throttle him. "It is her money to spend however she wishes."

"Except on the basic necessities?"

"I will provide the basic necessities," Nick said through clenched teeth. "But recall, if you will, that this marriage was not my idea. I have not come begging your approval. However, I will not have you thinking me a complete down-and-outer, Lord Henry. I am not."

"But you are very proud. Well, I can see that you and Prudence will have to work this out between you. But mind what I said, Parrish. I will not have her living like a church mouse when she has money that could make her life more comfortable."

Arabella and several of her cousins had obtained permission to use the duke's box at the theater for the evening. Coaxed and cajoled with

relentless enthusiasm by her niece, Pru finally
agreed that she and Nicholas would join them.
She was actually rather glad to do so. It put off a
bit longer the inevitable moment of being alone
with Nicholas for the first time as husband and
wife.

She watched him descend the terrace steps with
her father, and was bewildered to note the un-
characteristically grim look on his face. In fact, her
father did not appear particularly happy, either.
Oh, dear. What had they said to each other? Pru
did not care to think about it. The day's events
had already precipitated more emotional turmoil
than she'd endured in a lifetime, and there was
still the wedding night to face. She did not need
one more calamity to worry about.

By the time Nicholas reached her side, he was
wearing a polite smile. There was a hint of brittle-
ness about it, though, that seemed to mask something else. Was it anger? Had he and her father
quarreled?

She quickly told him of the invitation to the theater, and he gave a nod of acknowledgment,
though he said nothing. He stood quietly while
Arabella and two other young cousins of her own
generation tittered and giggled about who had already solicited dances for next week's ball. Arabella turned to Nicholas.

"And I trust we shall see you leading Aunt Prudence in the first dance, Mr. Parrish?"

He gave a little start, as though his thoughts
had been elsewhere, then flashed a more genuine

smile. "Yes, of course." He looked at Pru and once again wore an expression of mock devotion, remembering, apparently, that he was supposed to be in love with her. He took her hand and placed it on his arm. "I look forward to it with the greatest pleasure."

Soon afterward, some of the guests took their leave and the crowd began to thin. Pru's father pulled her aside to recommend that she return to his house and begin organizing the packing and removal of her things to Golden Square. Before she could respond, he was called away by his brother Frederick, and Pru was left alone to face the implications of his words.

That was it, then. The end of her life as the spinster daughter of Lord Henry Armitage. She was to quit forever the house she had been born in and grew up in, and make a new life, somehow, with Nicholas in the house on Golden Square. Today. Right now, and with very little time to accustom herself to the idea. Would her clothes share a wardrobe with his? Would her dressing gown hang on a peg next to his? Would his cook be able to make plum cake just the way she liked it? Was there enough room for her books? And what about music? How was she to survive without a pianoforte?

"It is a bit frightening, is it not?"

She looked up to find Nicholas studying her with concern. Had her thoughts been so clearly written on her face?

"To change one's way of life overnight," he

said, "to move away from all that is familiar. It is a shock. No less for me than for you. But we will get through this, my girl, I promise you."

"Yes."

"You will miss your family."

She smiled sheepishly. "Actually, I was thinking how peaceful it will be without all my brothers under the same roof. They can be a noisy bunch. I shall enjoy the quiet with just you and . . ."

"Just you and me."

"Yes." Just she and Nicholas. What could possibly be *less* peaceful? And more likely to set her emotions into wild disorder? A silent house would surely heighten her discomfort, providing no mask of noise and activity behind which she might hide. Nicholas was right. She would soon be missing that rackety household on Brooke Street, with all the bellowing and whooping and stomping about.

"Well, there is no rush to get everything done today," Nicholas said. "I do agree with Lord Henry that you should return home now and start getting your things packed. We can have the first of them brought over tomorrow. And since you will want to change for the theater, you will no doubt prefer to do that at home before you lose track of where you've put everything. I shall come by for you this evening."

"Will you come early and have dinner with us?" It was an impulsive request, but suddenly she did not want to face her family on her own, with her brothers' teasing and her father's forbearance.

Nicholas smiled. "Your last meal as hostess in your father's house? I would be honored. Come, let me take you there now. I am sure you have much to do."

And so her bridegroom deposited her at her father's house on Brooke Street, leaving her feeling stupidly alone and abandoned.

Chapter 5

Nick's head throbbed. He'd had far too much wine, and was well and truly foxed. Rather than blunting the anger that had roiled within his belly all day, however, the drink had merely intensified it.

Pru sat beside him in the carriage that was returning them to his middling little house on an unfashionable square barely on the fringes of Mayfair. How she must dread facing a life in such a modest setting. Her father's house, though not grand in scale, was beautifully elegant. Her sister's home was even more so, and he imagined every one of the aristocratic relatives he'd met today lived in fine style in houses much farther removed from the seamier side of town they were currently passing through. He was taking Pru to his pokey little row house no more than a stone's throw from the worst rookeries in town, and hated himself for feeling inadequate.

Ever since that awkward interrogation by Lord Henry, Nick had been quietly seething inside. He was angry about the forced marriage. He was angry about being connected now to a haughty, aristocratic family. He was angry at the way Pru was ignored, overlooked, or insulted by her own relations. He was angry at her father for assuming he would not take proper care of her.

Just about the only person he wasn't angry with was Pru herself. None of this was her fault. She was as trapped as he was. Yes, he hated the fact that she had some money of her own while he had so little, but he couldn't fault her for that. He couldn't even fault her for not telling him about her background. Nick could not recall a single time when he'd asked about it.

What he hated most of all, what he was most angry about, was that he'd let these high-and-mighty people get under his skin, with their fine houses and their elegant clothes and their expensive wine. He was every bit as good as they were, damn it all. No, he was better, for he had spent his adult life fighting to help the ordinary working-class people whose efforts allowed families like the Armitages to lead lives of privilege and indolence. Yet somehow these pampered aristocrats who'd done nothing of particular value in their lives had managed to make him feel awkward and inferior.

With Lord Henry, Nick had felt like an ineligible

suitor failing miserably to plead his case. He clearly thought Nick unworthy of Pru, which Nick supposed he was. But confound it, *he* had not been the one to force the marriage.

The strangeness of the day had carried through into the evening. He'd dressed carefully and arrived at Lord Henry's home promptly at seven, and then sat down to dinner with the five gentlemen who'd accosted him like a gang of ruffians that morning in his front hall. Their welcome had been surprisingly warm and friendly—the morning's contretemps either forgotten or forgiven. He'd been slapped genially, but soundly, on the back so many times, he was surely bruised.

He'd sat to Pru's right at a table where she was the only female. And none of the Armitage men, even her father, seemed prepared to modify his behavior in deference to feminine sensibilities. His sister, Edwina, would have applauded such equal treatment, as would Nick if he thought it had anything to do with the rights of women. It was no such thing. Pru was simply invisible to them. The talk was loud and general, the language sometimes rough, the drinking deep.

Pru said very little, but did not seem overly uncomfortable. Of course, she was probably accustomed to such rackety meals, having experienced them all her life. Nick had been so thoroughly aggravated with the way Pru was overlooked by this company of rogues, he had been on the verge of saying something when Lord Henry rose to his

feet. His commanding presence brought his boisterous sons to silence.

"I should like you all," he said, "to raise your
glasses to your sister."

Bravo, Nick had thought. Finally.

Everyone did as Lord Henry asked, after a footman had refilled all their glasses.

"She leaves us this day," Lord Henry continued,
"to begin a new life as Mrs. Nicholas Parrish. The
circumstances were not, I daresay, as upright as
she might have preferred. Or as romantic."

Her brothers chuckled and chortled until their
father's steely gaze shut them up.

"However, Prudence is respectably married
now, and I have every hope that she and Parrish
will make a good life together." He lifted his glass
high. "Here is to Mr. and Mrs. Parrish. May they
live long and happily together."

"Hear! Hear!" rang out in a chorus around the
table.

Nick had clinked his glass against Pru's, and
could swear there were tears building up in her
eyes. She had looked away, though, and quickly
composed herself.

"It will be downright quiet around here without you, Prudie," William said, eliciting howls of
laughter from his brothers.

Her shyness, her diffidence, was obviously
some kind of family joke. She smiled at her brothers' teasing—somewhat wistfully, Nick thought,
as though she might actually miss it.

Wine and more wine was poured until Nick wondered if he would be able to stand properly. Pru drank very little. Only he and William spoke to her. The others seemed to forget she was there. In fact, if Nick had not stood up, none of them would have noticed when she rose to leave the men to their port.

Nick had made his excuses soon after, since he and Pru were due at the theater.

"If you don't mind my saying so," Nick had said when they were on their way, "I believe I've had enough of your brothers for one day."

Pru gave a shy smile. "They *can* be overwhelming. But they're all good men. I do believe I shall miss them."

"And will they miss you?" Would they even notice she was gone?

She shrugged. "They are all very busy with their own lives, so I doubt they will have time to think about me." She gave a little chuckle. "Except, perhaps, when their morning coffee isn't quite right or the dinner menu doesn't include their favorite dishes."

Pru had no doubt run the household for them without their even realizing it. Nick could not feel sorry for them if their lives ran less smoothly from now on. It would serve them right, for taking her for granted for too long. She was the spinster sister who would always be there to take care of the tedious little details of their daily lives, and they never saw the intelligent, sweet woman so deserving of their regard. It quite cheered him up to know that they would no longer have Pru at their beck and call.

Before he realized what he was doing, he'd taken her hand and squeezed it.

The gathering in the Duke of Norwich's box at Drury Lane was no less boisterous than the one on Brooke Street. Arabella and her young friends and cousins were crackling with the excitement of a first evening in town. Their parents and aunts and uncles enjoyed themselves equally. The box was filled to bursting, and no one paid any attention to the performance on stage. Arabella, who seemed one of the few members of her family who truly appreciated Pru, gushed over the new marriage and insisted on celebrating, despite her mother's obvious reluctance to see anyone but her daughter, or herself, as the center of attention.

Arabella had swallowed whole the story of their supposed love match, and was agog with the romance of it all. Bottles of champagne were ordered and poured almost without stopping. Most of the women, save for young Arabella, ignored Pru and flirted outrageously with Nick. He, in turn, ignored them all, and downed glass after glass of champagne.

He had been embarrassed for Pru, but again, she did not seem at all offended to be so universally overlooked. She did not cower behind a curtain, but she might as well have done, for all the notice she was given. What was wrong with these people that they didn't appreciate Pru's gentle nature and quiet intelligence?

Nick had watched those women, dripping in hauteur and jewels, and hated them, and not only for their treatment of Pru. They flaunted precisely the sort of social arrogance the mobs in France had risen up against. Were these British elite so secure in their privilege?

Pru was looking down at the hands in her lap, still and silent as a nun, while the carriage bounced along the uneven cobbles of Coventry Street. No doubt, she was feeling just as discomposed as he was, frustrated at the turn her life had taken that morning. Nick had known her for four years, and all along quiet little Pru had been a part of the aristocratic world he disdained. He had never guessed, but wondered if he might have done, if he had not ignored her as thoroughly as did her own family. He was only now coming to realize he'd done that, and was ashamed for it.

One thing about Pru, though, was that she would never complain that his connections were far from noble, or that he was not a rich man. He knew that much about her. Or so he believed. As for his modest town house, at least it was one with which she was familiar. She had spent a great deal of time there these last few years. Perhaps it would not be too painful an upheaval—for Pru, anyway—for her to stay on permanently.

Nick studied her in the near darkness of the carriage. He could make out the rampant curls of her hair, the slender column of her neck, the slope of her shoulders. Out of that Viking horde of a family—tall, blond, boldly handsome—any one of the women was more striking than Pru. That morning he'd been concerned that he might not be able to conjure up enough desire to bed her. But that was because, like everyone else, he'd never paid her any notice. He had done so today, however, and found she was more attractive, in a quiet sort of way, than he'd imagined.

Even so, Nick was still uncomfortable about consummating the marriage. This was Pru, after all. She was almost like a sister. The notion of bedding her seemed so damned awkward. He kept watching her, trying to see her as someone other than a sisterly colleague, trying to imagine making love to a woman so shy, a woman who trembled whenever he touched her hand.

Pru seemed to sense his gaze on her and looked up. Even in the dark he could see the apprehension in her eyes. She must surely be dreading the same thing as he. Poor old Pru. She wasn't ready for physical intimacy with a husband she never wanted.

Nick wasn't ready, either. He was too drunk and too angry to make the effort. He'd done enough playacting for one day. No doubt Pru would appreciate a reprieve for the time being. In the meantime, Nick would have to figure out how he was ever to approach intimacy with this quiet, unassertive, little mouse of a woman whose background was everything he despised.

Pru's knees were actually shaking while Nick unlocked the front door. She was entering the house for the first time as his wife, and she was about to discover, at long last, what it was like to have a man make love to her. A man she had loved to distraction for years.

She had dreamed of such a night, but in the privacy of her own fantasies, Nicholas had been equally in love with her. In her dreams, she was transformed into a beautiful woman whose loveliness was irresistible to him. She had dreamed of his arms around her, of him loving her.

She'd always known the dream was foolish and fanciful. But then, she could never in a thousand years have imagined how things would turn out. Tonight was no dream. Instead, she must face the reality of what was about to happen—not with a man who returned her love, but with a man who did not love her and did not want her. The intimacy would be as forced as the marriage ceremony that morning.

How was it possible, she wondered, to want something so badly and dread it at the same time?

"I am sorry there is no servant to let us in," Nick said as he opened the door and stepped into the hallway to light a candle. "I've never had any live-in servants here, but perhaps you will want to hire someone."

"Oh." Pru could hardly speak for thinking of what was about to happen. Was her nightgown pretty enough? Would he snuff the candles and give her the advantage of total darkness? Would she die of embarrassment?

"We'll talk about all those practical matters in

the morning," he said. "It's been a long day. And a bit trying, eh?"

"A bit." She kept her voice as soft as possible in hopes he would not hear its tremor.

He led the way up the stairs, and Pru had to hold tightly to the rail. Oh God oh God oh God. It was really happening. She was going upstairs—all the way upstairs—with Nicholas.

When they reached the second floor, he said, "I had your bandbox brought up here, to Edwina's old bedchamber."

He stepped into the room and lit a small branch of candles. Pru had been here often, before Edwina was married. It looked more like a guest room now, with all her friend's personal items gone, including a beautiful picture of Psyche that Pru had admired. It had been painted by Edwina's mother, so of course she would have taken it with her.

The room had been made ready for her. Lucy, the part-time maid, had surely been at work here. Pru's bandbox, sent over from Brooke Street that afternoon, was tucked in a corner, and its contents already emptied. The one morning dress she'd packed was hanging on a peg inside the open wardrobe. There was a basin and pitcher of water set out, with linen towels and a bar of soap. A small vase of spring flowers sat on the dressing table, where her own toiletries had also been set out.

"I thought you would be most comfortable in this room," Nick said. After lighting the candles, he had moved to stand in the doorway.

"Yes, thank you."

Pru's cheeks flamed when she saw her night-gown had been laid out on the bed. It was the prettiest one she owned, with lovely lace edges and white-on-white embroidery. Had Nick seen it? She could not bear to look at him.

"Well, um . . ." He seemed nervous, unsure of what to do next.

He must be feeling as awkward as she was. Pru wished she could make it easier for him by an-swering in advance the questions he was no doubt trying to ask. Yes, she would like a few min-utes alone. Yes, she would be ready when he re-turned. Yes, he could join her on the bed. Yes and yes and yes.

But she would be too mortified to say any such thing, too nervous to do anything more than nod when he asked. But why did he not ask and get it over with? He still stood awkwardly in the door-way, a frown creasing his brow.

"Well, I will say good night, then."

Good night?

"Mrs. Gibb always sets out breakfast in the back parlor. I, um, wasn't sure if you preferred tea or coffee."

Breakfast? He wouldn't see her until breakfast? The air in her lungs suddenly felt thin, starving her of breath.

"Tea. Th-thank you." She had no idea where those words had come from, how she'd managed to form them with her mouth when she could barely breathe.

He wasn't coming to her. He wasn't going to make love to her.

"Tea. Right. So, I will, um, see you at breakfast. Good night, Pru."

He turned on his heel and left. Pru stood frozen in the middle of the room. She heard him open and close the door to the room next to hers.

He was not coming back.

She stood and listened to the sounds of him moving about. He would be able to hear her as well. He would know she hadn't moved. What a fool he must think her.

She forced one foot in front of the other and walked to the open door. She closed it, then tried to empty her mind of despair while she undressed. It was difficult without a maid to untie her corset strings in the back. But she could not have borne the presence of a maid, or anyone else, just now. She had to bear this humiliation alone.

A short time later, she lay in her bed and stared at the door. She couldn't keep her eyes from it. It was just possible she had misunderstood. He might come after all. He *might*.

No. He wasn't coming back.

She was a great goose to think Nicholas would walk through that door. He was a gentleman with a powerful sense of honor. It had driven him to marry her, and now kept him from her bed. At least, that was what she wanted to believe.

She wished he were not quite so honorable. But then, she did not offer much of a temptation to behave dishonorably. Even in her beautiful lace nightgown.

Was this to be the first of endless nights spent in the dark, staring at that door? Lord, how was she to bear this marriage?

She turned away, buried her face in the pillow, and wept.

Nick wasn't surprised to find Pru in the back parlor when he came downstairs the next morning. He'd heard her up and about early, but he deliberately stayed in his own bedchamber until he was certain she was gone. Cowardly, to be sure, but he had not wanted to run into her in the close confines of the upstairs corridor.

A tilt-top tea table was usually kept flat against a wall in the back parlor, but was opened and set in the middle of the room for meals. Ever since the Crimson Ladies—the colorists for the magazine's engravings—had taken over the dining room for their use, Nick and his sister had taken most of their meals either here or in the front drawing room.

Pru sat at the table sipping tea and reading some loose, handwritten pages. She looked up at his entrance, removed her spectacles, and blushed.

Damn. This whole business was so blasted awkward.

"Good morning," he said, and took a seat opposite her.

She scooted back her chair, and in a sudden rush of words, said, "I have just finished my tea. I have much to do today, having missed a whole day's work yesterday. I need to finish these edits and review some of the advertising contracts. I will leave you to your breakfast and newspaper." She rose to leave, as if she couldn't bear to be in the same room with him.

"Please stay a moment, Pru. Sit down. We have a great deal to talk about."

She looked thoroughly flustered, poor girl. He hated what this marriage had done to her. Theirs had been a perfectly comfortable friendship until yesterday. Now she could barely look him in the eye, so shy of him they might have been complete strangers rather than friends of several years.

She appeared to have had as little sleep as he did. There were purplish shadows beneath her eyes, which were reddened from lack of sleep. No, not that. She'd been crying. Damn, damn, damn.

"Please, Pru. It's important we talk about"—his hands made a vague gesture encompassing the breakfast table and the two of them—"all this."

She sat back down, perched on the edge of her chair like a governess, her back ramrod straight. "May I pour you tea?" she asked. "Or coffee?"

Nick had been about to reach for the coffee pot, but decided to let Pru do it for him. Her first wifely duty, he supposed. "Coffee, please. With just a touch of cream."

He watched her pour and was pleased to see that her hands were steady. She looked so uneasy, he had half expected the cup to rattle with her trembling. She had beautiful hands. He'd never noticed before. Slender, long fingers and perfectly shaped nails. Just like his mother's. An artist's hands. He wondered if she painted.

How little they knew each other, after all.

He filled his plate from the dishes of food that had been set out, and thought of what he wanted to say. He'd tossed and turned throughout the night, unable to silence the thoughts that agitated his brain. Anger. Frustration. Self-pity. Blame. In one day his life had changed so dramatically, it was difficult even to grasp it all. He had not wanted marriage in his life yet. He had certainly not wanted Pru. He had big plans, big dreams, and this marriage interfered with everything.

And it was his own fault. If only he'd taken more care about not being alone in the house with Pru. If only he'd insisted on driving her home before he left for the evening. If only he'd checked the office before going upstairs to bed.

If only.

The words had rung in his head throughout the night. After all that sleepless agitation, however, he'd come to a firm decision. He would *not* let this marriage ruin his life. Or Pru's. Wallowing in blame and self-pity wouldn't help matters. The thing was done. It had to be faced. Nick had determined to waste no more time feeling sorry for himself, and Pru needed to do the same. They needed to concentrate on making this marriage work, as unwanted as it was to both of them.

"I believe we must discuss how we are to go

on," he said. "We are married, Pru. I know you didn't want this any more than I did, but what's done is done. We must accept it."

"I know." Her voice was softer even than usual

"We've always been friends. That should count for something. We can make the best of this situation, over time."

"Yes, of course."

She still wouldn't look up at him. He needed to see her eyes. He reached across the table and tilted her chin until she was forced to look up. He almost wished he had not done so. The misery in those big blue eyes was almost palpable. Poor Pru. He had done this to her with his casual indifference to her presence in his house.

"I am dreadfully sorry." He kept his hand on her chin, stroking it with his thumb, trying to soothe the faint tremble that proclaimed her nervousness. "I know you must be heartsick about all this, but we will work it out. We will. But my dear, we should not waste time and energy lamenting what might have been, or resenting each other, or blaming each other. It is pointless in any case, since we cannot change what is done." He looked deep into her eyes, willing her to believe him. "Pru? Do you agree?"

She took a deep breath and nodded her head. He cupped her cheek briefly—Lord, what incredibly soft skin she had—and smiled. "Thank you," he said, and removed his hand.

"M-may I ask you something?"

"Of course."

"Was there . . . was there someone else you had hoped to marry? Someone you were courting?"

"No." Thank heaven for that. No others were hurt in this business. Or were they? Dear God, what if—

"But what about you?" he asked. "Was there . . . is there someone special?"

She gave a little smile tinged with self-mockery. "There was no one I dared hope to marry, I assure you."

"Well, then. At least neither of us is breaking someone else's heart. One less obstacle to overcome. Easier for us to make the best of things. I realize you have no choice, but are you willing to try?"

"Yes." Her voice was steadier than before. "Yes, I am."

"Good girl. I do think, though, we need to move slowly. It's all been so sudden, we should take some time to get used to the idea of marriage. Even though we're friends, there is much we do not know about each other. Small things, like whether we drink tea or coffee in the morning, for example. And larger things, like our expectations of life, our hopes, our dreams. Even our backgrounds and upbringing. Yours is still a surprise to me, and I need to become more comfortable with it. I'm sure there are surprises you will discover about me as well. So we should take it day by day, and learn to live under the same roof. Does that sound agreeable to you?"

"Yes."

He smiled. "I thought it might. But there are practical matters we must discuss. I spoke with your father yesterday about . . . money."

Her eyes grew wide. "Oh, you musn't worry about that. I should not be a burden on your income. I have a bit of money of my own. In fact I—"

"Yes, I know. Your father told me about your inheritance. But I want you to understand, Pru, that I would never touch your money. It is yours to use as you please."

"But I am happy for you to have it," she said. "I know you have plans and could certainly use it."

"No."

"But what about the factory in—"

"No, Pru. And that is final. Your money stays with you." It pained him to know that so much money was within his reach, but he could not, would not, take it from her. Besides, he was certain of some decent profits from Amsterdam very shortly, and that would help his project in Derby get off the ground. The warehouse there would not remain empty much longer, but it would be fitted out through his own efforts, not by relying on his wife's fortune.

"I will do my best to make you comfortable here," he said. "I have enough for that. But you must tell me if there are any changes you wish to make, or if there is anything you need. Servants, for example. I had thought perhaps to bring Lucy in on a full-time basis, if she will agree to it. And if you would like to hire a lady's maid, of course you must do so."

"That won't be necessary, if Lucy is here. Please do not think I am used to luxury, Nicholas. I am not. My father is not a rich man, you know. There were nine of us living on Brooke Street. It was quite cramped at times. And I never had a lady's maid of my own. I always made do with one of the housemaids. There is no reason I cannot do the same here. If you like, I can speak to Lucy about it."

"Thank you, Pru, that would be fine. And there is also the matter of Mrs. Gibb. She only comes in the mornings and prepares everything for the day. She has come in to cook a hot supper when we've asked, if we had guests, for example. But I thought we should ask her if she would like to expand her role in the kitchen, to come on full-time. There are servants' rooms on the top floor, so both she and Lucy could both live in."

"Are you certain, Nicholas? I do not wish to be the cause of more upheaval than necessary."

"It is no great upheaval to make things a bit more comfortable and orderly. I've been too careless of household matters since Edwina left, I'm afraid. I'm not very good with those sorts of details."

"If you are quite sure you want to make these changes, then you may leave it to me. I shall speak to Lucy and Mrs. Gibb. And I will take a look at the rooms upstairs to make sure they are ready for use."

"I can see you will take your wifely duties seriously." He smiled at her, and she blushed.

He knew what duties she was thinking of, and

it had nothing to do with the household help. It was something they needed to discuss, though. He took a deep breath.

"There is one more thing," he said, and felt uncommonly fidgety and anxious. "I intend to honor my vows, Pru. This will be a real marriage, in every respect."

Her blush grew brighter, spreading to her ears and all down her throat, and she shifted nervously on her chair. She didn't want this, dammit. Well, neither did he, but there was no escaping it.

"I know how difficult this is for you, my dear. It is for both of us. But if this marriage is to work, it must be a complete one. I think, though, that we should wait a while before . . . before taking that step."

She sucked in a sharp breath and seemed to hold it. Was she relived?

"It is all too new," he continued. "And we both need time to overcome the anger and distress over this unexpected union. We shall give ourselves time to adjust to the idea of being married. I shall not impose myself on you, Pru. I will wait until I am sure you are ready for . . . something more. All right?"

She nodded, but didn't look at him. She was such a shy little thing, this conversation must be mortifying for her.

"Don't worry, my dear," he said. "We shall rub along well together. You'll see."

She rose so abruptly, she had to grab the chair back to keep it from falling over. "I must go," she said. "These edits . . ." She picked up the pages and clasped them tightly. "I have work to do. If you will excuse me."

And she bolted from the room like a rabbit. Poor girl. If Nick was feeling awkward and angry, how much more so must Pru feel? Women gave up so much more in a marriage than did men. They lost their names and their identities as individuals, they were uprooted from their families, their fortunes and their bodies no longer belonged to them but to a husband.

Pru must know he would never subvert her needs to his own. He would never ask her to sacrifice her will to his. Surely she knew that. He would certainly never take away her fortune. As to her body . . . that was a different matter. He would take it eventually. He would have to, if there was ever to be a family. And he wanted children someday. It must be a mutual giving and taking, though, and so he would wait.

Nick found it difficult to imagine Pru as a bed partner. For one thing, he had no sense of the body beneath all those layers of muslin. She revealed very little, keeping herself all wrapped up in fichus and scarves and such. And she was so closed in and shy. Would she be too shy to express passion? Too inhibited to be truly involved? He had no experience with such a woman. He would not know what to do.

One of her cousins had made a snide remark about how the quiet ones always surprised you. He hoped to God Pru would surprise him.

Chapter 6

Pru dropped her forehead on the desk and wrapped her arms over her head, as though she couldn't bear to show her crimson face even to the empty room. She'd never been so embarrassed in all her life.

Nicholas must think her a complete goose for running away like that, but how could she be expected to speak of such things and not be mortified to her fingertips? Last night she had been perfectly willing to *do* the thing that would make their marriage complete, but she never in a million years expected they would actually talk about it.

She supposed she ought to be happy that he did, after all, intend to make love with her. Sometime. Later. When he was sure she was ready.

But she *was* ready. More than ready. She would,

of course, rather die than tell him so. She wondered how he was supposed to know when the time was right. Pru hoped with all her heart that he didn't expect her to walk up to him and announce, "I'm ready." If he did, she feared this marriage would never be consummated, for she could no more say such a thing than jump over the moon.

She groaned aloud. She was seven-and-twenty years old. It was high time she overcame such maidenly self-consciousness. Yet, no matter how hard she tried, she could not help blushing clear down to her toes at the very thought of making love with Nicholas. No, that was not entirely true. She could *think* about it. She had dreamed about it for years. But in her dreams he had held her in his arms and kissed her, and the only words spoken were words of love. He never spoke about what they were *doing*. And in her imagination it was always pitch dark when it was done, so she never had to actually visualize it.

If he thought she could openly admit to him that she was ready to do it, anxious to do it, *dying to do it*, then he didn't know her very well at all.

Or perhaps she had misunderstood. Pru was not particulaly knowledgeable about such matters, after all. Maybe men did have ways of knowing when a woman wanted . . . *it*. Perhaps there were signals of some kind. If there were, though, she certainly did not know them, and would probably be no less embarrassed to use them if she did.

She was doomed to be a spinster wife.

Pru lifted her head and sighed. The papers on the desk were now creased. Blast. As though it were not enough having one's life turned topsy-turvy overnight, there was still the magazine to publish. She had work to do.

For the next hour she forced aside all thoughts of marriage and Nicholas and *being ready*, and concentrated on the last of the edits due at the printer in three days. When those were finished, she sought out Lucy and Mrs. Gibb and discussed an expansion of their roles. Both were willing and happy to live in. Nicholas hadn't mentioned salary, but it must surely be increased if they were each to work longer hours. She offered what she thought was fair, and hoped Nicholas would approve.

The three of them had examined the garret rooms and found them dusty but adequate. Pru noted they could use new bed linens. She thought to ask Nicholas about it, but decided she would take care of it on her own. She had already cost him enough in added expenses. Since she would manage the household accounts, he need never know if she used her own money now and then when something extra was needed.

She returned to the office and had begun reviewing the advertisements for the next issue, when the door to the office was flung open. Mrs. Flora Gallagher, the *Cabinet*'s fashion editor, stood in the doorway.

Flora was the most infamous member of the magazine's staff. She had been a rather notorious demimondaine at one time, but was said to have retired from that "profession" before coming to work for the *Cabinet* last year. She had earned a small fortune over the years, so she did not work because she needed to, but simply because she loved fashion. And gossip. The fashion reports she penned for each issue frequently dropped names of who was seen wearing what at some society event.

Pru had always been rather in awe of Flora, but liked her a great deal. She was direct and outspoken, and harbored some of the same political and social ideals as the rest of them, though she was rather more cynical about it than hopeful of any real change. She was a striking-looking woman—tall, with bright red hair, and a rather impressive bosom. And for some inexplicable reason, she had developed a particular fondness for Pru. Theirs had become a rather unconventional friendship.

She locked eyes with Pru for a long moment as she stood in the doorway, then grinned broadly and said, "You sly puss."

Flora stepped into the office, closing the door behind her, and took a seat in the chair opposite the desk. She continued to stare, and Pru felt her cheeks flame.

"Is it true, then?" Flora asked. "You and Nicholas are married?"

"Yes, I'm afraid so."

"Afraid? My girl, you should be dancing in the streets. To have that delicious man all to yourself? My, what a coup."

"It was not a coup, Flora. More like a disaster."

Flora studied her with concern. "Tell me what happened."

And Pru did. The words spilled out in a bubbling frenzy, like champagne that had been shaken too much before the cork was released. Without Edwina to talk to, or her favorite cousin Joanna, Pru had bottled up everything inside her. It was a great relief finally to tell someone everything she'd been feeling since waking up in this office yesterday morning.

"He has not bedded you, then?"

"Flora!" Pru's cheeks flamed hotter.

"Well, obviously he has not, or you would not be in such a dismal state this morning. You would be walking on air. I have no doubt that man knows a thing or two about pleasing a woman. I can always tell, you know. He has a certain look in those lovely dark eyes."

"And I am just about the last woman on earth in whose direction he would ever cast those eyes. He's ten times more beautiful than I could ever be, Flora. It's monstrous that he should be saddled with a little dowd like me."

"A little dowd?"

Pru shrugged. "I know how to use a mirror."

"But not your brain, apparently. Good God, girl, do you think I managed to interest men with my looks alone? I've never been a beauty. But I recognize my best assets and know how to show them to advantage."

Pru's gaze involuntarily dropped to Flora's bosom. When she realized where she was looking, she quickly lifted her eyes to find Flora smiling. "That is, of course, one of my best assets. But not my only one, I assure you. My point is that you are foolish to assume you are not beautiful enough for Nicholas. You are a very attractive young woman, my dear. If you made a bit of an effort you could knock the man flat. Besides, you have more than beauty. You have brains. You have compassion. You are talented with your pen, and probably in other ways I don't know about. I will not have you believing you are not good enough for him. He is lucky to have you, whether either of you knows it or not. And so, you must take him to bed, my girl, the sooner the better."

Was Pru the only one uncomfortable speaking of such private matters? Nicholas, at least, recognized her uneasiness. She had a feeling Flora would not moderate her conversation no matter how embarrassing it was for Pru. Of course, Flora was a bit of an expert in this area. There could be no better confidante, if Pru needed encouragement or advice.

"H-he has suggested we wait," she said.

Flora raised her eyebrows.

"He thinks we were too rushed, and we should take time to become accustomed to each other."

"Hmm. And how long does he intend to wait?"

"I . . . I don't know." Until he realized she was *ready*.

"Well, let's hope it is not long. You must make yourself irresistible to him."

Pru gave a little bark of laughter. "Me? Irresistible?"

"Don't be a fool, my girl. Any woman can make a man take notice of her. It's a matter of self-confidence." She leaned back in her chair and narrowed her eyes. "You do have some small portion of confidence, do you not?"

Pru gave a little shrug. "I don't know. I suppose so."

Flora pursed her lips and shook her head. "This will not do, my girl. If you ever hope to make this marriage work, you must assert yourself. Nicholas will not want a timid little mouse of a wife. Show him you are made of sterner stuff. Show him you are more than worthy of him."

"How?"

Flora continued to shake her head in obvious frustration. "Heavens, Pru, are you that unsure of yourself?"

"Yes, I am." How pathetic she sounded. The sting of tears was building up behind her eyes. Before she could stop herself, in a tiny whisper of a voice she said, "Help me, Flora. Please."

She could not look up, ashamed at behaving in such an abject manner. Good Lord, she had sunk into a bog of self-pity. How foolish. Nicholas had said they should not waste time repining what could not be changed, and he was right. If he, who'd got the worst end of the bargain, was willing to make their marriage work, then by God, so was she. After a moment, she felt Flora's hand take hers and squeeze it. Pru lifted her eyes.

"I am sorry to sound like such a pitiful creature," she said. "Forgive me, Flora. My emotions have been running high, and I fear I have been feeling sorry for myself."

"And why is that? You have what most women dream of. You are married to a devilishly handsome man, someone you care for deeply."

Pru gave a little gasp.

Flora smiled. "You think I didn't know? You do tend to wear your heart in your eyes, my girl."

"Oh, dear." Was it so obvious? Did everyone know? Did Nicholas?

"Don't worry, Pru. I am sensitive to such things. Not everyone is."

"Oh, dear. You d-don't think—"

"Men are *never* that sensitive. He doesn't know, I assure you."

"Oh, Flora, I would die if he knew how I felt."

"You're not going to die, my girl. All you need to do is work on making him fall in love with you, too."

Pru gave an unladylike snort. "You should write fiction instead of fashion reports. You have as romantic an imagination as Simon Westover. Perhaps you should pen the *Cabinet's* next sentimental tale instead of him."

"Bosh. There's nothing to making a man fall in love with you. And you've got proximity on your side, which can only help matters. What you need, Pru, is to believe you are worthy of his love. And of course, you are."

"How am I? I'm not remotely beautiful. I'm too small. I'm too quiet. He hates my family."

"You have filled your ledger with too many liabilities, my girl. Let us balance them with assets. First, hardly any of us is truly beautiful, but we all have good features. You have lovely blue eyes. And creamy skin."

"I have freckles."

"Charmingly sprinkled across your nose. Your smattering of freckles is most endearing, and helps to keep you looking young. A definite asset. Your hair . . ."

"I know. It's a fright."

"Not at all. It's a bit untamed, but I do admire its color, a shade more red than blond. Very distinctive. Another asset, with help from a good hairdresser. Now, stand up and come over here. Yes, that's right, I want to get a good look at you."

Feeling foolish, and decidedly lacking, Pru walked around the desk and stood before the elegant, voluptuous Mrs. Gallagher. "I'm too short, I know."

"A lack of height in a woman can make a man extraordinarily protective, which can be used to your advantage. And a small woman makes a man feel taller. They like that, you know. It is another asset." Her eyes raked Pru from top to toe. "Your wardrobe, however, is not."

Flora circled her, lifting the white muslin of her dress, running the fabric through her fingers, examining seams and construction. "You often wear this type of ill-fitting garment," Flora said. "It is time I took you in hand."

Since Pru liked to sew and often made her own clothes, including this round gown and bodice, she winced at the insult.

"You really should wear more color, my girl. Your own special peaches-and-cream coloring is not set off well in white. I'm afraid it makes you look quite pallid."

"Most of my dresses are white."

"So I have noticed. Well, we shall need to add a bit of dash. The right cut and fabric, the right accessories can make all the difference. It would do you no harm to pay closer attention to our fashion plates, and my fashion reports. Now, as to your figure, you are delicate-boned and slender, which means you can carry your clothes with more flair. Let me see . . ."

Pru squealed when Flora grabbed the back of her muslin bodice and pulled it tight.

"Pru! You have a bosom!"

"Flora!"

"Well, one would never know it with all the fichus and tuckers and handkerchiefs you use as disguise. Most definitely an asset. Here, let me unpin this and see what we have."

Pru reached up to clasp the whitework fichu crossed over the bodice of her dress. "Flora, please!"

"For heaven's sake, girl, don't be such a ninny. If you won't remove a simple fichu in front of me, how do you ever hope to bare all in front of Nicholas?"

Pru gulped.

"You did ask for my help," Flora said. "I just want to see what we have to work with. Now, take your hands away and let me unpin this thing."

Pru did as she was asked. There was little choice with someone like Flora. The lace pins were removed and the fichu unwrapped. The bodice edge, cut low to allow a shirt or tucker, skimmed the top of her stays, exposing a great deal of bare skin. Pru shivered. She started to lift her hands to cover herself, but Flora took them and held them out to her side.

"My dear Mrs. Parrish, you have been hiding your light under a bushel. Mr. Parrish has a surprise in store. With the right dress, you could have him eating out of your hand."

"But I feel quite naked."

"Get used to it, my dear. Your husband will want to see a great deal more of you, I'm sure. Now, we must contrive some sort of evening affair where you can wear something suitably revealing."

"There is no need to contrive. My niece is coming out this Season, and my sister has a long list of events I will be expected to attend. A ball for Arabella is being held next week."

"Excellent. And do not tell me you already have a dress to wear. I am sure it is not at all the right thing. We must visit Madame Lanchester at once so she has time to make something up for you."

"Is she terribly expensive?"

"She can be. But we do have some influence with her, since we so often mention her creations in the *Cabinet*. I am sure we can work something out. Besides, I thought you said you had an inheritance."

"I do, but I hadn't thought to fritter it away on clothes. There are . . . other things I had hoped to do with it."

"Then I shall see that we don't fritter away too much of it. But you absolutely *must* have a decent ball gown. Think of all those cousins whose noses you could put out of joint. A beautiful gown, a beautiful husband. They will be pea-green with envy."

Pru chuckled. She had to admit, it would be rather nice. "All right. I defer to your judgment, Flora. Only please, nothing *too* revealing. I am not at all comfortable being so exposed, regardless of how fashionable it is."

"We shall see. But let us return to your assets."

Pru took a step backward. "I'm not taking off anything else."

Flora laughed and hitched one hip onto the edge of the desk. "Of course not. Whatever assets are hidden beneath your skirts will be for Nicholas to discover. No, I am talking about other assets. You will need every ounce of confidence you can muster if you truly want to engage your husband's affections. I daresay he is not the sort of man to appreciate timidity."

"I am sure you are right," Pru said. She crossed the fichu over her bosom once again, and began to secure it with the lace pins. "That is one reason I have been so anxious. I fear I can never be the wife he wants. I can't help being shy."

"There is nothing wrong with being shy. It, too, can be an endearing asset, if used properly. But to be too self-effacing, too meek, too timid, will not endear you to him. You can retain your public shyness, which he may find charming, but I do think you must make an effort to be open and comfortable when alone with him. To do that, you must believe yourself worthy of him. And you are."

Was she? Pru was not so sure about that.

"Yes, you are," Flora repeated, as though reading her thoughts. "You are well-educated and well-read. Nicholas appreciates that. You are remarkably well born. He may not like that so much at first, but he will learn soon enough the advantages to having a wife with such connections. Especially if he decides on a career in politics. Do not underestimate your value to him in that arena, Pru."

She had not considered that. He might find her connections distasteful, but they could be useful to him over time.

"So, you see," Flora said, "your assets far outweigh any perceived liabilities. You are a valuable person, a treasure to your friends, and more than worthy of any man. Even Nicholas Parrish."

Pru swallowed the lump in her throat and blinked back tears. "Thank you, Flora."

"It is perfectly true. Just don't let yourself forget it."

"I won't forget," Pru said. "I am not so insecure as all that. I have actually been quite content with myself for years, once I realized I would never be as glamorous as the rest of my family. It's just that being married to Nicholas, I have become more than ever aware of my shortcomings. I thank you for reminding me that I have something to offer."

"And I shall keep reminding you, I promise."

"What I don't know is how to to project that attitude you talk about. How to let him know that I am"—*ready!*—"interested. I get so shy around him. I'd like to know how to . . . flirt."

Flora sputtered into a laugh. "Flirt?"

Pru's cheeks flamed. "Yes. Don't you think I should?"

"Oh, I most definitely think you should."

"But I don't know how. I've always been too shy around gentlemen. Can you show me what to do?"

Flora tilted her head to one side as she studied Pru. "I suspect you will be a tough case, my girl. But I suppose it is worth a try. Shall I teach you a few tricks?"

"Yes, please."

"All right, then. Now, pay attention."

Some time later, their lesson was interrupted by a raucous explosion of voices from the front of the house.

"Ah. The Ladies are here," Flora said.

The Crimson Ladies were colorists for the magazine's engravings. Flora had hired the blowsy crew of street prostitutes last year to hand-color the fashion plates, and Edwina had christened them the Crimson Ladies, which they all thought a grand joke. Illiterate, bawdy, and coarse, they were nevertheless adept at coloring the fashion plates—in their own bold style.

"There is a lovely spotted muslin petticoat and jacket in one of this month's plates," Flora said. "I had better go make sure they understand it is not leopard skin."

She walked to the door and opened it, but turned again toward Pru. "Remember to save tomorrow afternoon. We are going to Madame Lanchester's showrooms. And mind what I've said, my girl. You *are* worthy of him. Repeat it to yourself like a litany, until it becomes second nature." She left the office and closed the door behind her.

I am worthy of him. It still didn't sound all that convincing to Pru. But Flora was right. If she continued to be intimidated by his perfection, she would never be a proper wife to Nicholas.

I am worthy of him. I am worthy of him.

Perhaps if she repeated it enough she would come to believe it.

Pru turned back to the desk, intending to resume her work on the advertising copy. But on her way to the desk, she tried the seductive walk Flora had taught her, with an exaggerated swing of hips that still did not feel quite right. Perhaps she should practice.

She walked back and forth across the room, again and again, hitching her hips from side to side with each step. But it felt silly, not at all right.

Why should it be so difficult to glide seductively across a room? She could dance well enough. In fact, she loved to dance. Maybe she ought to think of music, of walking and swaying in time to music.

So she hummed a tune and walked in time to it, swinging her hips with each step. This was easier. But it wasn't a normal way of walking, surely, all that bumping and swaying. Flora had not looked as ridiculous when she had demonstrated the walk. Perhaps Pru's legs were simply too short to do justice to it. But she continued to practice, humming an old song as she bumped and swished her way across the floor.

"Pru?"

She froze. *Oh, no.* Please God, let him not have been standing there long. She turned around very, very slowly. Nicholas stood in the doorway, a puzzled frown creasing his brow.

"Are you all right?" he asked.

She cast him a quizzical look.

"Have you hurt yourself? You were walking so strangely I thought you might have injured yourself in some way. Have you wrenched a muscle?"

Her cheeks flamed. The first full day of her marriage was turning out to be one humiliation after another. "I am quite all right, I assure you. I was just . . ." She could not admit that she was attempting a seductive walk. He would be certain to burst out laughing. She gave a vague gesture and said nothing more, then walked to the desk and sat down.

"Well, then," he said, and stepped into the room.

"I have just come from Simon's, and he asked me to deliver his Busybody column for the next issue." He took the pages from inside his waistcoat and placed them on the desk. "He said he will have the next installment of his latest romantic tale—I've forgotten the title—by tomorrow."

"Thank you."

He sank into the chair opposite the desk. "Have you had a chance to speak with Lucy and Mrs. Gibb?"

She told him of the arrangements she'd made, and he seemed pleased. He even approved the salary increases she had settled on the two servants, and Pru gave a sigh of relief. He was trying hard, she knew, to make everything as comfortable for her as possible. He was such a dear man.

"I have a meeting with Thurgood late this afternoon about the proposed factory bill," he said. "But I shall return home for supper. We are not promised somewhere tonight, are we?"

"No, not tonight."

"Good. Then I shall join you for supper later."

When he'd gone, Pru found it impossible to concentrate on her work. She could not stop thinking of how ridiculous she must have looked earlier when practicing Flora's walk. Nicholas must have thought she was limping. She giggled at the memory. It was probably best to stick to her normal way of walking.

Pru was prepared to heed Flora's advice on fashion and attitude, but she needed a few more lessons on flirtation before putting any of it into practice. She might end up scaring him off rather then enticing him.

Perhaps flirtation had been a foolish idea. How could she even think of flirting when she could barely look at the man without blushing? Especially after that mortifying discussion about waiting until she was ready. Every time he looked at her, he would be wondering, "Is she ready?" And she would know he wondered, and would blush and stammer and tremble so that he would never know how ready she was.

What a provoking situation.

It was amazing what a difference one quiet little woman could make. Nick had thought, had hoped, that Pru's presence in his house would not be too unsettling. She had always been so reserved and unassuming. She still was. But she nonetheless managed to keep Nick unsettled.

She had taken care of the new arrangements with Lucy and Mrs. Gibb. She had even suggested that Mrs. Gibb could use some help in the scullery, and he had capitulated. Until a few days ago there had been no full-time servants employed in the house. Now there were three. What next? A boot boy?

Nick was a bit irritated at the additional cost. It was not that he couldn't afford it, but he had hoped to buy more cargo shares in the shipments of sugar to Amsterdam on the *Ulysses*. He needed to recoup some of the losses of February, when storms had swallowed up two shiploads of profit.

One of the most aggravating aspects of this marriage was the fact that he could not simply do as he wished with his money and economize at home as necessary. He had a wife to consider now. He could not in good conscience ask Pru to cut back so he could buy cargo shares that might be lost in the end. He was perfectly willing to take the risk when there was no one to please but himself. He could no longer do that, now that he had a wife. Besides, he had promised Lord Henry he would not pauper his daughter.

So Nick had gritted his teeth and let the investment opportunity pass. In return he got hot meals and a well-ordered house. Sometimes, it did not seem such a bad bargain.

There was something even more unsettling, though, than Pru's competent housewifery. In the few short days she'd been ensconced in the house on Golden Square, Nick was constantly aware of her presence. If he'd been even half as conscious of her before, he would never have got himself into this mess. Now he was acutely aware of her every movement in the house, especially in the bedchamber next to his. He kept thinking of their conversation that first morning, and her skittishness when he hinted at consummating their marriage. He would stay true to his word. He would not rush her.

He could not, though, stop thinking about it, about what sort of bed partner she would be. He began to notice things about her. The graceful way she moved. The length of her neck. The line of her jaw. The clear blue of her eyes. The intriguing way her hair was never quite tamed, with soft, wayward curls bouncing out in all directions. He wondered what it would feel like to run his fingers through that hair, to bury his nose in it.

Such thoughts always stopped him in his tracks. Pru was not remotely the type of woman he desired. Was it a sort of perverse contrariness—because he had promised to leave her alone, he suddenly found her attractive?

What rubbish. She was Pru. Sweet, gentle, shy little Pru. His friend and colleague. It was difficult to think of her as anything else.

But she was his wife now, and at some point he was going to have to take her to bed. He could hardly be blamed for taking more notice of her in a physical way.

Nick often wondered if she could read his thoughts. It seemed she blushed every time she looked at him. And she was still so self-conscious with him, he wondered if she would ever truly be prepared to let him in her bed. It had become deuced awkward to be alone with her. Their comfortable friendship had descended into a cautious, fragile alliance. When they met at breakfast, she poured his coffee, always with just the perfect amount of cream, and quietly tended to some magazine business or read a book. They spoke little, and each seemed to rush the meal. They had shared dinner only on the first night after the marriage. It had been too painfully awkward to want to repeat. Nick had spent all subsequent evenings with his friends at the Scottish Martyrs Club.

They had been married almost a week when he was summoned one morning to the office. He could hear the Ladies chattering away in the dining room. He avoided that group as much as possible, as they tended to make an embarrassing fuss over him. The office door was open and he saw Pru at Edwina's desk. She was speaking to Robbie, the printer's apprentice.

"I know it's a last-minute request," she was saying, "but I really need that inside back cover printed. We have more advertisements than we can use in the standard pages. We must use that extra bit of space."

"It will mean an additional run," Robbie said.

"Yes, I know. Tell Imber I am aware of the added expense. But mind you, it's only half a sheet, so he'd better not try to charge double."

"Yes, miss. I'll tell him." He turned to leave and almost ran into Nick. "Oh, beg your pardon, sir."

"It's all right, Robbie. Be on your way."

Nick settled into the chair opposite the desk and studied Pru. It was odd how her shyness seemed to disappear when she worked on the *Cabinet*. She was always perfectly at ease dealing with distributors and printers and such.

"He still calls you *miss*," he said.

"Yes, I know. He has been told we are married. I suppose it is just habit. Madge does the same thing."

Madge was the "supervisor" of the Crimson Ladies. She had learned to read and had taken on more responsibility. Considering Madge's street-wise sense of humor, Nick wondered if she deliberately failed to acknowledge Pru's married state because she knew there had been no consummation of the marriage.

"I am glad you are free," Pru said. "I need your advice on these book reviews. I am not at all satisfied with them."

Nick pulled the chair close to the desk and took the sheets Pru passed to him. They spent the next hour discussing the merits of the prose and the opinions of the reviewer, one of their regular contributors, and collaborating on the necessary edits. It was their first entirely comfortable conversation since they'd married.

"It's a relief to have these done," she said. "There had been so much else to do, I simply couldn't find the time to think these over properly. I appreciate your help, Nicholas."

"Anytime, my dear, though you have such a keen editorial eye, I doubt you really need any assistance. You're doing a wonderful job."

She smiled and, for once, did not blush. Perhaps he'd discovered the key to breaking through her modest reserve. Always steer the discussion back to the magazine, where she felt some level of confidence.

"Take care, though," he said. "If you continue to do such a good job, Edwina may never come back. By the way, did you ever write to her?"

"Yes, I posted a letter two days ago. Had you wanted to add something?"

"Another time, perhaps." He smiled. "She will be surprised at our news, I daresay."

"Yes, I suppose she will. And you have written to your father?"

"I have." He chuckled as he imagined the look on his father's face when he read the news. "He'll be astonished to have both his children married within the same year. He will remember you from Edwina's wedding."

"Then he is sure to be doubly astonished." A definite twinkle lit those blue eyes, and Nick realized she was laughing at herself.

"He is sure to think I am a very fortunate man."

Pru grinned at him, and he felt a tiny cracking of the awkward wall between them.

"You do remember, I hope" she said, "that Arabella's ball is tomorrow night? I'm sorry to have to drag you along. I know you do not enjoy such things, but I really see no way to avoid it."

"Of course we shall not avoid it. She is your niece and, I believe, very fond of you. Besides, I've always rather enjoyed dancing."

"Have you? It is a good thing, then, because so many of my cousins will be angling for a dance with you."

"I was not thinking of your cousins. I look forward to dancing with *you*."

She raised her eyebrows. "How do you know I won't trample on your toes?"

"Because I know you will not. I rather imagine

you are a good dancer. You have a musical sort of grace about you."

She looked at him quizzically. "Do I?"

"Yes, you do. So, we shall dance together and make the entire company jealous with our terpsichorean efforts."

He actually *was* looking forward to dancing with Pru. Despite that odd moment when he'd caught her lurching about so awkwardly in the office, she really did have a graceful way of moving. More to the point, some of the dances could be quite sensual and provocative. He might be able to use them to accustom Pru to touching and moving together, as a prelude to some later intimacy.

And all the while, he would play the lovestruck bridegroom again, for the sake of her family. Then they would return home to their separate bedchambers, to sleep alone.

What an absurd marriage this was.

Chapter 7

"**Y**ou look awful pretty, ma'am."

"Thank you, Lucy." Pru studied her reflection in the mirror. "You have done marvels with this unruly mass of curls. I only hope they don't spring out in all directions before the evening is through."

"They are well secured by the bandeau. Mrs. Gallagher showed me what to do. But if one or two curls escape, it will still look pretty."

"Are you certain I should not wear plumes to make me look taller?"

"Mrs. Gallagher says this spray of short feathers is much more fashionable."

Mrs. Gallagher says. The woman was a spellbinder. Lucy had been in a state of awe ever since Flora had suggested she might lend a hand as Pru's dresser. The young girl had already absorbed more of Flora's advice than Pru. She seemed to have memorized every word. She'd done an excellent job with Pru's hair, which had never been easily tamed. But Lucy had tucked and braided and twisted the whole curly mess around a stiffened bandeau of gold-embroidered muslin, and Pru was quite pleased with the result. She looked almost passable.

I am worthy of him.

She stood and shook out her skirts. Madame Lanchester had rushed to create tonight's dress, complaining that she hadn't been given enough time to do a proper job. But she had acquiesced in exchange for Flora's promise to feature several of her designs in the fashion plates of the next few issues of the *Cabinet*.

Pru had not been a model client. She would not agree to the deep neckline Madame had wanted. Instead, she had insisted on an additional row of lace, which Pru thought looked rather pretty, and didn't leave her feeling quite so naked. Flora had been right about color. The pale green muslin did look better than her usual white. The open robe was embellished all along the edge with gold embroidered flowers, giving an added elegance to the simple line. Madame had suggested a cut slightly less full in the skirt than usual. The style, she had said, was better suited to Pru's short stature. There had been a muttered remark about pouter pigeons, but Pru let it pass without comment.

"Here are your gloves, ma'am. And your shawl."

Pru tugged on the gloves and took one last look

in the mirror. She was still no beauty, but she did look a bit less dowdy than usual. Now, there was only Nicholas to worry about.

I am worthy of him.

She found Nicholas in the drawing room. He looked more handsome than ever, in a dark blue coat, gray satin breeches, and sparkling white linen. He wore a waistcoat of fine silvery brocade with a stand-up collar framing the intricate pleating of his shirtfront. His nearly black hair and dark eyes were set off to perfection by the crisp white folds of his neckcloth.

The old, familiar fluttering began to thrum in her breast, and Flora's litany seemed suddenly ridiculous.

"Ah, Pru." His eyes widened slightly, then ever so discreetly scanned her from head to toe. He smiled and said, "How strange that I have never before seen you in evening dress. You look lovely."

She let out the breath she'd been holding. A flush of pure pleasure heated her cheeks. He thought she looked lovely. Or at least he was kind enough to say so. She smiled and walked toward him.

"I was just fortifying myself with a splash of brandy," he said. "May I pour one for you?"

"A small one, yes. Thank you."

"That's a very pretty dress," he said, talking over his shoulder as he poured. He handed her a glass and studied her as she took a sip. "And your hair is different, too. I like it."

"Thank you." Her instinct told her the words were false flattery, mere politeness, but she dismissed that thought. If she was to carry herself with the positive attitude Flora talked about, she must at least pretend to believe him. "I have discovered Lucy has a talent for hairdressing."

"She does indeed." A hint of something—anxiety?—flickered for an instant in his eyes, then vanished as quickly. "Are you thinking you might want Lucy to take on the role of a lady's maid? We could hire another housemaid if you like."

Pru shook her head. "That won't be necessary. I certainly do not need a personal maid. I will occasionally need Lucy's help with . . . with my hair and such. That is all." She had almost mentioned corset laces, and blushed at the very idea.

"You're sure?"

"Quite sure, thank you."

"Well, then."

He took a sip of brandy and continued to study her, making Pru exceedingly uneasy. Was he thinking that even dressed in her finest, probably looking as good as she ever would, she still wasn't remotely desirable?

Again, she dismissed those thoughts and tried to remember all the assets that were supposed to offset her liabilities. Perhaps she should not have insisted on that extra row of lace after all.

Flora had given her another lesson in flirtation, but Pru was a bit nervous about putting any of it into practice tonight. She was not at all confident that she could pull it off. Instead, she would simply try to walk tall—or as tall as she was able—and think about how jealous her cousins would be when she walked into the ball looking as good as she'd ever looked and with the handsomest man in the room on her arm.

"What are you thinking about?" His voice interrupted her reverie.

She looked up to find him smiling at her.

"You had such a look on your face," he said. "Your eyes were positively twinkling. What were you thinking?"

"Oh. I was just looking forward to the ball. It will be nice to have a dancing partner. That is, if you still mean to stand up with me."

"As many times as propriety allows a lovestruck bridegroom to dance with his wife," he said. "I am looking forward to it, too."

Ah, yes. Their supposed love match. At least that pretense was easy for her to do. She could wear her heart on her sleeve and he would never know it was not an act.

"I daresay we ought to be leaving. But first"— he held up his glass— "a toast to our first ball, Mrs. Parrish."

She clinked her glass to his. "Our first ball." She swallowed the rest of the brandy and allowed its smoldering fire to soothe those few nerves that still prickled along the edges of her composure.

He took her empty glass and set it with his on a sideboard. "We had better be on our way. Are you ready?"

"Yes." She'd been *ready* that whole week, for heaven's sake.

* * *

Nick led his wife onto the dance floor for the opening set. He was relieved to do so. He'd been introduced to even more Armitage family members and been faced with several prominent aristocrats he hadn't known were related to Pru. He'd been itching to challenge her uncle, Lord Gordon, on his recent harangue in the House of Lords on the Definitive Treaty, and to quiz her cousin Lord Caldecott on his position on the proposed factory bill.

But it was neither the time nor the place for political debate, so he kept his opinions to himself and tried to be charming.

He stood across from Pru in the line and locked eyes with her. They had maintained the fiction of a love match. It would have been impossible to do otherwise, with Arabella mentioning it at every opportunity. Pru, he discovered, was quite good at the game. Too reserved to make a big show of it, she nevertheless acted the part of a besotted bride to perfection. No one would guess that dazzled look in her eye was mere playacting.

His quiet little wife was full of surprises.

Nick watched her as the rest of the couples got into place. His earlier compliment had been meant to bolster her self-confidence before facing another public ordeal, but there had been truth in it, too. She looked surprisingly pretty. Before tonight, she had always seemed to be wrapped up in layers and layers of muslin, with scarves and handkerchiefs and fichus and whatnot draped all about. He could see now that she'd been hiding a nice, petite figure beneath all that swathing. Tonight's dress was simple and narrower in the skirt than usual, and—heaven be praised—lower cut in the neckline. Not as low as most of the women lined up beside her. There was a prodigious amount of lace obscuring any real glimpse of bosom, but Nick was intrigued nonetheless.

His gaze drifted to the woman standing to Pru's left. One of the cousins. Lady Bidwell, if he recalled correctly. She was staring openly at Nick and gave a provocative smile when his eyes met hers. She lifted her brows in question. Nick knew the look well. It was an invitation—and not the first he'd received that evening.

Nick was as susceptible as the next man to such encouragement from an attractive woman. But these were Pru's relatives, for God's sake. Did they really think he would abandon her so soon, and for one of her own family?

He ignored Lady Bidwell and glanced again at Pru, who wore a faint smile, rueful and self-mocking, as though she was fully aware of the actions of her female relations. What an odd little creature she was. Did she not care that they showed her such disrespect?

The music began, and they commenced the opening figure of the dance. Nick kept his eyes on Pru—to avoid any more blatant propositions from Lady Bidwell, and to lend credence to the love match fiction.

Pru's eyes gleamed with delight as she moved through the familiar steps of the triple minor set. She was an excellent dancer, as he'd expected. She glided through each figure with impeccable grace, and seemed to absorb the music right into her bones so that she moved in perfect synchrony with it. Her taller cousins and aunts all moved with a sort of stately elegance. Pru, on the other hand, was like a tiny fluff of down, softly floating along the floor. Nick was quite charmed as he watched her.

He gave her fingers a squeeze when he took her hand to lead her down the line, and he could feel the weight of his signet ring beneath her glove. A twinge of shame pricked his conscience. He really ought to have bought her another ring, but she had been so adamant that he not do so. She knew his financial situation, and always seemed to be cautious about spending his money. Everyone would see the damned thing when she removed her gloves for supper. Did she really have to flaunt it, so everyone would know he hadn't bought her a proper ring?

The dance was lengthy and vigorous, and most of the ladies were fanning themselves when it was over. He offered his arm to Pru, who was smiling and flushed pink with exertion, and escorted her from the floor.

"You enjoyed that, Pru?"

"Oh, yes. Thank you so much for leading me out. I've always loved to dance but never get many opportunities to do so. Oh, there's Uncle Randolph. He's a bit of an odd bird, but I'm quite fond of him. May I introduce you?"

"Of course."

Pru led him to an older man with a wild mass of grizzled gray hair and equally woolly eyebrows. He was tall, like all the Armitages, but was decidedly more stout. He smiled at Pru's approach.

"Prudence, my dear girl." His voice was almost a bellow, and the tiniest bit slurred. "I didn't see you arrive. Come here and give your old uncle a kiss."

He bent forward, and Pru rose up on her toes to kiss his cheek.

"How are you, Uncle?"

"Can't complain. Can't complain. But I heard something about you. What was it? Damn me, I can't remember."

"Uncle Randolph, you've had too many glasses of champagne again, haven't you?"

He waved his hand as though batting away a pesky insect. "Bah. A man can't get properly foxed on that fizzy stuff. But what was it I heard about you?"

"Uncle, I'd like to introduce you to someone. This is Nicholas Parrish. My . . . husband."

"Husband? Ha! That was it."

"Nicholas, this is my uncle, Lord Randolph Armitage."

"How do you do, Lord Randolph?" Nick held out his hand, and the old man grasped it tightly.

"Well, what do you know? You're Prudence's young man, then? Now I remember the whole tale. Never more surprised in my life. My wife told me all about it."

Nick thought the man, who grinned from ear to

ear and whose blue eyes twinkled with glee, would never stop pumping his hand.

"You remember my Aunt Julia?" Pru said to Nick, while deftly ending the handshake by placing her hand on her uncle's. "Lady Randolph?"

He did indeed remember the woman. She had not flirted with him but had glared at him down the length of her aristocratic nose, disapproval oozing from every pore.

"Something havey-cavey, as I recall," Lord Randolph said. "Julia said it was some sort of ramshackle business. Henry put a gun to your ribs, eh, my boy? Gun to your ribs?" He guffawed loudly, his belly shaking with laughter. "But I shouldn't worry. Prudence won't cause you a moment's trouble, I daresay. Quiet as a little mouse, that one." He leaned close to Nick. The smell of wine on his breath was almost overpowering. He lowered his voice to what he must have thought was a whisper, but was no such thing. "She'll be so glad to have a husband, she's sure to turn a blind eye to a bit of dalliance here and there. A blind eye." He winked, and nudged Nick on the arm.

Nick was about to object, to go into his speech about he and Pru being in love, when Lord Randolph spoke up again.

"Parrish? Parrish? Was that the name?"

Nick tugged Pru closer and placed her hand on his arm. If he couldn't convey the love match tale with words, he would do so with actions. "Yes, my lord. I am Nicholas Parrish."

"Now, where have I heard that name? Have we met before, my boy?"

"No, my lord, I do not believe so." He wondered if the man might have read one of his political pamphlets. Or one of the articles written under his own name in the *Morning Chronicle*.

"Well, I never forget a name. Can't always recall who or what it belongs to, but I never forget. Parrish. Hmm. It'll come to me. It'll come to me. Anyway, you got yourself a fine-looking young husband, my girl. You be a good little wife, now, you hear?"

Pru smiled and blushed. "Yes, Uncle, I will."

"Ah, there's Walsham. Must have a word. Good to meet you, my boy. Good to meet you."

Pru was grinning when Nick looked down at her. "I'm afraid he's a bit of a character," she said. "He's very sweet, though, even if he does drink too much and talk too loud."

"My dear *little wife*, you seem to be the only Armitage who knows how to speak softly."

She hid her face behind her fan and giggled.

Pru's cousin, Mrs. Shelbourne, strolled up to them. "Mr. Parrish, I do believe you promised me a dance."

There was no polite way to get out of it, so Nick led her onto the floor. While the set formed, he tried to keep his eye on Pru, hoping someone would ask her to dance.

"Watching out for the blushing bride?" Mrs. Shelbourne asked, a sarcastic edge to her voice.

"Don't worry about Prudence. She is quite accustomed to holding up the walls. I actually think she prefers it."

"I think you must be mistaken, Mrs. Shelbourne. My wife is a wonderful dancer, and she enjoys it immensely."

"My, my, what a loyal champion you are for our little mouse. I suppose that legacy of Aunt Elizabeth's makes it all worthwhile."

So, they *did* think him a fortune hunter. Damn and blast!

The music began before he could reply. Nick begrudgingly bowed to his partner and stepped into the figure. He noted that Pru had taken her place at the bottom of the line with her father. Thank God for that. He really did not like to think of her as a wallflower. And he rather enjoyed watching her dance.

When the set ended, Nick made his way to Pru's side, with Mrs. Shelbourne in tow. He was making small talk with Lord Henry when Lord Randolph burst upon them.

"It finally came to me," he said, addressing Nick in a thunderous voice. "I know where I heard the name Parrish. Took me a while to remember, but I ain't as sharp as I used to be, eh, Henry? Not as sharp."

"You're as sharp as you ever were, Randy," Lord Henry said, with a twinkle in his eye. "What is it you remembered?"

"I recognized the name Parrish. Couldn't place

it though. Couldn't place it. But I remember now. It was a painter."

"A painter?" Lord Henry said.

"Yes. Saw an exhibition years ago. Liked it. Very good paintings. Classical stuff and all that. Decided to buy one. But here's what I'd forgotten. The artist was a woman, name of Parrish. Helena Parrish."

Nick smiled. "She was my mother."

"You don't say?" Lord Randolph clapped Nick soundly on the back and laughed. "Your mother, eh? Well, what do you know about that."

Lord Henry turned to Nick. "I didn't know Helena Parrish was your mother. She was a very fine artist. I believe my brother, the duke, has a few of her paintings. And she did some decorative work at Beaufoy, his country seat. You remember, Randy? Those classical roundels in the new drawing room?"

"Quite so. And I have the one painting," Lord Randolph said. *"The Judgment of Paris.* Even Julia likes it, and you know what a high stickler she is."

Mrs. Shelbourne turned to Nick. "Well, Mr. Parrish, it seems you have a bit of cachet after all. Helena Parrish enjoyed a very elite patronage. She was quite successful, I believe."

"Yes, she was," Nick said, biting back the retort he would like to have delivered. "It is a pity she died so young."

Pru gave his arm a squeeze, and he patted her hand.

"I am very pleased to know you have the *Judg-*

ment, Lord Randolph," he said. "I remember it well."

"Look who I found." Pru's brother William stepped up to join them with a pretty young woman at his side. She was tall and blond and blue-eyed—definitely an Armitage.

"Joanna!"

Pru released Nick's arm and moved to stand before the woman, taking both her hands and beaming with pleasure. Her face changed when she was excited. It took on a sort of radiance so that she was almost pretty. No, that was unfair. She *was* pretty, in a sweet, soft, delicate way he had never really found appealing. Until now.

"You're back," Pru said to the other young woman. "I am *so* pleased. I have missed you."

"And I have missed you, too. But my dearest Pru, I understand there is big news." She looked up at Nick and smiled. "Is this the handsome bridegroom I've heard so much about?"

Pru released the woman's hands and tugged Nick forward. "This is Nicholas Parrish. My husband." She still managed to flush every time she said the word. "And Nicholas, this is my cousin Joanna, Mrs. Draycott. She is the daughter of my uncle, Lord Arthur, whom you met earlier."

Nick took the offered hand and bent over it. "Mrs. Draycott. It is a pleasure."

"I am very pleased to meet you, sir," she said. "I hope you know what a very lucky man you are."

There was a bark of laughter from William, quickly stifled by a poke in the ribs from his father, and a delicate snort from Mrs. Shelbourne.

Nick took Pru's hand and brought it to his lips. "I am very much aware of my good fortune, Mrs. Draycott."

She raised her brows, glanced at Pru—who blushed, of course—and then looked back at Nick. "Well, then. I am very happy for you both."

"I say, Parrish," Lord Randolph said, "I don't suppose you have any more of your mother's paintings lying around gathering dust?"

"Paintings?" Mrs. Draycott looked at Pru.

"Come," Pru said, "let us go find some champagne and I will tell you all about it."

She took her cousin by the arm and led her away. Nick suspected there was a lot more to be said between them than a discussion of his mother's pictures. He turned to Lord Randolph.

"Not gathering dust," he said, "but we still have quite a few paintings. My father has most of them up in Derbyshire."

"Dear God, Pru, he's gorgeous!"

Pru grinned. "I know."

"In all the times I've heard you talk of him," Joanna said, "you never once mentioned that minor detail."

Pru shrugged. "It never seemed important."

"Bosh. Well, I can see how you would become besotted with him."

"Shush, please, Joanna!"

"And it appears that he is equally besotted. The man is obviously in love with you, Pru."

"No, he is not."

"But—"

"Shush. Wait until we can be private and I'll explain."

Pru dragged her cousin faster along the perimeter of the ballroom toward a footman with a tray of glasses. They each grabbed one and walked out onto the terrace. Pru led the way to an empty stone bench farthest away from the few others who lingered outside in the cool night air.

They sat down, and Pru told her everything. Joanna was the only person in the world to whom Pru had ever admitted her infatuation with Nicholas. And only after her cousin had guessed. Pru had spoken so often of him and in such terms that Joanna had not been fooled. She, more than anyone, would understand the excruciating awkwardness of their marriage.

But she did not.

"My dear Pru, you are living a dream come true. Don't invent obstacles for yourself. My God, girl, you are married to the man you love. You should not be feeling sorry for yourself. You should be making the best of it."

"But he—"

"Now don't start up again about how he could never love you. Of course he can. You are very lovable."

Pru had to laugh at that. "Lovable?"

"Worthy of love."

I am worthy of him. It seemed all her friends were determined to encourage that litany.

"I don't mean to sound so self-deprecating, Joanna. I know I am not completely worthless as a human being. But he is everything I am not. We are dreadfully mismatched."

"Are you going to make me shake you, Pru? Heavens, just because a man is extraordinarily good-looking does not make him perfect. I am certain the man has flaws. I'll bet you can name one right now."

"A flaw?"

"Yes. Something about him that's less than perfect. You've been living with him for a week now. Surely there is something."

"Well . . . he is a bit stubborn about certain things."

"Aha. Like what?"

"Money, mostly. He is too proud to touch my inheritance, even though I know he could use it. He won't refuse me any household expense, even though I know he can ill afford it."

"There. You see? He sounds as pig-headed as my Oliver. Don't make him out to be a god. He is human, just as you are. And he will grow to love you in truth, I am sure."

Pru sighed. "I hope you are right, Joanna. Discounting everything else, it is still awkward to be so unevenly matched in affection. Love on one side only is almost worse than no love at all."

"Nonsense. He will love you in time. He *will*, Pru."

"I have a friend who . . . who is trying to help me."

"Help you how?"

"To be more attractive to him. To make him d-desire me." Pru could hardly believe she said such a thing aloud, even to Joanna. How thoroughly embarrassing.

"Well, she has done a good job. You look quite smashing in that dress. And your hair is lovely. I am sure Nicholas noticed, and others as well. Come, let's go back inside. There are gentlemen simply dying to dance with us."

As they walked back in, they practically collided with Nicholas. "I beg your pardon," he said. "I wondered if you would like me to fetch your shawl, Pru. These April nights can be chilling."

How very thoughtful he was. A gentleman to his fingertips. How could she not love him? "Thank you, Nicholas. But as you see, we have decided to come back inside."

"Pru has been telling me about how your marriage came about," Joanna said.

Pru gave a little gasp. *Be quiet, Joanna,* she wanted to say.

"I must congratulate you, sir, for doing the honorable thing. And for handling the situation so beautifully."

He took Pru's hand and tucked it into the now-familiar crook of his arm. She loved it when he did that.

"Pru has long been my friend. I could never have allowed her to be dishonored among her family. Despite—if you'll forgive me for saying so—the wretched way so many of them treat her."

"Yes, we Armitages can be exceedingly stupid at times."

"I was not, of course, referring to you, Mrs. Draycott. I can see that you are a true friend to Pru."

"I am. In fact, I suspect I am one of the few who realizes what she's been up to all these years, working on *The Ladies' Fashionable Cabinet.* Which means I am aware of your politics as well, sir. What a dreadful burden this rowdy, noble clan must be for you."

Nicholas smiled. "I am getting used to it."

"Good. For I fear you will be called upon to attend quite a few Armitage functions this Season, what with Arabella's come-out and all. In fact, I was rather hoping to coax you into coming to a little musical evening I will be hosting next week. And hoping to coax Pru into playing."

Nicholas gave Pru a quizzical look. "Playing?"

"I'm afraid I'm out of practice, Joanna. I'm sure you can find someone else."

Joanna's eyes narrowed. "How is it that you are out of practice? Oh, please do not tell me you have no pianoforte?"

Pru shrugged. It was not a subject she wished to discuss. One of the most painful aspects of moving out of her father's house had been leaving behind the pianoforte. She missed it dreadfully. It did not help matters to have Broadwood & Son, makers of the finest pianofortes in England, located just behind Golden Square on Great Pulteney Street. She could see the back of their premises each time she looked out her bed chamber window. It gave her such a pang of longing, though, that she had stopped looking out the window altogether.

She could have bought a pianoforte, of course. But she thought it might have ruffled her husband's proud feathers for her to make such an expensive purchase with her own money. And she certainly did not wish to make him feel obliged to buy one for her.

"There is no pianoforte in your house, Mr. Parrish?" Joanna asked.

"I am afraid not, ma'am. My sister never played, and I confess I had no idea Pru did."

"She not only plays, sir, but plays beautifully."

"Pru?" Nicholas gazed at her with sharp interest. "Why did you never tell me?"

She gave another shrug. "It never seemed important."

"And that is the biggest lie you have ever told," Joanna said. "I know you cannot be happy without your music. Well." She patted Pru's hand. "We shall just have to see what we can do about that. In the meantime, please do come to my little musicale. I'll send round a card. Oh dear, here comes Uncle Caldecott to claim his dance. Please excuse me."

When she'd gone, Nick looked down at her and said, "Pru? Have I just discovered one of those important things I didn't know about you? Music?"

"I play a little. That is all. So do thousands of other women. Most of the women in this room, I daresay."

"Only a little, Pru? Damn, I wish we had an in-strument, but—"

"Do not worry about it, Nicholas. Joanna exag-gerates. It is not all that important. Really. Oh, here is Lionel."

Joanna's brother approached, wearing a friendly smile.

"Cousin Prudence? Would you care to join me in the next set?"

No doubt his sister had sent him to make sure she did not sit out another dance. Frankly, she was glad he'd asked. She really did not want to talk about pianofortes anymore. "I would indeed, Li-onel. Thank you."

As she walked onto the dance floor, she turned back to see Nicholas wearing a puzzled frown.

Chapter 8

"**C**or lumme, would yer look at dat?"

The Crimson Ladies spilled out of the dining room and into the hall to watch the workmen maneuvering the new pianoforte up the stairs.

"Ooh, now ain't that a purty-lookin' t'ing?"

"Can yer play one o' them, Miz Nick?"

Pru watched the proceedings anxiously, terrified the workmen would damage the beautiful instrument. She was tempted to shout out, "Careful!" every few minutes, but the men from Broadwood & Son seemed to know what they were doing.

"Yes, Ginny, I can play the pianoforte. And I can hardly wait to play this one."

"Did Mr. Nick buy it fer yer, then?"

"No, it is a gift from my cousin. A wedding

present." An exceedingly generous one, too. She ought to have known Joanna would do something so extravagant. Pru had been tempted to send the workmen packing, to refuse to accept such a gift, until she read Joanna's note.

To my dearest Pru,

Please accept this wedding present from your cousin who loves you. I know you cannot be happy without music in your life, so this instrument represents my best wishes that your happiness may now be complete. And don't you dare insult me by sending it back. I want you to have it. Play it well and play it often. Don't forget to practice something special for my musical evening on Thursday.

All my love,
Joanna

Pru had blinked away tears after reading the note. Emotion was soon overcome, though, by pure childish excitement at the idea of having a brand new Broadwood five-and-a-half octave pianoforte of her very own. Joanna had chosen the instrument wisely. She had somehow known a grand would be too big for the small town house. But it was a beautiful large-sized square model in a satinwood case with boxwood and ebony stringing, and Pru's fingers were itching to play it.

"That's a right nice weddin' present," Ginny said. "I bet Mr. Nick'll be surprised."

No doubt about that. Pru only hoped he would not be angry to have a large pianoforte moved into the drawing room. And would not mind her playing now and then. She was more likely, though, to play when she was alone. She'd always preferred to play in private, to learn new pieces, to struggle and make mistakes without anyone else hearing.

"Watch yer step there, boyo," Bess shouted, "or ye'll be bouncing down them stairs on yer purty little arse."

The Ladies shrieked with laughter, and Pru began to worry that they might be too much of a distraction to the workmen.

"Perhaps we should leave the men to their work," she said, "and return to the dining room. How are those fashion plates coming along?"

She managed to herd the Ladies through the dining room door, though they made known their reluctance to do so. Pru had worked with them long enough not to be offended by any of their off-color remarks.

"Let me have a look at the plates," Pru said. The painted fashion plates were spread across the dining room table to dry. As always, every plate was slightly different as each Crimson Lady felt obliged to introduce her own notion of color. Flora always provided a master copy, colored to her specifications. The Ladies had finally been convinced to adhere to the main design, but would not be deterred from adding a bit of their own flair in the details. Shoes and fans and hats and scarves and shawls were inevitably brightened by the

Ladies' bold palette. Edwina had been wise enough to realize the unique plates would set the *Cabinet* apart from other similar publications, and had never discouraged the Ladies from adding their own bit of dash to the prints.

Ginny was partial to stripes. Madge could not resist a tiny splash of cherry red here and there. Bess, showing her Irish roots, loved bright greens. Daisy—who preferred to be called Marguerite—had a fondness for pattern and had become extraordinarily adept at painting paisley and floral designs on robe hems and shawls. Sadie liked any color, so long as it was bright, and had a penchant for unusual combinations, such as purple and orange.

And finally there was Polly. Rail thin and sickly, she had blossomed as a Crimson Lady, and Pru had hopes that she was no longer working the streets at night. She was the face painter, a very specialized and delicate job for which the girl had shown a special talent from the beginning. There was nothing bold about her work. Polly's faces were delicate, pink-cheeked, and utterly charming.

A huge stack of uncolored plates stood on the sideboard. They had just begun on the next issue's engravings, and there was still much to be done.

Pru picked up one of the finished plates. It was an afternoon dress of a particularly pleasing style. She looked at Flora's description. A short white gauze robe (painted pink) with vandyke lace trimming, wrapped at the waist with gold cord and tassels (painted sea green) over a white Cyprus petticoat. Yellow shoes (painted with pink stripes) and yellow gloves (actually painted yellow). The neckline dipped into a deep V and the cut of the robe across the shoulders and hips was especially flattering. Flora's description stated it was "invented by Mrs. Phillips of New Bond Street," one of the *Cabinet*'s frequent advertisers. Pru wondered—

"Miss?" Madge had come up behind Pru and peered over her shoulder. "Is there summink wrong wif the paintin'?"

Pru turned and smiled. "No, not at all, Madge. I was simply admiring the dress."

"Aye, i'nt it loverly? It'd look real nice on yer, miss. That is, missus. Cor lumme, I can't git used ter it. Yer bein' Missus Nick, I mean."

Pru laughed. "I can't quite get used to it myself." She replaced the print on the table and eyed the pile on the sideboard. "These are fine, Madge, but there are lots more to paint. I need them done by Wednesday. Can you manage it?"

" 'Course we can, miss. Missus. Ma'am. Oh, crikey!"

Pru left them to their work and hurried up the stairs to see if the Broadwood had made it safely to the drawing room. The workmen had apparently just deposited it inside the doorway. They were all bent over and huffing like steam engines. She told them where to place it, then sat down and tested the tone. After some minor adjustments, it was perfect.

When the workmen had gone, Pru dashed to her bedchamber, fell to her knees, and crawled under the bed where she had stored her box of music. She really ought to go downstairs and work on the page proofs for the next issue. She really should.

But the Broadwood beckoned.

She had no idea how long she sat there playing all her favorite pieces. It was as though she had been dying in a desert and suddenly came upon an oasis. She had not realized how thirsty for music she'd been, and she drank her fill. Nothing difficult. Nothing new. But all her best pieces, the ones her fingers knew practically by heart. She played and played and played.

With the last note of a Mazzinghi air, she dropped her head onto the smooth satinwood, exhausted.

"That was beautiful, Pru."

She sat up with a start to find Nicholas seated on a chair across the room. Dear heaven, she'd been so lost to the music she had not even noticed he'd come in.

"How long have you been there?" she asked.

"For the last three pieces. My God, Pru, you had me completely spellbound. I'm no expert, but you really are good, aren't you?"

She shrugged. "Passable. But I enjoy it."

"I can see that. You were in another world, my dear."

"Nicholas, isn't it wonderful? Joanna sent the pianoforte as a wedding present."

"It's quite wonderful. That was very kind of her. Madge told me all about it when I came home."

"Madge? Oh dear, I forgot all about the Ladies. Are they—"

"They are gone for the day. Madge was just straightening up when I came in. They'd been enjoying your playing."

"Oh, but I have wasted the entire afternoon. Only look, it is dark out already. I had no idea."

"You were lost in the music."

"I suppose so. You do not mind, do you, Nicholas? About the pianoforte, I mean. I didn't know where else to put it, and—"

"Of course I don't mind. I want you to be happy here, and I can see now that your cousin was right about music being necessary to your happiness. It was very kind of her to send it. I am glad to know that *someone* in your family appreciates you. Come and sit down, Pru."

He gestured toward the settee adjacent to where he sat. Pru stood, shook out her skirts, and arched her aching back. How long *had* she been playing?

When she was seated comfortably on the settee, Nicholas said, "Do you mind if I ask you about your family?"

"No, of course I don't mind. What would you like to know?"

"If you'll forgive me for asking, I'd like to know how you can bear the way most of them overlook you so completely. I listen to you play, Pru, and I am in awe of your talent. And yet your own family seems to dismiss you out of hand. They tease you about your shyness and your small stature, or they ignore you altogether. And you seem to take it all in stride. How on earth have you managed to live with them and not turn into a quivering, craven mass of nerves?"

"It's not been as bad as all that," she said.

"I don't know how you do it, Pru. I know that you're shy and quiet, but you're not spineless. You have a self-possession I would never expect from the treatment of you I've witnessed. I'm sorry to speak so disparagingly of your family. But it makes me angry to think they don't recognize how special you are."

Special? He thinks I'm special?

"Tell me how you have survived, Pru. It's another one of those important things I want to learn about you."

She shrugged. "I don't know what to tell you." Especially with her mind preoccupied by the notion that he thought her special. But appreciating her playing was not the same as finding her desirable, or falling in love with her. It was perhaps foolish of her to wish for more than admiration or respect. She knew many marriages were not blessed with even as much as that. She ought to be content.

"I've never found it all that difficult," she continued. "I've always known I was different, of course. I was the only one who took after my mother. She was small like me, and yet she was a bit of a spitfire. I suppose I had her as an example. But I was always quiet. I could never be as outspoken as she was. Yet she taught me to accept who I am."

"I wish I'd known her."

Pru smiled wistfully. "You would have liked her, Nicholas. She was a true bluestocking. She probably would have dashed off to France, like you did, to be a part of the Revolution, if she had lived long enough."

"Ah, so you get your republican sensibilities from your mother?"

"Certainly not from my father. Or my brothers." She chuckled. "Tories to the tips of their toes."

Nicholas got up and moved to sit at the other end of the settee. "And she also taught you how to survive among the Viking hordes?"

Pru gave a crack of unladylike laughter, then covered her mouth in embarrassment. "The Viking hordes? Is that how they appear to you? Oh, I like that. It's a perfect image. But yes, I suppose I did learn from her how to survive as the least Viking-like of them all. I've always known I would never be as tall or as beautiful or as gregarious or as witty as the rest of them. But I never felt envious."

He watched her with such an intense expression in those dark eyes, she had to wonder what he was thinking. Did he not believe her? And was she indeed being completely truthful? Hadn't she been wishing she was beautiful like a true Armitage so she wouldn't feel such a dowd beside Nicholas?

I am worthy of him. I am worthy of him.

"Actually," she said, "I . . . I am not the most self-confident person who ever lived. Being the runt of such a grand litter does take its toll. But I must confess that my work for the *Cabinet* has given me more confidence than anything I've ever done."

His eyes brightened. "Really?"

"Oh, yes."

"More than music?"

"Yes. Music is just for me, you see. An indulgence, really. But the *Cabinet* is something of real value. Working with Edwina, and for this short time on my own, has been the greatest pleasure of my life. I feel like I have really and truly accomplished something."

"And yet you must have felt some confidence before you joined the *Cabinet*. When you submitted your first essay, for example. You had to have believed in yourself."

"Yes, you're right. I was prepared for it to be rejected, but I was exceedingly proud of it." She smiled as she remembered the exaltation she'd felt when the essay had been accepted, the thrill of knowing her words would be printed for anyone to read. It had been a heady moment. "I may be small and plain and quiet—a mouse among a family of lions—but I have always known I had a brain, and a few talents, and that has been enough."

Nicholas reached out and touched her cheek, ever so lightly. "Small and quiet, or petite and soft-spoken. But never plain."

He did not think her plain? Her pulse rushed, and she trembled beneath his touch. Was he just being kind once again?

He held his hand against her cheek and smiled into her eyes. "Never plain," he repeated.

Oh, how she wanted to believe him. If she had moved up a notch from plain, was she inching closer to desirable?

Flora's lessons began to race through her mind. If ever there was a time to flirt, to entice, it was now. Perhaps she should try one of the eye tricks. *One must not flutter one's lashes rapidly as though assailed by gnats, but slowly and seductively like the wings of a butterfly.*

Pru tried it. Close. Open. Close. Open. Again and again.

He dropped his hand from her cheek, leaving her bereft. She fluttered more urgently.

"My dear, do you have something in your eye?"

She closed her eyes and stifled a groan.

"Pru?"

"No, no, I am fine. There is nothing in my eye." How mortifying.

"You know, my dear," he said, "you should not be afraid to wear your spectacles if you feel the need."

Spectacles? Dear God, what a hopeless excuse for a flirt she was. She could not even flutter her

lashes properly without him thinking she had a
squint. Flora would be ashamed of her.

"I know ladies do not like to wear them but—"

"I do not need my spectacles, I assure you. I
only wear them for close-up work." Now she
sounded petulant. Lord, what a mess she'd made
of things, and after he'd been kind enough to tell
her she was not plain. She felt as if she had taken
one step forward and two steps back. "I am a little
tired," she said, grasping at the one excuse she
could think of.

He rose and walked across the room to the sideboard. "You should make an early night of it,
then. How about a brandy to relax you?" he
asked.

"Yes, pl-please." Never had she needed it more.

Nick squirmed in his seat while the Italian soprano shrieked through an aria. It was bad
enough that he had to mingle once again with
Pru's Vikings, but to have to sit through such cat-
erwauling was almost more than he could bear. It
was a wonder all the windows and mirrors hadn't
shattered in protest.

He looked at Pru, to see if her more sophisticated musical ear allowed her to enjoy the performance, but she was studying the hands in her lap.
She seemed to sense his gaze and looked up. Nick
rolled his eyes and she chewed her lower lip to sti-
fle a giggle. Her eyes twinkled with amusement.
The soprano hit a particularly shrill high note and

Nick grabbed Pru's hand, then had to look away or he would have started laughing.

When the aria ended, Nick lost no time in tugging Pru from her seat and leading her away. In the hallway outside the drawing room, he collapsed against the wall and gave in to laughter. Pru's softer, melodious laugh—like the tinkling of little bells in the wind—soon joined his.

"That really was dreadful, was it not?" he asked when he could finally speak. "Or is it my unsophisticated plebeian taste that amuses you?"

"She was a bit screechy," Pru said.

She covered her mouth with her fan as she laughed again, and Nick was thoroughly charmed by the sound of it, by the way it transformed her face. "I haven't seen you laugh like that," he said, "since that escapade with the misprinted magazine last year."

An embarrassing printing error, for which Nick had been to blame, had not been caught until the evening the issues had been distributed. They had scurried about in teams all over London retrieving every copy. Nick and Pru had been one team, and they'd had a wild and adventurous time of it.

"You ought to laugh more often," he said, and ran a knuckle softly along her check. "It suits you."

He should have realized his touch would ignite a rosy blush. Damn. She was still so skittish whenever their conversation took a more personal direction. Or when he touched her. But he could not seem to help himself. She had the softest skin. He was gloved tonight, but the other day when he stoked her face with his bare fingers, she had actually trembled. How in blazes was he ever going to make her feel comfortable enough to share his bed?

"I am glad to see you two are enjoying the evening."

Joanna Draycott smiled at Pru, who raised her fan to cover her face. Hiding her blushes, no doubt.

"What did you think of Signora Gambiatti?" Joanna asked.

A choking sound came from behind Pru's fan.

"She was . . . incredible," Nick said, trying desperately to keep a straight face.

"Really?" Joanna said. "Frankly, I found her shrill and highly overrated. I'm rather sorry I was convinced to invite her. What? What is so funny?"

"Oh, Joanna," Pru said, her voice quivering with mirth, "she was perfectly awful. Nicholas and I had to flee the room so we wouldn't embarrass her with our laughter."

Joanna grinned. "Ah. Well, just be sure not to flee too far. You're up next."

Pru sobered instantly. "Oh, dear."

Nick realized he still held her hand. He brought it to his lips. "You'll be brilliant, I am sure." He noticed once again the bulge of his signet ring beneath her glove. "Oh, but hadn't you better remove that ring? It's far too big and might get in your way."

"Not to worry," she said, and began to remove her glove.

Nick was startled by the unexpected pang of desire brought about by observing the simple act of unbuttoning a glove and sliding it down her slender, pale arm.

"I am quite prepared," she said. When the glove was removed, she slid the ring off her finger. As always, it was wrapped in ribbon in order to fit her small hand. She unwound the ribbon, which was threaded through the ring, and slipped it over her head. Nick's signet fell into the hint of cleavage revealed by the V-neckline of the dress.

"Excellent," Joanna said. "It shall be your good luck charm."

Pru's hand went to her head and touched the bandeau of twisted fabric and pearls that did its best to hold her hair in place. "Is this thing on straight?"

"It's perfect," Joanna said. "You look very fine, in fact. I do like that dress. It is very becoming."

"Do you think so?" Pru smoothed the folds of her skirt and shook out the short train. "You will see it, or something very much like it, in the next issue of the *Cabinet*."

"Really?"

"Yes," Pru said, her voice tinged with a hint of self-satisfaction. "It was created by one of our advertisers."

"In exchange for extra publicity?" Joanna asked. "And you get to be in the first stare of fashion. A tidy little bargain, my dear. Well done."

Nick wondered how much the dress really cost. Though Joanna had made the assumption, Pru never said it had been a quid pro quo transaction. She was dipping into her inheritance. He could hardly disapprove, but damn it all, he wished she didn't have to do so. He would like to be able to clothe his own wife properly. But she was a duke's granddaughter. It galled him to know he could never afford to provide her a wardrobe suitable to her station.

"Aunt Prudence!"

Arabella came dashing up, breathless as ever. "You are playing next! Come on! Let's get you settled." She turned to Nick and added, with pride, "I am her page turner."

"And my moral support." Pru took a deep, shuddery breath. "Come along, then, Arabella. Let us get this business over with."

Nick's eyes followed them as they made their way down the hall to the drawing room. Arabella was half a head taller and beautifully blond, but it was Pru he watched. She looked remarkably pretty, especially when she had laughed earlier, and Nick realized with a jolt that it had been some time now since he'd thought of her in any other way. When had he stopped thinking she was plain and mousy?

Her apricot-colored hair was gathered full and high in the back and confined with the twisted bandeau, but it was too curly to be completely tamed, and several little corkscrew curls had fallen loose and bobbed delicately against the nape of her slender neck. He watched her walk away, and a swell of white-hot lust surged through him as he contemplated kissing that pale neck.

Good God, where had that notion come from? This was Pru, for God's sake. He'd known her four years and never found her attractive before. As she disappeared through the drawing room door, he realized what a blind fool he'd been. Just like all the rest of her family. How could he have never noticed how pretty, how desirable she was?

"Don't worry, Mr. Parrish, she'll be fine."

Nick turned to Joanna. "I beg your pardon?"

"You were frowning. I thought you might be worried about her, about performing in public. You needn't be concerned. When she plays I believe she forgets the audience and plays only for herself. She forgets to be self-conscious."

"So I have discovered. She is very talented, isn't she? It was extremely kind of you to send the pianoforte."

"Yes, she is talented. I wanted to give her the Broadwood so she would perhaps feel more comfortable in her new home with you. I want her to be happy, Mr. Parrish."

Her tone suggested she spoke of more than just the pianoforte. "So do I, Mrs. Draycott."

"Good. I should be exceedingly disappointed to learn otherwise. Pru is very special to me."

And to him as well. It was actually quite astonishing how special she was becoming to him as he grew to know her better.

"Tell me," he said, "has she never had suitors?"

Joanna raised her eyebrows at his question. He wasn't quite sure what had prompted it, except that he wanted to know more about Pru. Perhaps if he understood more of her background, he would be able to more easily break down the barriers to intimacy, would be better able to gauge the anxiety behind her skittishness.

"None that were given any encouragement," Joanna said. "She is painfully shy with men in that sort of situation, as you must know."

He did indeed, damn it all. "How is it that she became so shy of men while living in a house full of brothers?"

Joanna smiled. "I believe that is part of the problem. She has heard them talk quite candidly about women, since they so often tend to forget she is there. Knowing her brothers as I do, I have no doubt she heard a great deal more than she wished. I believe it has caused her to be so anxious about what men may think or say about *her*, that she makes herself miserably uncomfortable in their company. I believe the whole business of men and women and what they . . . do together simply embarrasses her. Of course, I am not telling you anything you haven't already discovered, I'm sure."

Nick wondered just how much Pru had told her cousin about their marriage.

"I remember her Season," Joanna continued. "She would get so flustered if a man showed an interest that she could hardly get a word out without stammering awkwardly. She hated the whole ordeal so much she refused any additional Seasons. Uncle Henry fussed and fumed that she would never find a husband, but Pru claimed she didn't care, that she wasn't interested in marriage. Or so she said."

She tilted her head to one side and studied him. "Frankly, Mr. Parrish, I think marrying you is the best thing that ever happened to her."

"Why? She did not want it any more than I did."

He could have bitten off his tongue. Theirs was supposed to be a love match. But he suspected Joanna knew better.

"But it is perfect, don't you see?" she said. "Pru already knows you as a friend, she can speak to you—even laugh with you—without getting flustered."

That ought to have been true, but quite the reverse had happened. To be sure, they were comfortable together speaking of impersonal matters. But whenever the conversation turned personal, or whenever he touched her, she became more shy and nervous than ever.

"There was no awkward courtship, no social games," Joanna continued. "As a fait accompli, she did not have to face the agony of the marriage mart and a grand family wedding. Instead, she is married to a friend with whom she can be comfortable. I know it is not what *you* wanted, sir, but I can think of no better husband for Pru. And you, Mr. Parrish, are a very fortunate man, for you will ultimately get to know the real Pru, more than any ordinary suitor could have done. You will come to realize what a precious gem you hold in your hands."

The real Pru. He was learning more of her every day, and found he rather enjoyed the adventure of discovery.

"Come, sir. Your wife is about to play. Let us take our seats."

"I dropped a note in the allegro."

"And you are the only one who knows that, I assure you. My God, Pru, you were amazing. Absolutely brilliant. I was so proud of you."

Pru flushed with pleasure. Nick's words were a balm to her soul. "You are very kind to say so."

"Dammit, Pru, I wish you would stop thinking it is mere kindness when I compliment you. We've known each other far too long for me to offer you cheap flattery."

"I do not think your flattery cheap, Nicholas. On the contrary, it is quite dear." She could hardly believe she said such a thing. The darkness of the carriage must have emboldened her.

"Ah, Pru." He took her chin in his hand and leaned toward her.

Dear God, he was going to kiss her. Wasn't he? Please please please let him realize how much she wanted it, how *ready* she was for it. He leaned closer. She leaned closer. His eyes drifted over her shoulder.

"What the devil?"

He dropped his hand from her chin and looked out the window.

No!

"What's going on?" he said, peering around

her. "There is light at every window. Something's happened."

The carriage slowed. Pru could barely breathe for choking back the sob of frustration lodged in the back of her throat. She didn't care what was going on out there. She was dying inside.

Nick bounded over her and out the door before the carriage came to a complete stop. He looked around and was ready to charge up the front steps when he seemed to remember her. He turned back and handed her down.

He was right. There was candlelight coming through the drawing room curtains and the fan-light above the door. "Nicholas, someone is here. Look, there's a traveling carriage. Who could it be?"

"I'm not certain, but I have a hunch."

He led her up the front steps, and the door opened before he had time to get out his key. Lucy, wide-eyed and anxious, held open the door.

"I didn't know what to do, sir," she said. "He said it was all right, that it was his house, but I never seen him before in my life, so I wasn't sure."

Before either of them could reply, a man came bounding down the stairs. A man she had met once before. An older version of Nicholas.

"There you are!" he said.

"Father!" Nicholas grabbed him in a bear hug. "What on earth are you doing in London?"

"Since no one bothered to invite me to the wedding, I figured I'd come and offer my warmest congratulations in person. Prudence?" He took both her hands in his and smiled. "I couldn't be more pleased. Welcome to the family." He bent and kissed her on the cheek.

He really did seem pleased. Pru wondered what Nicholas had said in his letter. Would his father be so happy if he knew his son had been forced into the marriage? Or perhaps he did know the truth, and was simply as kindhearted as Nicholas.

"Well done, my boy. Well done. Come upstairs. It is still early and we have a great deal to catch up on."

Batholomew Parrish was a very handsome man. He had the same dark eyes and brows as both his children. His hair had likely once been as dark as theirs, too, but was now sprinkled with gray. Pru had met him at Edwina's wedding and had liked him at once.

But was he staying here? In the same house with her and Nicholas?

Of course he was. It was his house, after all. But it was not a large house, so he would know . . . he would know . . .

Pru had to force her legs to carry her up the stairs. How thoroughly mortifying for Mr. Parrish to know the true state of their marriage. For they could not hide it. All the bedrooms were on the same floor. He would know they slept separately.

She stifled a groan. And they would continue to sleep separately as long as he stayed, for Pru would rather die than have him know . . . to have him hear . . . Dear God, she hoped he did not plan to stay long.

They entered the drawing room, where Lucy had laid out wine and cakes.

"I cannot believe you came all the way to London," Nicholas said. "I know how you hate it here."

"You must wish me to the devil for barging in on your privacy, but I promise I will not intrude for too long. I confess I wanted to get to know my new daughter-in-law. Now, let us have a toast."

He poured three glasses of claret and handed one to each of them. "Here's to you both. May you have a long and happy life together."

They clinked glasses, and Pru downed her wine in a single gulp. She gave a little hiccup and a sheepish giggle when she realized what she'd done. "I beg your pardon."

Nicholas stared at her. Mr. Parrish refilled her glass. She would take it slower this time, though she was sorely tempted to get thoroughly foxed.

"Come and sit down," Mr. Parrish said. "I have something for you."

Pru sat on the settee and Nicholas sat beside her. "Mr. Parrish," Pru said, "I am sorry we were not here to welcome you. Has Lucy taken care of settling you in properly?"

"She has indeed. But please, you must call me Bartholomew." He walked to the other side of the room. "This is new," he said, and ran his fingers along the smooth finish of the pianoforte. "It must be yours, Prudence."

"It was a wedding present from my cousin," she said.

"Ah. And I have brought you a small present,

too, my dear." He reached for something propped against the wall, and Pru could see it was a painting, though its front was turned away from her. He hoisted it with some difficulty, and Nicholas rose to help him.

"One of Mother's?" he asked.

"Yes, I thought Prudence might like it."

They dragged it to the center of the room and turned it around.

"Oh, I say!" Nicholas beamed with pleasure.

"Yes, I thought it fitting for a marriage gift," Bartolomew said. "I know your mother would have approved."

Prudence stood and stared at the huge picture, beautifully painted in a classical style. She was dumbstruck. Even if she had been able to form the words, she had no idea what she would say.

It was a painting of Mars and Venus caught in the act of making love in full naked splendor.

Chapter 9

"And so, it really was all my own fault, you see."

Nick poured himself another cup of coffee and took a long swallow. His father frowned as he stirred his own coffee. Over breakfast, after Pru had excused herself to work downstairs, Nick had told him the full details of the situation that had led to his marriage, everything he had judiciously left out of the letter he'd sent. He had not, however, told him anything of the unconsummated state of the marriage. His father would guess enough, living under the same roof.

"It is good of you to take responsibility, Nick, and I am pleased you did right by Prudence. You behaved just as a gentleman ought."

"Then, what is troubling you, Father?"

"I like Prudence."

"So do I."

"She is a sweet little thing."

"Yes, she is."

His father looked up from his coffee, his brow creased with concern. "I would not like to see you break her heart, my boy."

Nick shook his head and buttered another slice of toast. "You may rest easy on that score, Father. Her heart is no more engaged in this marriage than is mine. She did not want it any more than I did. In fact, she has been saddled with the worst part of the bargain. She has left a fine Mayfair home and an aristocratic family to live here with me, in considerably less splendor. She has forfeited whatever other options she may have entertained. No, if Pru's heart is broken it is because of what she had to give up."

"Are you quite sure? There is a certain air about her. A bit demure. Bashful, even. She seems like a blushing bride to me."

"It is only her natural shyness you are seeing. She would seem that way to you even if we were not married. She is not a tongue-tied, lovesick girl, I assure you. Do you not remember her from Edwina's wedding?"

"I remember she was quiet, and a bit nervous. But I confess I was not paying much attention to Prudence that day."

"No one has ever paid her much attention, I'm afraid. Including me, I am ashamed to admit. That shyness has made it all too easy for her to blend into the background, and all too easy for everyone else to ignore her. You should see the way her family treats her, Father. It makes my blood boil."

"It goes against your grain to be connected to such a highborn family. I believe you would find them irritating under any circumstances."

"Most likely. But their blue blood does not excuse them for so thoroughly disregarding one of their own, just because she is small and quiet. There is so much about her that should make them proud."

His father smiled at last. "She is lucky, then, to have found a husband who appreciates her."

"Anyone with half a brain would appreciate her. You should hear her play the pianoforte, Father. She is quite brilliant."

"Indeed? And she writes very good essays for the *Cabinet*, I understand."

"She is an excellent writer. And a smashing good editor. Edwina could not have left the magazine in better hands."

"And she is pretty."

Nick stared at his father and tried to determine if he was merely being indulged. He did not completely trust that smile. "She is, isn't she? I admit I had never noticed before, but she does have the most remarkable blue eyes and such lovely skin. When she isn't blushing."

His father nodded as though he was in complete agreement, as though those eyes and that skin were not a revelation.

"And her hair is quite unusual. Your mother would have loved to paint it. It is the color of—"

"Apricots," Nick said. "Yes, I know. And all those curls. It is quite unique among her family. It should make her stand out among them, if only she weren't so tiny. They are all Vikings, you know. Great tall, hulking things, every one of them."

"Well, then." His father leaned back in his chair, chuckled softly, and looked altogether well pleased, as though he savored some sort of private joke. "It seems I am worrying over nothing," he said. "I can see you are not likely to break the girl's heart, after all. I am sure you will make the best of this marriage, despite its inauspicious beginnings."

"That is certainly my intention. Yes, it put a crimp in my plans for the Derby project, and no, Pru would not have been my choice of bride. But what's done is done."

"Indeed."

"And I will do what I can to make a comfortable life for Pru. None of this is her fault, after all."

"She is comfortable here?"

Nick considered the question. There were many kinds of comfortable. "It's an effort for her, I think, to adjust. Even though her father claims not to be a rich man, Pru is used to a grander style of life. And there is . . ."

"What?"

Nick shrugged. How to explain it? A once re-laxed and comfortable friendship turned awk-ward and self-conscious? But was that really true? Had there ever really been much of a friendship between him and Pru? How could he have been her friend and not known so many basic aspects of her life? He hadn't known she was highborn. He hadn't known she had a large family. He hadn't known she played the pianoforte like an angel. All he'd really known was that she shared many of his views on politics and social reform. And he knew that much from her writings more than from actual conversations.

He hadn't really known Pru at all.

As for relaxed and comfortable, Nick was no longer so sure about that, either. When he thought back, he realized he could not state with any certainty that Pru had ever been entirely relaxed in his company. With Edwina, yes. But not with him. Not really. He recollected the words of her cousin Joanna, about Pru's general uneasiness with men. Well, Nick was a man, so she could never have been completely at ease with him. She had always been a bit bashful, always blushing.

Since their marriage, though, she had seemed even more self-conscious. Well, of course she had. There was, after all, a new level of relationship to endure. Even though she had not yet been forced to endure the physical aspect of it, there was a constant awareness of it between them.

And that damned painting of Mars and Venus had only added emphasis to the uneasiness of the situation.

His father's eyebrows lifted in question, awaiting Nick's response. "There is what?" he prompted.

Nick sighed. "An awkwardness between us. She is . . . ill-at-ease. She is not . . . not yet comfortable with . . . living under the same roof with me. Being married to me. She is embarrassed by it all. It has been a bigger change for her than for me, you know."

"Ah. I suspected as much."

He would, of course. There was no hiding the sleeping arrangements in such a small house.

"And my presence," his father said, "is not helping matters is it? Well, I promise to stay out of your way as much as possible. I have a few friends here in Town I wish to spend some time with."

"You do? I had wondered what brought you back to Town again so soon."

"Your marriage brought me back, of course. I wanted to get to know my new daughter-in-law. I suppose it was rude of me to barge in so soon after the wedding, but I was anxious to . . . to see how things went on."

"Well, you did surprise me, Father. When you came for Edwina's wedding, it was the first time you'd been to London in years. I know you hate it here. I am sorry you felt the need to return again so soon."

"Nothing to feel sorry about, my boy. I wanted to come. I enjoyed my last visit. I'd quite forgotten what delights London has to offer. I am looking forward to . . . enjoying them once again."

"You are?"

How extraordinary. Was this his country squire, bookish father speaking, the one who'd spent most of Nick's life railing against the frivolities, and expense, of life in London? There was a distinct gleam in his father's eye, though, and his mouth twitched up at the corners.

"Enough about me," his father said. "You mentioned the Derby project. Tell me how those latest investments of yours are doing."

"Has he noticed?"

Pru stifled a groan. Flora was not only ready to give an endless stream of advice on how Pru could captivate her husband, but she wanted to know every detail of the campaign as well.

"I haven't given him much to notice," she said.

Flora pulled a face and leaned over the desk. "And why not? Do not tell me you have never worn any of the new dresses you had made up."

"Oh, I have worn some of them. But . . ."

"But?"

"Well, you must remember, Flora, that I am not outgoing like you. I really cannot bear to be stared at."

"What have you done, my girl?"

"I, um, added more lace to fill in the necklines."

Pru shrank back as Flora looked ready to lunge across the desk and throttle her. "You didn't!"

"I am afraid I did. I couldn't help it, Flora. I felt so . . . exposed."

"But that is the whole idea, you silly goose. How do you expect to catch your husband's eye if you hide all the best attractions? And those dresses were designed with specific necklines. You no doubt ruined the line completely."

"I really do not think so. Actually, I thought

they looked rather nice. Nicholas complimented me. So did my cousin Joanna."

"Did they? Well, that is something, I suppose. But I'd be willing to bet it was the color and cut that drew the praise. Neither of them would be so rude as to tell you that your bosom was overflowing with too much lace. Tell me, exactly how much lace did you add?"

"Only an extra row. Or two."

Flora shook her head and groaned. "Whatever am I going to do with you?"

"I am a lost cause."

This time Flora did reach across the desk, but instead of throttling Pru, she took Pru's chin in her hand and gently raised it. "Never say that, Prudence. It is not true. Remember what I told you."

"I know. I am worthy of him."

Flora smiled. "You are indeed. And don't ever forget it. You *are* making progress. Just at a slower pace than I would like."

She gave Pru's cheek a pat and then sank back into the chair opposite the desk. "Suppose we approach this . . . transformation in small steps. Lucy is dressing your hair?"

"When we go out in the evenings. She is quite talented."

"Yes, I thought she might be. Have you thought of having her dress your hair every day?"

"Every day?" Pru reached up to find the inevitable curls that had fallen loose. "Why? I spend most days here at my desk. Who's going to see me?"

"Your husband, silly."

"Oh."

"You have lovely hair, Prudence, but it does tend to fly about somewhat. Why don't you ask Lucy to come up with something neat and tidy and easy for every day? Perhaps you could make more use of combs."

"All right. I'll ask her."

"And now, let's consider how you dress during the day."

"I do not wish to invest in a whole new wardrobe, Flora."

"There is no need to do so. Your muslins and cambrics are good quality and well maintained. As are your accessories. There are simply too many of them."

"I beg your pardon?"

"I mean that one lightweight fichu or handkerchief will do the job. There is no need to wear so many of them at once."

"Oh." Her mother had always wrapped herself in layers of scarves and lace and such, and Pru had thought she looked marvelous. She supposed she had unconsciously tried to emulate her mother's flair.

"And when you wear a habit shirt, my dear, there is no need for a fichu at all. When you over-drape yourself, there is a perception of plumpness, especially in one of your small stature."

Pru remembered Madame Lanchester's comment about pouter pigeons. Was that what she'd meant?

"Besides," Flora continued, "all that compli-cated layering is . . . well, to be quite blunt, my dear, it is somewhat outré. Those styles were fash-ionable several years back, but styles are simpler now. As you would know if you paid more atten-tion to the content of my fashion reports, instead of only grammar and word counts."

"I don't wish to be unfashionable." Especially now that people paid her more attention—at least they did whenever she had Nicholas on her arm. And she did not want to embarrass him with her lack of modishness. "What do you suggest? Within reason, of course."

"Come over here and let's have a look."

Pru rose, walked around the desk, and stood in front of Flora. She remembered the last time she had done so, and kept her distance. Nicholas was still at breakfast, after all. He might come down-stairs at any moment.

"I think we can dispense with the handkerchief, pretty though it is."

Pru carefully unpinned the folded square of fig-ured muslin and removed it.

"You see?" Flora said. "Better already. Now that nice little habit shirt with its dainty pleating is shown to its best advantage. And you are quite covered up enough, what with all those little but-tons up to your throat. The handkerchief was a bit excessive. Now, pin that little brooch up under the collar, and voilà. A whole new look. Very pretty. Let's make a new rule."

"What rule?"

"From now on, whenever you come downstairs each morning, remove one item. I guarantee it will not be missed."

"Are you sure?"

"Trust me, Pru. I know what I'm talking about. Was I not hired as the *Cabinet*'s fashion editor? Now, let's have a little chat with Lucy about your hair, shall we? Someone is coming down the stairs. Perhaps it is Lucy."

Pru went to the doorway. "No, I believe it is Nicholas and his father."

A sharp intake of breath behind her caused Pru to turn around. Flora had risen to her feet and wore a strange expression on her face—a mixture of curiosity and anticipation.

"Bartholomew Parrish is here?"

"Yes. He arrived last night. Shall I introduce you?"

"Oh, we've already met," Flora said, and a smile tugged at her lips. "At Edwina's wedding."

"Yes, of course. I'd forgotten."

Pru stepped into the hallway and waylaid her husband and father-in-law. "Mr. Parrish . . . that is, Bartholomew, would you step into the office for a moment. If you don't mind."

"Of course, my dear. Nick has been speaking highly of your work on the magazine. I should be pleased to have a look." He followed her through the doorway, but came to a halt when he saw Flora. His eyes widened.

"Actually," Pru said, "I wanted to introduce

you to our fashion editor, and my friend, Mrs. Gallagher. But she has just reminded me that you met at Edwina's wedding."

Bartholomew stepped forward and took the hand Flora held out to him. "We did indeed. It is a pleasure to see you again, Mrs. Gallagher."

"The pleasure is all mine, sir. And what brings you to Town again so soon?"

"I had a notion that I would like to get to know my new daughter-in-law. And I thought to look up a few . . . old friends. In fact, I was on my way just now to call upon one of them."

"Well, then. It was nice to see you again, sir. Perhaps our paths will cross once or twice while you are in Town?" She turned to Pru. "I'm afraid I must dash. I promised Mrs. Phillips I would stop by to see some of the gowns she would like to feature in our next issue's plates."

How odd. Flora had been ready to stay long enough to chat with Lucy about hairstyles, but now seemed anxious to leave.

"And don't forget that new rule we discussed," Flora said.

Pru smiled. "I won't forget."

"May I drop you somewhere, Mrs. Gallagher," Bartholomew said. "I'd be happy to share a hackney."

"I thank you, sir, but I have my own carriage waiting outside. Perhaps I might drop *you* somewhere, Mr. Parrish?"

"I would be delighted, ma'am. Prudence, my

dear, I will most likely be out all day and will dine with friends. If you and Nick have plans for the evening, do not worry about me."

He offered his arm to Flora, and led her out the front door.

Both Pru and Nicholas stared after them in silence. They turned toward each other at the same moment, wearing matching expressions of puzzlement.

"That was certainly odd," Nicholas asked. "But Father has been in a strange mood all morning."

"Has he?" Pru could not suppress a grin.

"What? Why is everyone so damned merry this morning? What's going on?"

Pru felt the color rise in her cheeks. "It really is none of my business."

"What is none of your business?"

"Your father and Flora."

Nicholas stared at her wide-eyed and incredulous. "You don't think . . . ? No. I won't believe it."

Pru shrugged. She did not know Bartholomew Parrish very well, and so would not presume to understand his behavior any better than Nicholas. But she did indeed believe there was something going on between him and Flora. When he had first come into the room and seen Flora, the air had fairly crackled with . . . something.

"Not Father and Flora," Nicholas said. "No, Pru, I simply will not believe it. It is too ridiculous."

She gazed at him, puzzled by his attitude. "Why? Why is it ridiculous? Do you disapprove because of Flora's past?"

He frowned. "No. No, of course not. It is just not like Father to . . . Well, he has always kept to himself."

"Maybe he has discovered a reason not to. She is a rather extraordinary woman."

His frown twisted up into a smile. "She is that. I do think, though, you are being a bit hasty. He's only just arrived. How can there be something between them?"

She supposed it was difficult to think of one's parents as human. Pru certainly did not like to imagine her own father with another woman. She would not press the matter with Nicholas. He was clearly unsettled by the notion of Flora with his father.

"I am sure you are right," she said.

"But tell me," he said, "what is this new rule Flora mentioned."

"Oh." Her cheeks burned and she knew they must be flushed with ugly crimson patches. She looked away. "It was nothing."

"Pru? What is it? You're blushing."

"I'm always bl-blushing."

Nicholas chuckled. "It's your fair coloring. Just like Simon. Never knew a man to pink up as much as he does. But what is it, Pru. What is this new rule that makes you blush so?"

"It is just some silliness," she said, "about my . . . my manner of dress."

"Your manner of dress?"

"Flora has taken it upon herself to be . . . my fashion adviser."

"Has she indeed?"

Pru heard the smile in his voice, though she continued to look away from him.

"She is very stylish, you know," Pru said. "And I am . . . not. I believe she sees me as a sort of project."

Nicholas took her chin in his hand and turned her face so that she was made to look in his eyes. He was smiling. "It is a successful project, my dear."

"It is?" Her voice came out in an embarrassing little squeak.

"A fine success. You look very pretty. Is that a new dress?" He gave her cheek a brief stroke with his knuckle, and released her chin.

"This? Oh, no, it's not new." It was difficult to speak with her heart thumping so hard in her chest. His touch always did such strange and amazing things to her body. "I've w-worn it a hundred times before."

"Have you? Funny. It doesn't look familiar."

"It's the new rule."

"I beg your pardon?"

"Flora's rule. She says I wear too many accessories, and I am to remove one of them before coming downstairs. She made me take off my handkerchief."

Nicholas, still smiling, passed a hand over his mouth as he muttered something under his breath. She could not make it out, but it sounded like "Goodness Flora." Or maybe it was "God bless Flora."

"It seems like a fine rule to me," he said aloud.

"Then I shall follow it. I would like . . . that is, I have felt . . . badly, that you have been saddled with such a dowdy female for a wife. I do not wish you to be . . . ashamed of me."

Good Lord, had she really said that? She stifled a groan at her own stupidity. She sounded like a pathetic, abject creature. How was she to make him desire her if she behaved like such a ninny?

"Pru? Is that what you think? That I'm ashamed of you?"

She dropped her gaze and studied the toes of her slippers. "I'm sorry. I should not have said that. You are too much a gentleman to be ashamed of me." Or to say so if he was.

He lifted her chin again. "Don't say such things, Pru. There is nothing about you to be ashamed of. Nothing at all. Quite the contrary, in fact."

And then a miracle happened. He bent his head and gently touched his lips to hers. Ever so softly. Ever so briefly.

It was the first time in her life a man had kissed her on the lips. Even at their wedding, Nicholas had merely given her a chaste salute on the cheek. But this . . . this was different. This was wonderful.

She gave a tiny gasp when he pulled back, startled that it was over so soon. She had wanted it to last forever. Embarrassed at her reaction, she brought a hand to her mouth, and found her lips tingling. It was as if she could still feel him there, as if his lips had left an imprint on hers. The notion sent a tremor of excitement through her body.

Nicholas had kissed her!

He released her chin and stepped back. Pru looked up at him, wide-eyed with joy.

"I'm sorry, Pru. I shouldn't have done that."

And the joy crumbled at her feet. What was he saying?

He wore a look of chagrin and stepped back a few more steps, deliberately putting more distance between them. More distance, when she wanted him ever so much closer.

"I promised to give you time. I promised to move slowly. I can see I have moved too quickly. I've frightened you. Startled you. I should never have imposed. You aren't ready. I am sorry, Pru. It won't happen again. I . . . promise. Please forgive me."

He turned on his heel and left the room. A moment later, she heard the front door open, and close behind him. He had fled. Because he thought he'd offended her.

You aren't ready.

If she were any more *ready*, she'd burst.

She sank into the nearest chair before her knees could give way. She touched her lips again. How was it she could still feel him there after such brief contact? How was it such a simple, almost chaste kiss set up such a longing in her for something more? And how was it he didn't know that?

She closed her eyes and tried very hard not to cry. This marriage was turning out so much more difficult than she expected. She had thought, at least for that first day, that Nicholas would take what was now his, even if the imposed intimacy was feigned. Instead, he played the honorable gentleman and left the pursuit of a physical relationship in her hands. And she was too stupid and too shy to take the control he'd given her and let him know she would welcome his touch.

She could not help being shy. Modesty was a part of her nature. Nicholas no doubt equated her behavior with prudery. She was easily embarrassed by the whole business, but she was not a prude. She wanted to experience the full physical aspect of marriage. She longed for it more than anything. It was just so difficult to imagine how she was ever to let him know that. And so he would think her a prude and put off consummating their marriage as long as he could.

She didn't know what to do.

Yes, she did. Flora had taught her, but she'd been too shy and embarrassed to put the lessons in action. Perhaps it was time to swallow her pride and make another attempt at flirtation.

Pru was going to have to flirt in earnest with her husband if she ever wanted more than a simple kiss.

Chapter 10

Nick opened the front door to the sound of raucous, but definitely feminine, laughter. The Crimson Ladies. He smiled as he wondered what had set them off this time. When he stepped into the entry to see his father fleeing full speed up the stairs, his smile faltered.

What had they done?

He thought to follow his father upstairs. He'd seen very little of Bartholomew since he'd arrived a few days earlier. But perhaps he should first find out what the resident doxies had been up to. He walked to the dining room, where the Crimson Ladies worked, and poked his head in the doorway.

" 'Ello, dearie." Sadie's voice rose about the din of chatter and laughter. "Come on in 'ere and give us grotty old tarts a rare treat, jus' ter look at yer."

The chatter ceased, and six pairs of eyes pinned him to the spot. Suggestive smiles, winks, and thrust bosoms were aimed in his direction.

"Ladies." He stepped into the room, accustomed to their bold manner, unaffected by it. "Have you been misbehaving again?"

Barks of laughter filled the air, as they poked one another in the ribs and wiggled their bosoms provocatively.

"Wotcher mean, then?" Madge asked. The erstwhile supervisor of the colorists, she was always quick to rein in their raucousness and set them back to work. "We done summink wrong?"

"I suspect you spooked my father," Nick said. He smiled as he spoke so they would know he was only teasing. "I just saw him bolt up the stairs as though running for his life."

"Yer da?" Bess still had a bit of Ireland in her voice. "That feller was yer da?"

"Yes. What did you say to send him dashing off like a scared rabbit?"

"Nuffink much," Sadie said. "D'int give us time. Took one look an' was orff faster'n a bride's nightie." She giggled. "Beggin' yer pardon, sir."

"Nice-lookin' man, yer da," Ginny said. "Clear as day where yer got t'at pretty phiz of yers."

"I suppose you said as much to him?" Nick asked.

Ginny shrugged, her frizzy brown curls bouncing at the movement. "Dunno. Mighta done."

"Don't yer listen to 'er, Mr. Nick," Daisy said above the laughter that once again filled the room.

"Ginny tol' 'im what corner she worked an' what time ter come by. Offered 'im a cut rate, too."

Dear God. No wonder his father had fled. Nick bit back a smile.

"I'm dreadful sorry, Mr. Nick," Madge said, and sent Ginny a steely glare. "We d'int know 'e was yer pa. I tries ter keep th' girls in line, but sometime it be like 'erding cats. I keeps tellin' 'em while we're in yer 'ouse, we gotter act nice, like."

"It's my father's house, actually. And he's just a simple country gentleman. He's not used to the likes of you ladies." Nick flashed a grin. "Try not to frighten him to death, will you?"

"Sweet Jaysus, yer don't t'ink 'e'll t'row us out, do yer?" Bess had sobered at that thought. The Ladies needed this work. It kept them off the streets. For the most part.

"I will speak to him," Nick said, "and explain what you're doing. You won't lose your work, I promise you. Just . . . try to behave while he is staying here."

"Yessir, Mr. Nick," Madge said. "We won't be no more trouble. Else I'll box me a few ears, I will."

"Thank you, ladies."

Nick grinned as he turned to leave. Lord, what must his father have thought, finding a group of old bawds occupying his dining room? He was grinning at the thought when he entered the hallway and ran smack into Pru.

"I beg your pardon," he said, and instinctively

reached out to steady her. He dropped his hands when he felt her stiffen beneath his touch. She colored up and gazed at the floor.

"I'm s-sorry," she said.

Damn. He had learned she stammered when she felt at her most awkward. That foolish little kiss the day before had only increased the uneasiness between them instead of chipping away at it. Damn, damn, damn.

"I am just going upstairs to speak to my father," he said, trying to keep his tone easy, not giving away the frustration he felt. "We've seen so little of him, I was hoping he might be free this evening. Perhaps we could have a nice, quiet dinner here at home? Just the three of us?"

"That w-would be lovely. I'll go d-down and talk to Mrs. Gibb about the menu."

She looked ready to bolt, but he was determined that his wife should learn to be comfortable with him, and so he kept her talking. "Father is partial to roast lamb," he said.

"Oh. Is he? I will send Mrs. Gibb to the butcher if she doesn't have lamb in the larder."

"That would be very nice, Pru. By the way, I have a favor to ask."

"A favor?"

"Yes. I was working on a pamphlet yesterday about the state of parish apprentices, and I fear I got a bit carried away with my invective. You are much better at this than I am. I was wondering if you'd take a look. You always seem to know the right words, to persuade with subtlety rather than bombast. I've often admired that about your work."

A rosy pink hue flooded her cheeks, but Nick sensed it was a glow of pleasure and not embarrassment.

"That is very kind of you to say," she said.

"It's not kindness. It's truth. I need your help, Pru. Will you have a look at it tomorrow?"

"Yes, of course."

"I knew I could count on you." Without thinking, he reached and touched a wayward curl that had sprung loose from its comb and danced fetchingly beside her eye.

She gave a little start and reached up to tuck the curl back into place, but Nick captured her hand instead.

"Leave it," he said. "It is charming."

She seemed thoroughly flustered and stared at their joined hands. He brought her fingers to his lips and kissed them. "I adore your hair, Pru. Every defiant little curl."

"You do?" Her voice was almost a whisper.

"I do. You know how I am drawn to rebellion." He smiled, hoping to put her at ease but failing. She seemed barely able to breathe. He released her hand and stepped back.

She expelled a shuddery breath and said, "I must speak with Mrs. Gibb."

Before he could say another word, she had bolted past him to the door leading downstairs to the kitchen.

Nick heaved a weary sigh. Things were not going at all well with this marriage. He kept bungling it by moving too fast. The awkwardness between them had intensified since yesterday's innocent kiss. He had so hoped a simple, uncomplicated kiss would have helped to make her more comfortable with him, but quite the reverse had occurred. Pru had trembled and gasped and stared at him wide-eyed with terror. He'd frightened her, damn it all. Perhaps she had sensed his own reaction. He had not expected a simple kiss to affect him so profoundly. But the instant his lips had met hers, a jolt of pure desire had shot through him with surprising force. He'd recognized it for what it was and pulled back at once, not wanting to take advantage of her. Her innocence had been a powerfully erotic temptation.

But he must honor that innocence and move more slowly. He must not crowd her. Their forced union was difficult enough for her without him pressing her with unwanted attentions. Besides, he had promised to wait until she was ready. He would have to be patient. Unfortunately, patience was not one of his strong suits.

He trudged upstairs and found his father in the drawing room, reading a newspaper while seated on the settee above which *Mars and Venus* was now hung, in pride of place. Nick studied his mother's painting, in which pearly white limbs were entwined and discreet folds of deep red drapery hid very little of what the lovers did. The face of Venus was rapturous with release. Nick wondered if he would ever see such a look on his wife's face. Would he ever know such unbridled sexuality in his own home? Or would he be forced to seek it elsewhere? He had not yet done so. He had wanted to give this marriage, and Pru, a chance. But how long was a man expected to wait?

He tore his gaze away from the lusty and illicit lovers and stepped into the room.

"Hullo, Father. Did the Ladies give you a fright?"

Pru smiled as she listened to her husband and father-in-law reminisce about Nicholas's boyhood in Derbyshire. She took another bite of Mrs. Gibb's excellent apple tart and watched her two dinner companions. Her eyes were most often drawn to her husband. She was encouraged by recent developments. Even though he had backed away and apologized for kissing her yesterday, today he had taken her hand and kissed her fingers. He had done so many times before, of course, but only in the presence of her family, when he was trying to give credence to their supposed love match. There had been no one watching today, though, and so she could only surmise he had done it because he'd wanted to. And he had not apologized.

It gave her hope.

Father and son were chuckling over some remembered tale. They looked very much alike, especially when laughing and smiling, and both were equally charming. It would be no surprise if Flora had fallen under Bartholomew's spell. Just as Pru had—

"Is it true, Prudence," Bartholomew said, interrupting her wayward thoughts, "that you have fifty-two cousins?"

"First cousins, yes."

Bartholomew smiled and shook his head in disbelief. "Good Gad."

"I have already apologized to Pru," Nicholas said, his dark eyes twinkling, "for aligning her to such a paltry little family as ours. You could populate a good-sized town with Pru's relatives."

"You must, then, be accustomed to a very busy household, my dear," Bartholomew said.

"I suppose so," Pru replied. "With five brothers and a sister, plus a constant flow of visiting cousins, it was always a bit crowded. But I didn't mind. It was just the way things were. I never knew any other way to live."

"Well, I must confess I have grown accustomed to my solitude," Bartholomew said. "I have lived alone for so long that all the comings and goings here are a bit disconcerting at times."

Nicholas laughed. "It is the Crimson Ladies that disconcert you, I believe."

"Oh, dear," Pru said. "Have the Ladies been bothering you, sir?"

Bartholomew gave a sheepish grin and hunched a shoulder. "Let us just say they startled me a bit. I had not expected to find such . . . colorful characters in my dining room. But it is not just the Ladies. There is a great deal of activity here, which I have found somewhat surprising."

"It is the *Cabinet* business," Nicholas said. "What with printers' apprentices and binders and engravers and distributors and advertisers, there is always someone about."

"So I have noticed," Batholomew said. "I confess I hadn't realized how busy it could be. But of course, I am accustomed to my solitary existence in the country and not used to the noise and bustle of city life."

"That's why I am still surprised you returned to London so soon after your last visit," Nicholas said. "You are always welcome, of course. And it *is* your house. But I don't wish for you to be unhappy, or uncomfortable here."

"I am nothing of the sort," Bartholomew said. "In fact, I am enjoying my stay in Town more than I could have imagined. Getting to know my new daughter-in-law. Renewing old acquaintances. It is all rather pleasant, actually."

Throughout the rest of the evening Pru was unable to shake off the uneasiness brought about by Bartholomew's offhand comment about the busy atmosphere of the house. It belonged to him, after all. Was he too kind to admit that he did not want her and Nicholas and the *Cabinet* to remain there?

Nick could not concentrate. He was trying to write an article in support of the new factory bill under discussion in the House, but his eyes kept

drifting across the room to where Pru sat working at the desk. Normally, when she escaped into
her work on the *Cabinet* she seemed to relax, to
be more at ease than at any other time. But she
was not relaxed at the moment. There was tension in the way she held her shoulders and in the
set of her jaw. It pained him to see her so on edge.
He wished he could break through, or help her
break through, the awkward barrier still between
them.

"What's troubling you, Pru?"

She looked up at him, her blue eyes large behind the spectacles she wore when she worked.

"Is it something I can help with?" he asked.
"You've taken on so much in Edwina's absence.
Please don't hesitate to delegate something to me.
I am happy to help."

"Thank you, Nicholas, but I believe the next issue is under control. As long as you finish that article you promised. No, I was thinking of
something else. I was thinking of your father."

"Father? What about him?"

"I realize he is your parent and I don't know
him very well, but . . ."

"But?"

She started to say something more, stopped,
seemed to consider it, started again, and
stopped again. What was it she was finding so
difficult to say?

"Don't tell me you are still thinking about him
and Flora?" he asked. "I shouldn't worry about
that if I were you."

"No, I wasn't thinking of Flora." She pulled a face, as though considering the idea, and added, "Not exactly."

"What, then?"

"It's just . . . I don't think he likes us using his house for the *Cabinet*."

"You are thinking of what he said last night."

"Yes. And I know he said it was just that he is not accustomed to being in Town, but Nicholas, it *is* his house."

"And?" He did not like the direction in which he feared this conversation was headed.

"And it is a bit crowded, what with all the magazine work and the Ladies coming and going. And . . . and with the three of us living here. He did say he was accustomed to more privacy. I was just wondering if . . . if he would prefer it if we moved into a place of our own."

Nick looked down at the half-written page in front of him. His spine prickled with annoyance. He was not going to listen to such nonsense. "I am sorry, Pru, but I cannot afford to buy us a house of our own."

"But I can."

He looked up sharply. "No. I have told you I will not take your money."

"But—"

"I said no, Pru and I mean it." His voice had risen with anger, but he could not help it. This was not a subject for discussion. He had told her from the beginning how it would be and she had agreed. Or so he had thought. But he'd been wrong. She had no doubt been waiting for the right moment to broach the subject again. And his father's presence in the house and his comment about the busy atmosphere was the perfect opportunity.

Well, he would not be cajoled or shamed or bullied into using his wife's money like some toad-eating freeloader. He had never wanted to marry an heiress. He was *not* a fortune hunter.

"I did not marry you for your money, Pru, as you well know. I am sorry," he said, his voice dripping with scorn, "that you are forced to live in such a small, crowded, unimpressive little house on such an unfashionable square. Something so far beneath your fine aristocratic upbringing. But you are stuck with both me and this house. I suggest you get used to it."

Her face crumbled and tears filled her eyes. Without a word, she jerked to her feet and fled the room.

Good God, what had he done?

He folded his arms on the table and dropped his head on them. Damn. He hadn't meant to make her cry. He despised himself for doing so. He wished he could take back his words, that he hadn't spoken so harshly, so sarcastically. But, dammit, she'd made him angry. Why did she have to bring up her money again? He hated being reminded that he had none of his own. Not yet, anyway.

The sound of music caused him to lift his head. She was playing. Something loud and angry.

* * *

Pru sent all her emotion into her fingers as they flew across the shiny new keys of the Broadwood. She would not think of Nicholas or what he'd said. She ignored the hard lump in her throat and the sting of tears in her eyes. Never very good at expressing her feelings in words, she had learned to use music to cleanse her soul.

And she did so now as she pounded out the allegro movement to one of Herr Beethoven's recent sonatas. Pru did not know the piece well and played it badly. But she did not care. The notes perfectly expressed the turmoil of her emotions and would ultimately, she knew, soothe her tattered nerves.

She played and played, lost in the passion of the notes, until she felt a presence at her side. She stopped abruptly when she realized Nicholas was standing next to the bench, watching and listening.

She dropped her hands into her lap. She could not look at him. She recalled his words again—she had not quite yet purged them from her mind— and did not want to see him.

"Don't stop," he said. "Please finish the piece."

"No. I don't wish to play anymore." She made a move to rise, but he placed a gentle hand on her shoulder. There was such warmth in his touch, she wanted to lean into it, to absorb his heat into her skin. But he had said hateful things to her, and she should not be wanting anything of him just now.

"Please, Pru. I know I hurt you with what I said. And I also know you will never tell me so. But your music. Ah, Pru, such emotion! Finish the piece. Send your anger into the music. But please, let me stay and listen."

She did not look up at him. It shook her a bit that he knew what she was doing. It was cowardly, she supposed, to use music as an escape, but she had done so all her life. Besides the simple enjoyment of entertaining herself, she played for two reasons. One was to challenge herself. She played well enough, but always sought to improve. Even if no one heard, there was a keen thrill of accomplishment when mastering a difficult piece. Afterward, she would often reward herself with a simple country song or ballad, which she loved. But pushing her considerable skill to the limit helped to make her real world—where all was awkwardness, strain, and uncertainty—recede for a short while.

The second reason she played was to give vent to feelings she could not express verbally. As she had been doing a moment ago. Could she do it with Nicholas listening and knowing what it meant?

She was not sure.

Her fingers crept back up to the keyboard, almost of their own volition. She rested them softly on the keys a moment, then started the allegro once again.

No longer as angry, she played with more skill. But the power of the notes soon overwhelmed her again, and she was lost to their passion as the music moved from somber to frenetic and back again. When she finished, she took a deep breath and realized the allegro had done its work. She had been soothed. She was no longer angry or hurt.

"Pru?"

Lord, she'd almost forgotten Nicholas was there. Such was the power of Herr Beethoven. She looked up and was surprised when he sat down beside her on the bench. It was a small bench. Their bodies touched all along one side, from shoulder to thigh. She gave an involuntary little shiver.

"What was that piece, Pru? I don't believe I've ever heard it."

"It is part of a sonata by Herr Beethoven. It is known as"—she gave a little smirk at the appropriateness of it—"the *Pathétique*. Edwina sent it from Vienna."

"Edwina knows you play? Am I the only one who didn't know?"

"She didn't know, either, until I asked if she could procure some music for me. Herr Beethoven's music is not yet published here in England. But I am very fond of his work and hoped Edwina might be able to find copies for me."

Pru was drawn to modern musical works, especially those of Beethoven, when she wanted to vent her emotions. She used earlier works of the last century to hone her technical skill, but sometimes they were too mechanical, almost mathematical, and did not stir any passion in her.

These latest sonatas by Beethoven were something quite new. She could not play their rich tones and chords without great feeling and passion. She often wondered what sort of man he was, to be able to compose music with such honest, even raw, emotion.

"It is powerful music," Nicholas said. "And you play it beautifully, even turning your own pages. Pru, you truly are an artist."

"No. I just play a little, for my own enjoyment."

"And to let out your anger. At me. I was horrid to you, Pru. I had no right to say such things. I am dreadfully sorry."

Pru shrugged, and her shoulder rubbed against his. "It's all right. I shouldn't have brought up the subject."

"Listen to me, Pru." He touched her cheek and turned her face toward his. "I really do not want your money. Truly. I have investments that are due to pay off any day now, and then I will be able to support you in better style. You may spend your money on yourself in any way you like. But for us together, I am responsible. Please allow me to take care of our living expenses. All right?"

She nodded her head. "All right." She wondered what he would think if he knew how much of her own money she'd already spent on various small household necessities. He was obviously very sensitive about such things, so she would simply take care that he did not find out. What he did not know could not hurt him.

Then he did something quite unexpected. He put an arm around her shoulder and gave a squeeze. "You're a good sport, Pru. Have patience with me, and I have no doubt we'll work out all these little kinks in this marriage of ours." With his free hand he reached up and rubbed a thumb beneath her eyes. "And I promise never to make you cry again."

"Oh. I do beg your pardon."

Pru dragged her gaze from her husband's beautiful dark eyes to see Bartholomew standing in the drawing room doorway. To her regret, Nicholas dropped his arm from her shoulder, stood, and walked away from the pianoforte.

"Come in, Father. You just missed a superb performance."

"I am sorry I missed it. You must play for me sometime, Prudence."

"I would be happy to," she said, and rose to her feet. "But just now, I think I shall ring for tea. I hope you will join us, sir?"

After ringing for Lucy and giving her instructions for tea, Pru excused herself for a moment and dashed upstairs to her bedchamber. She splashed cold water on her face, hoping to erase any signs of her earlier tears. When she looked in the mirror, she instinctively reached up to adjust her hair, which, even with Lucy's skillful arrangement with combs, was never entirely tamed. But then she remembered what Nicholas had said yesterday.

I adore your hair.

She had always found her hair a trial, and so it was quite unbelievable to her that Nicholas liked it. If he adored her hair, might he someday grow to adore the rest of her? She studied her face with its too-big eyes and smattering of freckles. Would it ever be tempting enough for him to want to kiss her again? She had hoped he had been about to do so when he'd apologized so prettily and put his arm around her. But instead he had simply called her a good sport. She did not have the sort of face to tempt a man.

Foolish girl. It wasn't about her face, as Flora was quick to point out. It was attitude and confidence. She had lost a bit of confidence when Nicholas had spoken so harshly to her. But she was determined to not allow his stubborn pride to impact her self-assurance. She was still madly in love with him, but she was no longer blind to his faults. And knowing he wasn't perfect somehow made her love him all the more. What a foolish coil.

I am worthy of him.

She stared at her reflection and repeated the litany a few more times until she felt more sure of herself. She had taken Flora's rule about accessories to heart and removed a fichu this morning before coming downstairs, allowing the V neckline of the bodice to remain open. She did feel a bit bare without some sort of handkerchief or scarf to fill in, but had boldly gone forth without one. And looked better for it. Flora had been right about that.

She shook out her skirts, made one quick adjustment to her bodice, and returned downstairs to the drawing room. Lucy followed close behind and Pru helped her set out the tea service. She poured a cup for Bartholomew and for Nicholas, and passed them a plate of small cakes before pouring her own cup and settling down to enjoy it.

"I hope you will not think it presumptuous," Bartholomew said, after savoring a bit of cream cake, "but I do believe I have come upon the perfect wedding present for the two of you."

"But sir," Pru said, "you have already brought us the painting."

"That was a gift to you, Prudence. No, I have wanted to give something to both of you and I hope you will approve of what I have done."

"Father?" Nicholas eyed him suspiciously. "What have you done?"

"I have found offices for the *Cabinet*."

"Offices?"

A rush of panic danced down Pru's spine. He *had* been angry about the magazine business taking over his house. Was he going to ask her to give up the *Cabinet*? "But sir," she said, "I . . . that is, we . . . that is . . ." She took a deep shuddery breath to compose herself. "It is no tr-trouble to work on the *Cabinet*. I . . . enjoy it."

Batholomew reached across the tea table and patted her hand. "I know you do, my dear. And I am proud of what you and Edwina and Nick have done with it. Exceedingly proud. But it is high time the magazine had offices of its own, don't you think?"

"Oh." As the full implication of his words sank in, the tiniest twinge of exhilaration began to flutter in her breast. "Oh."

Batholomew smiled. "I can see you agree with me, Prudence. With the magazine business growing so much, it seems to me it is time to move it to its own premises. So you no longer have to share your home with a business, like some shopkeeper in Cheapside. So you can dine in the dining room again. So the library can be a restful place again.

So you can have the house all to yourselves—once I have returned to Derbyshire."

Pru did not know what to think. She knew it was meant kindly and was in fact very generous of Bartholomew. The idea of having a home all to themselves was really quite . . . exciting. Before today's confrontation, she had hoped, had dreamed, that someday she and Nicholas could have a real home together, either here at Golden Square or somewhere else. The skeptical look on her husband's face, however, was enough to keep her excitement in check and her tongue between her teeth.

Please, God, don't let him be too stubborn to accept his father's offer. It was not as though it involved her money this time.

"It's very kind of you, Father," he said, "but we have always run the *Cabinet* from the house. For years now."

"I know, and you have all done a wonderful job. But you have a wife now, Nick, and hopefully will have a family one day soon."

Not all that soon, Pru thought, and felt her cheeks color up.

"It no longer seems right to keep the business here," Bartholomew said. "So, I took it upon myself to secure a set of offices for you in St. Paul's Churchyard. As a wedding gift."

"St. Paul's Churchyard?" Pru could barely keep the excitement out of her voice. "But that is where many of our booksellers are, as well as our printer and binder. And lots of other publishers."

"Yes, I know," he said, his eyes twinkling a little in triumph. "That is why I thought it the perfect place for *The Ladies' Fashionable Cabinet* to be published. So, it is a wedding present for the two of you, by way of freeing up this house, and also for Edwina."

"Oh, she will be thrilled," Pru said. "Proper offices!"

Bartholomew chuckled. "Yes, with shelving and storage and lots of work space. Not to mention a good deal of furniture that I convinced the previous owner to leave behind. It's all yours, now. Or the *Cabinet*'s."

"Oh, sir, what a wonderful gift. How can we ever thank you?"

"It is my pleasure, Prudence. It is time this house was simply a home and not a business."

Pru looked to Nicholas, who had said nothing and did not look thrilled about the idea. Why should he object? Surely he could not reject a gift from his own father?

"Nick?" Bartholomew must have sensed the same uneasiness in his son. "You are very quiet. Have I done something I shouldn't? Ought I to have consulted with you first?"

"No, of course not," Nicholas said, and he finally offered a smile. A genuine full-blown smile that reached all the way to his eyes, the sort that made him look his most handsome. "It is exceedingly generous of you, Father. And quite the most perfect gift. Of course, the magazine is not mine.

Pru is the editor in Edwina's absence. And if the editor is happy, then so am I."

The editor was definitely happy. It just might be the first real step toward a life of their own, a life together and apart from the business. A chance to make this marriage work.

Oh, yes, the editor was most excessively happy.

Chapter 11

"Well, what do you think, Pru?"

She turned to Nick, who sat beside her as they bounced along the road back to Golden Square in a hackney coach. Her blue eyes shone with excitement.

"Oh, it's simply wonderful," she said. "It feels more like a professional publication, now that it has its own offices. Don't you think so?"

They had spent the entire day moving boxes full of books and papers from the house to the new magazine offices. Bartholomew had had the rooms thoroughly cleaned, and a crew of laborers was on hand to move furniture about or install more shelving. His father had done everything possible to make the move easy and painless, and Nick was grateful.

He had to admit that at first he'd been skeptical. Coming so soon after the unpleasant confrontation with Pru over moving out of the house, his father's offer had seemed almost too coincidental. Nick's first thought was that the whole thing had been Pru's idea: that they—or she—buy a house of their own, and also arrange to have the magazine business moved elsewhere. All because of some misguided notion that his father wanted the house to himself.

It had not taken long to realize he'd been wrong. Pru's initial panic that his father somehow meant to take the business away, and then her controlled but obvious delight at the prospect of moving into real offices, had convinced him she had nothing to do with it.

Nick had also experienced a momentary niggling concern that moving the business was not perhaps a good idea. With the exception of that afternoon, working together on the magazine was the only time he and Pru seemed entirely at ease together. He had wondered if removing that comfortable haven would put a further strain on their marriage. But a moment's reflection convinced him that it was, instead, a brilliant idea. Keeping home life and business life separate might be just what they needed to forge a new level of intimacy.

"Yes, it does seem more like a real business now," he said. "I hope Edwina won't return from the continent and discover she cannot find where anything is." Pru and Nick had spent most of the afternoon going through boxes and organizing files. "She is so disgustingly organized, you know."

Pru gave a little chuckle. "Yes, I do know. That is why I was so careful to keep things in order. Just a bit more spread out. Oh, I cannot wait to get started! It will be so good to have enough room to line up a whole set of page proofs on a large work-table, rather than reviewing them in bits and pieces. And a whole room set aside for the Ladies. And a private office for meeting with advertisers and such. Oh, Nicholas, it is all so wonderful. How very kind of your father to procure the lease for us. And to pay the first year in advance. With the increased circulation and new advertising, we have more than enough to cover the rent after that."

Nick nodded in agreement. He loved it when Pru forgot to be shy and burst into these little explosions of words. She was so quiet most of the time that it was a delight to hear her chatter.

And to watch the excitement light her face. She positively glowed with it. Nick marveled at how pretty she looked, with those big blue eyes and radiant smile. He could not tear his eyes away, and still marveled that he had ever thought her mousy and dull. What a fool he'd been.

Her eyes were his favorite feature. As clear a blue as summer skies, and framed in lashes that were thick and curled, but very pale. Most fashionable women would have darkened such fair lashes, but Nick was glad Pru had never done so. Somehow her eyes appeared bluer and bigger with that surround of pale apricot fringe.

Or perhaps it was her hair he liked best. It was so beautifully wild. Even now an apricot tendril curled frivolously against her cheek. The fact that is was not artfully done but quite natural made it even more intriguing. Lord, but he could not wait to see it loose and falling about her shoulders.

He thought, too, about how she looked when she played, when she seemed to forget about everything and everybody. It wasn't so much her prettiness that struck him then, but the physical signs of the passion she felt for the music. Her facial expressions ran the gamut from dreamy to pained, her body swayed and tensed, moving into the music as though making love to the instrument.

He had once feared Pru would be too shy to express any physical passion, assuming they ever took their marriage that far. But Nick no longer worried about that. Pru was a woman of passion, even if she did not realize it. He hoped one day to release that sense of abandon between the sheets.

If he could ever be sure he wouldn't frighten her to death.

He had not yet tried to kiss her again. He could not forget that sweet little salute and the wide-eyed look of terror on her face afterward. But he had begun touching her more often, and he noticed she had not flinched or stiffened quite so much when he did.

It gave him hope. But he knew he must still move slowly. In the meantime, he had been working out his frustrated desires with increased physical activity. He'd taken to fencing at Angelo's Academy several times a week. It helped, but it wasn't the cure he needed.

He suddenly realized she'd been talking and he hadn't heard a word. "I'm sorry, my dear, I was woolgathering. What was that you were saying?"

She flashed an indulgent smile. "I said we will need to send out notices to all our vendors and advertisers, alerting them to our new direction. I must start writing them out first thing tomorrow."

"Why not have Imber print up an announcement? That would certainly save you a great deal of time."

"Oh, what a good idea. Another sign of how professional we have become. Isn't it marvelous that Imber is only a few doors away now? I shall pop round to see him in the morning."

Nick happened at that moment to look out the window on Pru's side of the carriage, and saw a pair of unpleasant-looking characters fighting over a jug, then one of them sank laughing into the gutter. He realized how close they were to the worst rookeries in London.

He turned to Pru and reached for her hand. "My dear, you must promise me something."

She looked down at their joined fingers but did not pull away. It was a good sign. She was becoming accustomed to his touch.

"Yes?"

"You must never leave the offices alone at night or in the late afternoon. If I am not there with you, then you must let me know when you would like to be fetched, and I will bring a hackney. I don't want you out alone in these neighborhoods. It's not safe."

"Oh." She looked out the window, where by now there was nothing more to be seen than ordinary people out and about on ordinary business. She turned to Nick, a quizzical look on her face.

He squeezed her hand. "Promise me, Pru. The streets closer to the offices border on some rather unsavory areas. And you practically skirt the rookeries on the way back home. It's not safe for a woman alone."

"But you would have to drive all this way to fetch me," she said. "It seems like a great deal of bother."

"It is no trouble at all. I am happy to do it. I want you to be safe, my dear. We'll simply agree on a time for me to come by the offices, and if you aren't quite finished for the day, I will wait until you are. All right?"

"All right. I had not considered it, but I suppose we will be spending a great deal more than usual on hackney fares."

Nick winced. Just because he could not afford to buy a house did not mean he was a complete pauper. Lord, but he could not wait for the *Ulysses* to come in with, quite literally, a boatload of profit. It was slightly overdue, but not enough to be a concern. He promised himself that when it did come in, he was not going to send every penny up to the Derby project. He was going to buy something nice for Pru. He stroked her long, soft fingers and came up against his signet ring with its wrapping of ribbon. When the *Ulysses* came in, perhaps he would buy her a proper wedding ring.

"Well, isn't this cozy."

Flora looked about her as she stood in the part of the office that had been screened off into a small reception area. Pru had even brought in a few plants to make it seem more inviting.

"Do you like it?" she asked.

"I do. It's quite clubby, isn't it? Very comfortable, my dear."

"There is a small office for you, Flora."

"For me?

"Yes, of course. The fashion editor needs her own space, don't you think? Come, let me show you."

It was little more than a cubbyhole with a desk, but Flora beamed. "Oh, it is positively cunning! I shall pin fashion plates all along the walls. What fun we shall have! I *knew* this would be a good idea."

"What do you mean?"

"Moving the offices here. I knew it would be the perfect wedding gift."

"Flora? What are you saying? Did you have something to do with all this?"

"Well, of course, my dear. Didn't Bartholomew tell you? No, I suppose he wouldn't. It was my idea, ducky." She leaned close to Pru and whispered in her ear. "I thought you and that handsome husband of yours needed to have the house to yourselves. Or at least you will when Bartholomew leaves."

"Flora? You talked him into doing this?"

"Well, to be quite frank, I just put a little bug in his ear and let it buzz around a bit. In the end, it was all his doing."

"It doesn't matter whose idea it was, I am grateful. The business has grown so that it had taken over the entire ground floor of the town house."

"Yes, which made you little better than a shopkeeper."

Pru narrowed her eyes. "That's exactly what Bartholomew said."

"I'm sure he did."

"Flora? When has all this scheming taken place? Have you and Bartholomew been—"

"He is a charming man, is he not? And quite as handsome as his son."

"Flora?"

"Look to your own business, Pru. I am doing quite well on my own."

Pru's cheeks flushed. Apparently she had guessed correctly. Flora and Bartholomew *were* involved. How extraordinary. She wondered what Nicholas would think. He seemed not to believe it was possible. But why not? They were both attractive, unattached adults. So long as they were discreet, what should it matter?

"Stop thinking about it, Pru. You're putting

wrinkles in your brow, and that will not do. Show me around instead. Let me see what you've done."

And so Pru gave her a brief tour. There were four small private offices: one for Edwina, with all the editorial files and account books; one for Pru, with all the subscription files and advertising contracts; one for Flora, with all her fashion files; and one that could be used by Nicholas, or Simon Westover, or any other contributor who might need a place to work, or as a private office for meeting with advertisers and vendors. And there were two workrooms, each fitted with several large tables. One would be for the hand-coloring and the Crimson Ladies. The other would be for putting together mock-ups and reviewing page proofs and any other work that needed a large space. There was even a tiny kitchen area near the back, so they could at least make a pot of tea whenever they wanted. It was all quite compact but sensibly and efficiently arranged. Pru could not wait for Edwina's return. She would be astonished.

Flora was suitably impressed with how quickly everything had been installed, and approved of the general layout.

"I especially like your little reception area," she said, "with all the framed mastheads and fashion plates in the window. An inspired choice of decor."

"They were all hung in Edwina's office back at the house," Pru said.

"Yes, and lost among the clutter. Here, they

stand out and showcase what is accomplished inside. The other publishers on the street will be green with envy. Well done, my girl."

Pru smiled. "Thank you, Flora. And you might be pleased to know that I have asked Madge to expand her role. Starting tomorrow, she will be installed behind a small desk in the reception area and will be charged with determining the business of anyone who enters."

"She will be your entry clerk?"

"More or less."

Flora frowned. "My girl, are you sure that is wise? Most businesses use a young man for that role. And Madge is still somewhat . . . colorful."

"She has learned to read and write, and is working hard to make a better life for herself. She can direct visitors to the right office just as well as any man, Flora."

"Touché, Prudence. Edwina will certainly approve." She flashed a wicked grin. "I do believe you ladies will cause a stir in St. Paul's Churchyard."

They went into Pru's office together. Just as at the house on Golden Square, Flora took the chair opposite the desk and made herself at home. Even though she now had her own tiny office, Pru suspected she would nevertheless continue to spend much of her time in Pru's office. If truth be told, however, they seldom discussed business when they sat together. The conversation was more often of a personal nature. From the look in Flora's eye, this time would be no different.

"And so, how are you, my girl? How are things progressing?"

Pru did not pretend to misunderstand. "I think I need a few more lessons."

"Oh?"

"I'm not very good at this, Flora."

"Nonsense. You just need more practice. But let's try something easy." She pulled a fan out of her reticule and snapped it open. "It is time you learned the language of fans."

"La! What a crush."

Nick slanted a glance at Pru, just to make sure it was actually his wife on his arm and not some stranger. She'd been acting a bit oddish ever since they'd arrived at her cousin's rout party. Nothing he could put his finger on. Just the occasional word or expression he would never have expected from her.

He wondered if she was nervous, though he could not imagine why she should be. She was well acquainted with their hosts, Lord and Lady Russell. The viscountess was the daughter of Pru's uncle, Lord Phillip Armitage, and had been friendly enough when she'd greeted them. A touch too vociferous, but so were all Pru's relatives. And of course, the place was full of them. Nick could spot them now, even without an introduction. Tall, blond, and loud, and with some variation of what he'd come to recognize as the Armitage nose. A few of the uncles had prodigious honkers, and some of the women had perfect little noses with only the merest hint of aquilinity. The rest, like Pru, fell somewhere in between. But there was a similarity quite obvious when so many family members were gathered together.

"Ah, Prudence. How lovely to see you."

A middle-aged female blessed with one of the more beaky versions of the nose had joined them. Nick was sure he'd met her before, but could not remember which Armitage she was. Her eyes darted quizzically between him and Pru.

"Good evening, Gertrude. Nicholas, you remember my cousin, Lady Stockton?"

"Yes, of course." He took her outstretched hand.

They engaged in small talk for a few minutes before Her Ladyship was hailed by another turbaned matron.

"I declare, Nicholas," Pru said, working her fan vigorously, "I have never been noticed quite so much as I have been since marrying you. It is rather marvelous what a handsome husband can do for one's consequence."

She stopped fanning, brought the open fan up to her face, and poked herself in the eye.

"My dear, are you all right?" Nick kept his hand at her elbow while she blinked rapidly and dabbed at the corner of her eye.

"I'm fine," she said. "I'm fine. It is nothing, really."

After a moment, she looked up and smiled, then brought the closed fan to rest on her right cheek. He wondered if she knew that it was a signal, and a rather suggestive one at that. No, Pru was not the sort of woman to know anything about flirting with fans. And even if she was, he could not imagine she would ever flirt with a man she had been trapped into marrying against her will. No, it was simply a natural gesture, more shy than provocative. And utterly charming. With her eyes still a bit watery, they seemed more blue than ever. He wanted to drown in them.

"You look very pretty tonight, Pru." It was not mere flattery, he realized. He meant it. She could hold her own tonight with any of her more stylish relatives. Her hair was dressed with a large gold comb in the back, over which spilled carefully arranged cascades of apricot curls. She wore a short blue tunic over a white petticoat, and for once the neckline was not smothered in lace. There was a hint of cleavage on display. Only the merest hint—nothing anywhere near as daring as most every other woman in attendance, some of whom wore bodices so low-cut there was little left to the imagination—but enough to make Nick anxious to see more. It was definitely a welcome change. And the color perfectly matched her eyes. The eyes that looked up at him, drawing him, making him want to kiss her then and there.

It seemed ever since he'd promised not to impose upon her, he'd thought of nothing but imposing. This surprisingly powerful lust he'd developed for his wife, the lust that he was honor-bound to keep in check, was driving him to distraction.

Her eyebrows lifted slightly. Did she know what he was thinking? Was she, for once, not going to shy away like a frightened little mouse? She snapped her wrist to open the fan.

And it flew out of her hand across the room, smack into the head of a footman carrying a tray of glasses.

The fellow bobbled the tray precariously, but righted himself quickly before disappearing into the crowd.

Nick chuckled softly as he crossed the room to retrieve the fan. By the time he found it on the floor, it had been trampled upon more than once.

"I'm sorry, Pru," he said when he returned to her side and held out the broken remains. "I hope this was not a favorite fan. Every stick is broken."

"Oh, dear."

She was flushed pink all the way to her ears. His mother would have loved that rosy hue, would have known just how to capture it on canvas. Lord, he was close to being well and truly lost. Even Pru's blushes had become an object of desire.

"How mortifying," she said. "Did anyone see?"

Nick could not help but smile. She was so charmingly embarrassed. "I don't think so. And if they did see a fan in flight, they would not have known who launched it. No harm done, my dear. Except, of course, to the poor fan."

He would buy her a new one. When the *Ulysses* came in, he would buy her a dozen new ones.

"Perhaps a glass of champagne would be in order," he said. "Shall I hail a footman?"

"So long as it is not one with a suspicious lump on his head."

Nick grinned, gave her a wink, and turned to find a footman. He was pleased that Pru hadn't shriveled up like a hedgehog in her embarrassment. But then, she never did. She was quiet and shy, to be sure, but never immobilized with fright. Except on occasion with him. But that was a different matter. And, heaven be praised, he sensed a slight loosening of her guard in that respect. There was hope for him yet.

He located two glasses of champagne and passed one to Pru. "To what shall we toast? The *Cabinet*'s new offices?"

"Yes. To a new beginning." She clinked her glass against his and took a dainty sip.

Should he dare to hope there was more meaning to her words? He saluted her with his glass and swallowed the contents in a single gulp. It was a very small glass.

Another cousin stopped to greet them and pulled Pru into conversation. Nick was looking about when he was approached by a slightly tipsy Viking. After an awkward moment of trying to sort through all the names and titles he'd learned and match one to this particular face, the Viking helped him out.

"Christopher Gordon, Prudence's cousin," he said, then gave a loud bark of laughter. "That isn't much help, is it? I am the son of Jane, Lady Gordon, sister to Prudence's father."

"Of course. How do you do?"

The man waved a limp hand as though dismissing the polite question. "Glad you married Prudence," he said. "Put my sister Alison's nose quite out of joint, you know. One less spinster in the family. And since Prudence was the youngest among their ranks, it ain't as though her marriage is encouraging to the rest of 'em. Ha! Poor old Alison's been scowling since she heard the news. Well done, old boy."

The fellow wandered off chuckling to himself. Nick shook his head in disbelief. If Pru had never been noticed before, she was certainly getting her fair share of attention now, for all sorts of reasons. All because she'd married him. He liked to think he'd done her a favor, but he wasn't entirely sure that was true.

He returned to Pru, who was speaking with her elderly aunt Mary, the Countess of Walsham. After exchanging a few polite words with Nick, she walked on. He turned to Pru. She was looking at him over the rim of her champagne glass. Her eyes were blinking strangely, as though trying to dislodge a piece of grit. Then he remembered the fan.

"Is your eye still smarting from being poked with a fan stick? Poor girl. That must have hurt. Do you have your spectacles in your reticule? Perhaps they would help."

She rolled her gaze to the ceiling—there really must be something wrong with her eye—and uttered a little groan. Maybe it wasn't her eyes at all.

"Are you feeling ill?" he asked. "It is excessively crowded in here. Perhaps we should find our way to the terrace and get some fresh air."

"Yes," she said and gave a weary sigh. "Let's do that."

She took his arm and he maneuvered them through the crowd. He acknowledged greetings, but did not stop to chat with anyone. He really was a bit concerned about Pru. She did not seem at all herself tonight.

"Ah, Prudence."

Damn. The one person who would not be content with a mere nod of greeting.

"Lady Daine," Nick said.

"Hullo, Margaret," Pru said.

"I am looking for Arabella," her sister said without acknowledging their greetings. "Have you seen her?"

"We saw Arabella earlier and she looked quite beautiful. I do believe Sir Leonard Gedney is showing a marked interest. You must be very pleased. He is quite a charming young man."

"She can do better. The Season is still young. And I must say, Prudence, that you are looking remarkably well yourself." She slanted a glance in Nick's direction. "Remarkably well."

"Oh. Thank you." Pru beamed a smile at her sister, obviously pleased to be complimented. From

what little Nick knew of Margaret, it was likely a
rare occurrence.

"I do like that tunic you're wearing," Margaret
said. "Who is your modiste?"

Pru looked down at her dress, fluffed the tunic,
and straightened the train. "Madame Lanchester
made this one."

Margaret's fair brows shot up to the edge of her
exotic turban. "Indeed? She is rather exclusive, is
she not? Well, I can see Aunt Elizabeth's legacy is
finally being put to good use."

So, Pru's new fashionable look was apparently
an expensive one. And it would not, of course,
occur to anyone that her husband could afford to
dress her in such style. They would all know
that she used her own money, that she was
forced to do so since she had married so far beneath her.

Damn them all.

"If you will excuse us, Lady Daine, I am taking
Pru out to the terrace. She is in need of fresh air."

She narrowed her eyes as she studied Pru. "Are
you? Do not tell me you are increasing already?"

Pru sucked in a sharp breath, then blushed all
the way down to that provocative little swell of
bosom. Frankly, Nick would not be surprised if
his own face were as red as a lobster. Leave it to
Margaret to hone in on the one thing certain to
embarrass both of them. But at least he could feel
comfort in the thought that Pru's family was not
privy to the secrets of their marriage.

Even so, the thought of Pru increasing led to thoughts of getting her in that state. He wondered how much longer it would be before she was ready, and how the devil he was to bear the wait.

Chapter 12

How the devil was she ever to let her husband know she was *ready* if she couldn't even manage to flirt properly? Pru stopped staring at the closed bedchamber door and pulled the covers over her head.

What an unmitigated disaster the evening had been. It was bad enough that Nicholas did not even notice her pathetic attempts at flirtation. He must now think her squint-eyed and clumsy as well. That was the last time she would try to be something she was not, lessons or no lessons. It was too dangerous. She might truly injure someone next time. The image of her fan sailing across the room made her burrow deeper beneath the covers. How thoroughly and completely mortifying.

How had she ever thought she could pull it off? She had never been flirtatious in all her life. Quite the contrary, in fact. She'd always been twitchy and uncertain around men. She remembered her one Season with painful humiliation. The whole marriage mart business where young girls paraded themselves before the entire population of eligible bachelors for inspection, like horses at Tattersall's, was simply embarrassing.

She had not fared well. It had been a thousand times more disastrous than tonight's disgraceful ineptitude. At least Nicholas had not run as far away as possible, as had every gentleman presented to her during her Season. Of course, Nicholas could not run away. He was stuck with her.

He had been charming and solicitous, and he had laughed. Not *at* her, though, which made all the difference. He was still fond of her, she knew, if in a brotherly sort of way.

Perhaps friendship was all they could ever share. It would be enough. Or almost. Pru wished they could return to the camaraderie they had once shared, before he was forced to think of her as anything but a friend and colleague. There had always been a certain amount of pain on her part, because she had secretly loved him. But he had been ignorant of her feelings, and so he had been completely at ease in her company.

Now, however, there was this great *thing* between them, this incomplete marriage that changed everything. Pru fell asleep wondering how she might recapture that friendship, at least, so they might go on more comfortably together.

The next morning, just as she was leaving for the office, a letter arrived from Edwina. She took off her bonnet and stepped into the disconcertingly empty library to read it in private. Knowing Edwina must be responding to the news of Pru's marriage to her brother, Pru was a bit slow to break the seal. She was not certain how her friend would react, and was anxious that she not be too disappointed. Pru had been quite frank in her own letter about how the marriage had come about.

She sat down behind the desk, broke the seal, and unfolded the pages. "My dearest Pru," it began, and she breathed a sigh of relief.

I could not have been more astonished by your news. But once I picked up my jaw from the floor, where it had dropped, I quite terrified Anthony with a shriek of pleasure. What could be more delightful than having my two favorite people in the world (discounting my dear Anthony, of course) joined in marriage? And better still, I may now call you "sister."

How extraordinary. In all that had happened, Pru had never even thought of that. Her closest friend was now her sister. What a wonderful notion. Her own sister, Margaret, was a trial at best. Edwina would make a much better sister. Pru adored her, and admired her more than any other woman of her acquaintance.

And now, as Nick moves closer to putting his
Grand Scheme into action, or so he assures me,
how wonderful it will be for him to have you at his
side—someone who understands and will appre-
ciate his efforts as no other woman could.

Oh, dear. Pru was suddenly reminded of every
extra expense incurred on her behalf. Yes, she had
taken on many of the household expenses herself,
but only inconsequential things that were easily
hidden from him. There were so many other expenses he'd taken on—the additional scullery
maid to help Mrs. Gibb, and more recently an additional housemaid to assist Lucy, and all four servants requiring room and board. Then there were
all those social functions he was forced to attend
requiring hired carriages or hackneys. He always
dressed beautifully when he accompanied her,
and she had no idea if that meant he had had to
expand his own wardrobe.

In any case, Pru knew she had cost him a great
deal by falling asleep in the downstairs office.
And all of it eating away at Nicholas's savings for
his project. She wished he wasn't too proud to
take her money. She would gladly give it to him.
She knew something of his factory project and
certainly supported his efforts. Even knowing she
shared his ideals, he would not take her money,
and that was the source of a great deal of
heartache. She was hurt—foolishly so, but there it
was—that he preferred to keep their capital separate, with no partnership between them.

Perhaps it would have been different if theirs had been a love match. He might have been more willing to share everything, to make his wife a true partner in his enterprise, if he had loved her.

But of course, money was simply one more thing they did not share. Theirs was not a true marriage in any sense of the word.

On the other hand, she had never told him that she, too, had plans for a project. Nothing as grand as his, but it had been a nice project to dream about. She had never told anyone about it, though, and now probably never would. She would much prefer to spend Aunt Elizabeth's legacy in helping Nicholas achieve his goal. If she could only figure out how.

He had married her out of honor, and he refused her money for the same reason. But there must be other ways she could help, without giving him the money outright. She needed to understand more about the factory project before she could decide what to do.

She picked up Edwina's letter and read on. There were more good wishes about the marriage, about Pru's future with Nicholas, followed by reports of Edwina's own happy union. Pru tucked the letter in her reticule, retrieved her bonnet, and set off for the *Cabinet* offices. Once inside the hackney, she began to ponder how she could find out more about her husband's project and his investments.

"Ready, Pru?"

She gave him such an odd look, he checked to

see if he'd forgotten to button his waistcoat or tie his neckcloth.

"Yes, I am ready."

"Come along, then." Nick turned to leave her office, but was stopped at the door by her next words.

"Oh. Just a moment. I want to finish logging these expenses in the account book, if you don't mind waiting."

"I thought you said you were ready to go?"

She blushed scarlet and looked down at the open ledger on her desk. "I b-beg your pardon. I m-misunderstood. I will only be about fifteen minutes, probably less. Do you mind?"

"Not at all. I'll just see if the jarvey will keep the hackney waiting. If not, I'll send him on his way and call another when you're finished."

Nick popped outside to talk with the hackney driver. For an extra shilling, he would wait, he said. Nick told him it would be at least a half hour or so, since women generally had no sense of time. He tossed the extra shilling to the jarvey and told him to go have a pint of ale, so long as he was back in half an hour.

Nick wandered about the new offices, amazed at how easily, and quickly, they had filled up a space several times the size of the office at home. Edwina would be so pleased. He had wondered what she planned to do when she returned from Europe, if she would want to continue working out of the Golden Square house or move the offices to her new home with Morehouse. This new arrangement was by far the best solution.

He trusted his father had not gone into debt to finance the lease. Though he had the manor house in Derbyshire and the town house in London, he was not a rich man. Nick had a feeling that Edwina, who was now married to a very rich man, would secretly pay back their father when she returned. The business belonged to her, after all.

Nick peeked his head in the door of Pru's office, only to find her closing the ledger and replacing her pen in the stand. "You're finished? Already?"

"I told you I only needed a few minutes. We can leave now."

"Actually, we can't. I sent the jarvey away to have a pint. He'll be back in half an hour."

"Half an hour? You thought I'd be that long?"

Nick gave a sheepish shrug. "If I'd thought about it long enough, I would have remembered you are always on time. Unlike Edwina and every other woman I've known. It's just another one of those things I need to learn about you, is it not?"

Pru smiled. "Sit down, Nicholas, and be comfortable. Since you mention it, and since we have a bit of time to kill, there is something about you I'd like to know better."

Nick pulled the guest chair close to the desk, turned it around, and sat on it backward, his arms resting on the back rail. "What would you like to know?"

"Tell me about your Grand Scheme."

"The factory project?"

"Yes. I know about it only in the most general way. I'd like to know more. It is to be a sort of utopian factory, is it not?"

"Yes. A factory complex, to be precise. A textile factory with decent working conditions, an adjacent village for the workers with clean housing, a school for the children, and a resident doctor as well. Everything to make the workers' lives comfortable and productive."

"Because a happy worker is a more productive worker?"

"Precisely. And since I believe the future of our economy lies with industrial rather than farm products, we must not allow the current horrendous work conditions to continue. The inhumane conditions of some of our factories are costing workers their lives, especially the children. How can we be a productive economy if we're killing our workers?"

"You are quite right, of course," Pru said. "We cannot allow the current factory situation to continue."

Nick smiled. "You have an excellent understanding, my dear."

"For a woman, you mean?"

"For a woman of such aristocratic lineage."

"Are you mocking my background, sir?"

He grinned. "I would not dream of doing so. I have no wish to find another angry Viking horde on my doorstep."

"Actually," she said, "I believe my 'aristocratic

lineage' allows me a better understanding of what you propose."

"Oh? How so?"

"You would set up your own industrial community, and see that the workers and their families are treated well. Correct?"

"Yes, that is my hope."

Pru cocked her head to one side in a quizzical manner. "Then what you are saying is that you wish to set yourself up to emulate the great landowners."

Nick flinched. "Not at all. My enlightened community will be a republican utopia, with no connection to the old ways of the grand estates."

"But those grand estate holders—like my own family, the dukes of Norwich—have always taken responsibility for the people who work their land and depend on their largess. It is actually very clever of you, Nicholas, to use the landed gentry as a model for the new industrial complexes. It was the old estate system, after all, that made England a strong country. It makes sense that the same methods could keep us strong in an industrial economy."

Nick gazed at her in wonder. By Jove, she had a point. "My dear, you have rendered me speechless. I have no argument against your wisdom."

She smiled in triumph. And looked very pretty for it. "I've always been appalled to think of young children in some of the textile mills I've heard about. But at least there is talk of a factory bill in the House, one that would not allow children of a very young age to be employed. And to reduce the hours of older children. My cousin, Lord Caldecott, has spoken in favor of it in Lords."

"Yes, I know. One day, if I ever have the opportunity to meet him in something other than a purely social situation, I should like to discuss it with him. We need all the support we can rally for that bill."

"Will it make a difference to your plans if it passes?" she asked.

"Whether it passes or not, there will be no young children at my factory. We will build them a school to attend instead. Even the older children will be required to attend part of each day."

"Has anyone ever tried this sort of utopian factory before?" Pru asked.

"Yes, Robert Owen did, with New Lanark Village. In fact, it is his humane model that I strive to emulate. But if I am to succeed where he did not, I must be the solitary investor. He failed because his investors did not trust his progressive labor ideas and feared loss of profits."

"And so you have been trying to increase your capital through investments?"

"Yes."

"How far along is the project? You have the land?"

"Yes, I own a large area of land outside of Derby, as well as one large warehouse waiting to be fitted up as the first factory. And that is one of the primary expenses. The latest equipment will cost a small fortune. Then we have to build the cottages or other housing for the workers. We need a school and a market and a church. There is much to be done."

"It sounds like a life's work."

"It might be. But I have investments that are due to pay off soon. That will give me the capital to purchase the machinery."

"And you do not wish to solicit investors," she said, "so you are not funding it all on your own?"

"No. I want to retain full control, otherwise I cannot be certain things would be done exactly as I wished. Look at what happened to Owen. He had to buy out his investors when they disagreed with him. If I decided to rely on outside funding in order to get this project off the ground, I would likely never be able to buy out anyone if necessary. I will have sunk all my capital into my portion of the partnership. No, I do not want to take on investors who would try to tell me what to do."

"I would not."

He sighed. "Pru."

A frown creased her forehead. "I would be happy to invest my inheritance in your project, Nicholas. But you would not accept it, would you?"

"No, as I have told you. It belongs to you, Pru. I shall not allow you to sink it into a project that may fail. I do not wish to be responsible for bankrupting both of us, if it comes to that."

She gazed at him for a long, quiet moment, then said, "If you will not take my money, will you allow me to give you some advice?"

He shot her a skeptical look. "What sort of advice?"

"Investment strategy."

He smiled. "Your father told me you managed your own investments. You have discovered a strategy for success, have you?"

"I have increased my capital."

"How?"

And she proceeded to tell him, in great detail, how she had used government securities and five-percents to slowly build her nest egg. It was all very impressive, and he admired her research and determination. But as far as he was concerned, it was all "spinster and widow funds." Much too moderate for his needs.

"But, Pru, it can take years to make enough profit with such conservative methods. I don't have years. I need capital now."

"What are you currently invested in, if you don't mind telling me?"

He told her of the cargo shares and canal projects and industrial patents. He even admitted to the serious losses in cargo shares because of the huge storms in February that had swallowed up ships whole. Not to mention the failed investment in Irish linen imports last year, after trade expanded when the Union was created. Unfortunately, linen turned out not to be at all profitable.

"Cargo shares and imports are rather risky investments," she said.

"But the returns can be tremendous."

"Not if the ships are lost or the trade declines."

He shrugged. No amount of dissuasion would convince him to give up his cargo shares. There was simply too much money to be made.

"Nor if the canal is never built," she continued.

"Some aren't, of course. But projects like canals can bring so much prosperity to a region."

"But too many canal projects have failed. May I suggest an alternative."

"Of course."

"If you prefer building projects, you might look into some of the dock expansion enterprises. The dock in Hull, for example. I have purchased shares in the London Dock Company. As the new dock at Wapping nears completion, the premiums have been significant."

"Really? You impress me, Pru. I had no idea you were so knowledgeable about financial investments."

She offered a shy little smile, obviously pleased with his praise. "I've done a great deal of research since I came into my inheritance."

"Have you simply been trying to secure your future? Or have you some other purpose for increasing your capital?"

"You mean, do I have a project, too?"

He smiled. "Do you?"

She colored up. "As a matter of fact, I have had a sort of dream. Not a real project. Just a . . . dream."

"Pru! You are full of surprises. Tell me."

"You will think it silly."

"No, I won't. If it is something you want, that you dream of having, it cannot be silly. What is it? Tell me."

"It is . . . a school."

"But that is wonderful. What sort of school?"

"For poor children, here in London. Children who have no opportunities, who will otherwise make their way on the streets."

"But that is a wonderful idea. Why have you not done it? Surely your inheritance would be enough to fund a school."

"Not the kind of school I have in mind. I will still need a great deal more capital if I am to do what I want."

"And what is that? What sort of school?"

She chewed on her lower lip, as though afraid to answer.

"Pru? What is it?"

"You will think I am foolish."

He rocked the chair forward, reached across the desk, and placed a hand on her arm. "Never. Tell me, Pru."

She was becoming more accustomed to his touch and did not stiffen or tremble, thank God. She looked into his eyes a long moment before she answered, as though weighing what she should say.

"I want to open a music school," she said, and lifted her chin a notch as though daring him to find fault.

He sat back and studied her. It was not quite what he expected, although it ought not to have been a complete surprise. "You wish to share your love for music with children?"

"Yes. Poor children. Children of the streets who have no future. But it would not be a school only for music. It would provide a full education, but with an emphasis on music. The goal would be to train them to find employment in orchestras or as music teachers or copyists."

"It's a lovely idea, Pru, but—if I may be so bold—do you not think music is one of the last things an impoverished child needs? It is almost more of a luxury than a necessity."

"Of course it is not a necessity. But music is more than a luxury. It is a door—to creativity and expression and self-discovery. It can enrich lives of children who have known nothing but want and emptiness and despair. It can change their lives forever, lifting them out of the gutter through their own talent—talent that would otherwise remain undiscovered and untrained."

Her eyes had brightened with the zeal of her cause. She was animated and without a glimmer of self-consciousness. This was what music—even talking of music—did to her. It was a mesmerizing transformation.

"Music is a great equalizer," she continued. "A poor little street urchin can be taught to make the same beautiful music as the highest-born nobleman. They can even make music together, with no thought to rank. It makes us all the same, don't you see? Imagine how that notion could change a child's life?"

"I do see," he said. He was so caught up in her enthusiasm, he was ready to believe her. It all sounded very admirable. There was even something almost republican about the concept.

It was an intriguing and perfectly commendable idea. Then why did he have this niggling, traitorous little notion that it was a frivolous plan? Was he so selfish that he thought his own project more worthy? Was he so envious of the fortune she had for her dream when he had none for his? He really did respect what Pru wanted to do. He really did. But she might be able to change the lives of only a few dozen children, while his factory scheme could change the lives of hundreds, even thousands. He hated such disloyal thoughts, but damn it all, he couldn't help it. The factory project had been the focus of all his energies for too long. He really did think it was the more important project of the two, deep in his heart. He hated that he thought so, but there it was.

He would, of course, cut out his tongue before he would say such a thing to Pru.

"Have you done anything yet," he asked, "to put your plan in action?"

"Not really. I have located a building in Clerkenwell that I think would be perfect. But it would have to be completely rebuilt inside to accommodate studios and classrooms and dormitories and kitchens and such. Then there are instruments and furniture and sheet music and teachers. Oh, and one more foolish little notion of mine. I do not even know yet if it makes any sense. But I thought it would be lovely if each child, upon completion of his or her studies, were presented with an instrument. Something, besides an education, with which to begin a new life."

She gave a sheepish smile. "Do you think me horribly silly?"

"Not in the least. I think it's a wonderful idea. I have come to know how important music is to you."

"It has fed my soul and brightened my days. It gave my life meaning when I felt lost among my larger-than-life family. I would like to be the instrument, if you will forgive the pun, through which other children might find a similar happiness."

"And so you shall be. It is a splendid plan, my dear." And it really was. It was so quintessentially Pru. So perfect. He could not begrudge her using the inheritance for such a school. He really could not.

The little bell on the front door jangled as someone entered. "Hullo in there. Yer comin' or not? Can't wait all day."

Good Lord, he'd forgotten all about the hackney. "Come along, Pru. We'd better hurry. You can tell me more about the school on the drive home."

He waited while she collected her shawl and bonnet, and locked up the offices, then led her outside to the waiting hackney. After lifting her inside, he had an idea. "You said the building you were interested in is in Clerkenwell?"

"Yes, in St. John's Square. It's a nice enough area without being too far removed from the parts of town where the students—the potential students—would have grown up. It did not seem appropriate to locate such a school in Mayfair. Clerkenwell, I thought, was a good compromise."

"An excellent plan. Let's have a look, shall we?"

Her eyes widened with anticipation. "Do you mean it?"

"Of course. Give me the direction and I'll tell the jarvey."

Twenty minutes later, Nick stood on the pavement with Pru, looking up at a sturdy old brick building of three stories. It was in very good repair, with all its sash windows intact, and an intricate Gothic-influenced fanlight above the entrance. It was also quite obviously empty.

"You have met with the owner?" Nick asked.

"Yes. And I have walked through with him on two occasions. But it is still a bit beyond my reach. There is no sense buying a building if I can only afford to leave it empty. I shall wait until some of my investments grow, and will hope that it will still be available. If not, there are other buildings. But I do like this one, don't you?"

"It is a fine building. Quite perfect for a music school."

Pru chuckled, and Nick noticed a touch of self-mockery in it. "I confess," she said, "that I have dreamed of one day seeing a discreet little brass sign beside the door: The Prudence Armitage School of Music. Oh!" She blushed. "I should say The Prudence Parrish School of Music, should I not?"

He smiled. "You should indeed, Mrs. Parrish."

"Nicholas, tell me truthfully. Do you think it is a foolish scheme?"

"No, I think it is a perfect project for you, my dear."

She began to tell him of all she would like to do to make the building into a proper school. As she talked, she grew almost giddy with excitement and looked ready to shout out loud and twirl in joyous circles. Pru would never do such a thing, of course. He rather wished she would. It was something he would have liked to see. In fact, he heard little of what she said, thinking of how much he wished she would look at him someday with such ardor, how he would like to be able to put that shine in her eyes and that glow in her cheeks himself.

On their way back to Golden Square, he questioned her more about the school, for the pure pleasure of hearing her chatter and watching her face glow with enthusiasm. All shyness was gone, for the moment. Nick hoped he could keep awkwardness at bay, and so he let her ramble.

When he thought back to a few weeks earlier, when he'd seen Pru only as a mousy little colleague, he could hardly believe the change in his perception of her. It was true what they said about not judging a book by its cover. Pru was a slim little volume packed full of intriguing information. And the cover was not so plain on closer inspection. This music school idea really was admirable. With her enthusiasm it was bound to be a success.

He could not, however, shake the selfish notion that his own project was so much more worthwhile. It was disloyal, but he could not help it. He simply could not accept the idea that poor children would benefit much from a musical education. Better to train them in a trade so they could earn a living as skilled laborers. Or better to spend the money on a utopian factory in Derbyshire.

It suddenly occurred to him that Pru had offered to forgo her dream to fund his own. In that, she was infinitely more noble than he.

Yet he could not allow himself to dwell on such selflessness, such undeserved loyalty, or he would be shamed into doing something rash. He supposed that made him a bad person. Certainly unworthy of Pru's regard. But if he did not maintain a singular focus on his project in Derby, he would never reach his goal, and young children would continue to work themselves to death in unregulated factories.

Perhaps one day, if they were lucky, both their dreams would come true.

Chapter 13

"**Y**ou're joking."

Flora lifted her chin and said, "I am quite serious, I assure you."

"You want to print a list of the worst-dressed women in London?"

"Yes."

"And name them outright? Not just hint at their identities?"

"That's correct. Isn't it delicious? We will follow it the next month with the best-dressed list. By then, women will be clamoring to see who's on it."

"I don't know, Flora." Pru stood on the small dais in the center of Madame Lanchester's fitting room as she was pinned into a new ball dress. "It sounds potentially libelous."

"Nonsense," Flora said. She stood beside the

dais with arms crossed, scrutinizing every adjustment made to the dress. "I guarantee you, if we
make it an annual feature, it will become a badge
of honor to be named on the worst-dressed list.
Worst or best, both lists will give notoriety to a
chosen few. Everyone will want to see their names
on one of the lists. It hardly matters which."

"Mrs. Gallagher is correct," Madame said. "A
woman whose taste in fashion is not merely unin-
spired but truly frightful—and I could name a
few, if you like—is asking to be noticed. She will
secretly gloat at being singled out for dressing
badly. And naturally, you could suggest she come
to me for a complete renovation."

"The plates of your designs will speak for themselves, Madame," Flora said. "This one, especially."

"Yes, it will be a stunning creation, once we
have all the rosettes in place. See how lovely this
lavender crepe flows against the body. You will be
the belle of the ball, Mrs. Parrish. Now, don't
move. I'll be right back. Annette, come with me."

Madame and her assistant disappeared through
a curtain, leaving Pru and Flora alone.

"I cannot believe I let you talk me into this,
Flora."

"What? Modeling for a fashion plate in your own
magazine? What could be more appropriate?"

"A taller woman, for one thing. I do not remotely resemble the Amazonian creatures in most
of the prints."

"Raisbeck's drawing will make you look like a
queen, I promise you. Remember, it is the dress on

display, not the model. He will adjust the model as necessary to make the dress look best. Even if that means stretching your legs a bit to give a more dramatic line to the dress."

"But why me, for heaven's sake?"

"Madame was quite taken with how your dress came out and wanted to feature it. Just think, the dress you will wear to the duchess's ball will be immortalized the next month in the *Cabinet*. It's a beautiful dress, my girl."

Pru lifted an edge of the crepe tunic, marveling at its gossamer softness. The white lace trim was subtle and delicate. The tunic was cut at knee-level in the front, revealing a white muslin underdress edged at the hem with lavender ribbon, and sloped into a long train in the back. When she moved, the crepe floated about her like a cloud. It made her feel like a fairy queen.

"It is pretty, is it not?" she said. "I want to look my very best at the ball."

"For Nicholas? Or so you can flirt with other men and make him jealous?"

Pru frowned. "I will *not* be flirting with anyone, I promise you. Never again. But I would like to look nice. I know I'll never be as beautiful as Edwina, or most of my female cousins. Heavens, I will never be as beautiful as Nicholas. But I *would* like to look pretty for him."

"Merely pretty?"

"Well . . . I suppose I'd like him to look at me and sort of gasp. Not with horror, but with—"

"Desire?"

Pru felt her color rise. "Yes."

"Let the dress work for you, then. It has a very sensual movement about it. You will not need to flirt at all. Just move gracefully, as I know you can do, and let him gaze in wonder."

"I hope you are right, Flora. And besides, it is important to look my best for my aunt's ball. It is our most important family event of the season."

"My dear girl, the Duchess of Norwich's ball is *the* most important event of the season. I was quite stunned to receive an invitation. I won't ask how you did it, but I am terribly grateful, Pru. It will be a perfect occasion for spotting those who will go on the best-dressed list."

"That is true. Everyone will be looking quite fine, I am sure."

"And as for the worst-dressed list, I shall get a good start this evening. I am attending the opera. It is an important production, and everyone will be there. I have high expectations of a few perfectly horrid dresses."

"Oh, Flora, are you really going to do this?"

"Of course. With your approval, of course. You *are* the editor, after all."

Pru sighed. "I hope Edwina will not have my head for this, but all right. It might help increase our numbers. We go to press in two days. Can you have it ready by then?"

"I have no doubt I can find a wealth of fashion disasters at the opera tonight. I will write it up tomorrow. It will be a great success, I promise you."

"Here we are," Madame Lanchester said as she swept back into the room, with her assistant trailing behind. "The lace rosettes. The final touch, and then we will be ready for the impatient Mr. Raisbeck. Now, stand up straight Mrs. Parrish."

The two women began to pin tiny lace rosettes at intervals along the lavender ribbon at the hem of the underdress. Then the sleeves of the tunic were gathered at the shoulders and pinned with rosettes, revealing the lace-edged and ever-so-slightly puffed sleeves of the bodice. Finally, Madame grasped the front of the tunic and pulled it down to a deep, plunging V, pinning it in place with a slightly larger rosette at the high waistline.

Pru let out an involuntary squeal. "No, please. That is much too low."

"Au contraire, Mrs. Parrish. It is very fashionable, I assure you."

Pru groaned. "But it seems indecent."

Madame shook her head. "Not at all. In France, it would be even lower, deep enough to show the nipples. This simply shows off your lovely bosom. Be sure to lace your stays tight so there is a nice swell of cleavage."

"Oh dear."

"We are ready for Mr. Raisbeck, I think. Mrs. Parrish, follow me into the showroom, if you please."

Pru did not please, but saw no way out. She put a hand to her exposed flesh, but Flora batted it away.

"Remember what you told me," she said,

"about wanting Nicholas to look at you and gasp? This, my girl, will make him choke. Now, don't be a ninny. You look stunning."

Pru spent the next half hour standing still as a statue while the famous academician, Lionel Raisbeck, drew her picture. Madame Lanchester hovered nearby, making sure his drawing would highlight the best features of her creation. He posed Pru standing at a slight angle, with her head turned to look over her shoulder. She was painfully aware of the expanse of her bosom on display for all to see. But as she stood there, she tried to imagine she was posing for Nicholas and that he found her beautiful.

"Perfect," the artist said. "Don't move a muscle."

Later that afternoon, back at the magazine offices, Pru and Flora pored over the drawings made at Madame Lanchester's, as well as a few made earlier that week at a different showroom. They were all quite lovely, as always. Mr. Raisbeck was one of the reasons the *Cabinet* had become so successful. The engravings made of his drawings, hand-colored by the Crimson Ladies, were finer than the prints of any of their competitors.

"This is an excellent likeness," Flora said, holding up the drawing of Pru in the lavender tunic. "He has captured you perfectly. I hope the engraver will do it justice."

Pru rather hoped the engraver would muddy the features so it did not look quite so much like her. She was not at all sure she liked the idea of her face being displayed in the magazine. And her bosom. Though she had to admit, Mr. Raisbeck had made her look almost beautiful. Of course, as a portrait artist, that was his job. Here, though, it was the dress that was of most importance. Perhaps no one would notice the face of the model. Most readers probably did not even realize that real models were used, that the fashion prints were drawn from life.

There was no sense worrying about it now, though. It was done, and she had other work to do.

"Mr. Jarvis will be by later to pick up the drawings to be engraved," she said. "Have you decided on these two?"

"Yes, these will do nicely."

Naturally, one of them was Pru's. "All right, then. I need to finish editing some of the essays, so I must get to work. I have wasted altogether too much time today."

Pru spent the next several hours reading through all the submitted essays, determining which would be printed and which rejected, then editing the ones chosen to accommodate the required length. She became lost in her work until she noticed the sound of church bells ringing the hour. It was dark outside.

She looked at the clock on the shelf and saw it was seven o'clock. Nicholas always came to fetch her at six, unless she arranged for a different time. She had not done so today, and yet he was not there.

He must have been detained. It really was not fair to ask him to plan his days around her schedule. It was not at all necessary. But he had so far been very conscientious about bringing around a hackney to take her home.

Pru wondered if she should wait. He was already an hour late, though, so perhaps he wasn't coming at all. And Mrs. Gibb, accommodating their late schedule, always had supper ready at eight. If Pru waited much longer, supper would be ruined. Or simply cold. Since it was to be only she and Nicholas—Bartholomew had mentioned he would be attending the opera tonight—it would not be so horrible to have a cold dinner. Mrs. Gibb would be upset, but such things happened.

How long should she wait?

She went to the reception area and opened the door, hoping she might see a hackney pulling up with Nicholas inside. But the streets were empty.

It seemed foolish to wait. He had told her not to go out alone after dark, but surely he was being overly cautious. After all, St. Paul's loomed just outside. How dangerous could it be in the shadow of London's largest church?

She went back to her office and collected her bonnet and shawl. It occurred to her that she should leave a note, just in case Nicholas did show up. She scribbled a few lines on a scrap of paper and blew the ink dry. She took a quick look at the schedule she kept tucked under the inkwell on her desk, reviewing what needed to be done tomorrow. Satisfied that the next issue was under control, she snuffed the candles, grabbed her reticule, and headed out the door.

After locking up and tucking the note inside the doorframe, she looked about for a hackney, but the street was deserted. She walked around to the great pillared portico at the front of the church. It was less deserted as people milled about here and there, but no hackney was in sight.

She began the walk up Ludgate Hill, the broad and busy street that terminated at the church, certain she would find a hackney eventually. There were several dark, narrow streets leading off Ludgate Hill, filled with ominous shadows, and Pru began to get a bit nervous. When one of the shadows moved, and a man stepped out of Creed Lane, she gasped aloud.

"Well now, what 'ave we 'ere?"

Nick could not believe he had been so stupid. He supposed he wasn't yet accustomed to having a wife to worry about. But that was no excuse for being so late. Poor Pru must be beside herself, wondering what had become of him.

He had simply lost track of time.

There had been a meeting of the Scottish Martyrs Club at a tavern in Shoreditch, and the discussion had gone on longer than he'd realized. He had been so involved in the plans to lobby various MPs for support of the factory bill, he had quite forgotten about Pru.

How he could have done such a thing, when she had been so much on his mind, was a mystery.

Just before leaving for the meeting, he'd received a letter from Edwina. He knew Pru had also had a letter, but it must have been private, for she had not shared it with him. And here was his private letter, which he could not share.

His sister was surprisingly pleased about his marriage. Or perhaps not so surprising when he considered how close a friend she was to Pru. What unsettled him, though, was Edwina's repeated caution not to break Pru's heart.

Why did everyone seem to think Pru's heart was involved in this marriage? It was not as though she had wanted it any more than he had. Despite the pretense of a love match he maintained for her family, his own close friends and family must know there was never anything between them. Neither of their hearts was involved, beyond the general affection of friendship. And that affection had deepened since their marriage, at least on his part, as he grew to know her.

It galled him to think people worried that he would break Pru's heart. Did they think him such a cad? Hadn't he done his honorable duty and married her when it was the very last thing he'd wanted to do?

Nick had cogitated on Edwina's warning all afternoon, before meeting with his business agent and arranging to buy shares in the Hull Dock Company. He had thought about what Pru had said regarding the value of her own dock shares, and he figured it was worth a try. He would not tell her, though. He would wait and see how profitable an investment it was before he admitted anything to her.

And so he still had Pru on his mind when he went to the Scottish Martyrs Club meeting. Yet he managed to become so involved, he forgot about her and left her waiting for more than an hour. What an idiot he was.

The hackney turned from Cheapside into St. Paul's Churchyard, and slowed to a stop in front of the *Cabinet* offices. How strange. It looked completely dark inside.

A prickle of anxiety ran down his spine.

He jumped down from the carriage, hoping to discover a glimmer of candlelight somewhere deep inside, but instead he found a scrap of paper slipped into the doorframe. His name was scrawled on the outside. He ripped it out and unfolded it.

Damn! She had already gone. He'd been so late, she had left without waiting. But she said she had waited until seven, and it was now only ten minutes after. He'd just missed her.

Blast it all, he wished he had been on time. Or that she had waited. He did not like to think of her on the streets, a woman alone, hailing a hackney. When he got home, he would first apologize, then he would scold her for taking such a risk. He did not mean to be a bully of a husband. It simply wasn't safe, and she needed to understand that.

He shouted to the jarvey to take him to Golden Square, then bounded back inside the carriage. They had just turned onto Ludgate Hill when Nick looked out the window and felt his blood freeze. In the shadows of a narrow lane, two large, rough-looking men were accosting a woman. A small woman with curly reddish hair.

Oh, my God!

He pounded on the ceiling for the jarvey to stop, and without waiting he flung open the door and jumped, stumbling to the pavement before the carriage had come to a halt. One man had his hand on her breast as she tried, kicking and screaming, to fight him off. The other man held her from behind. Nick lunged toward them without conscious thought.

"Nicholas!"

He grabbed the first man by the shoulders and pulled him away from Pru, then threw his fist in the blackguard's face with more force than he had ever used in his life. A sickening crunching sound preceded a howl of rage from the brute. The second man dropped his hold on Pru, spun around, and disappeared into the dark. She gave a little cry and reached out to Nick. He pulled her to him with one arm, holding her tight, but kept the other hand free to grab the bloody-nosed miscreant by the collar.

"I should kill you for daring to touch my wife."

The man held his hand to his nose and glared at Nick. He made some sort of gargled, inarticulate response, shrugged out of Nick's grasp, and took a step backward.

"Get out of here," Nick said, "before I call for the night watch and have you taken up for assault. Go on. Get out of here. Go!"

The man turned and ran into the dark lane, his footfalls echoing on the damp cobblestones.

Nick put his other arm around Pru and held her tight.

"My God, Pru. My God. Did they hurt you?"

She shook her head, but kept her face buried against his chest. She was trembling like a leaf.

He looked over her head to see the hackney had stopped a few yards away. The jarvey looked wide-eyed with shock. Nick signaled to open the door, and the man bent down and did so. Nick swept Pru into his arms and carried her to the coach. He did not lift her inside and set her down, but kept hold of her. He stepped up and inside clutching her to him like a baby. He did not want to let go of her. His blood still ran cold at what had almost happened.

Nick sat down and held her on his lap. The hackney lurched into motion, and the brim of Pru's bonnet struck him in the face. He reached under her chin, untied the ribbons, and somehow managed to get the bonnet off her head. He flung it on the seat beside him, and tossed off his own hat to join it. Then he placed a hand on her head and held her against his shoulder, stroking her hair.

He could feel the frantic beating of her heart. Or perhaps it was his own.

"Pru, I'm so sorry. I'm so sorry. I should have been there. I should not have made you wait. If only I'd been on time, this never would have happened. Oh, my God, Pru."

She did not speak, but burrowed closer. Her tiny body curled into his, so fragile, like a frightened bird. They might have killed her. His Pru. His little Pru. And that scoundrel had touched her breast. What else had he done?

"Are you sure they did not hurt you, my dear?"

She muttered something, but he could not hear. He tilted her head back so he could see her face.

"Did they hurt you?" He stroked his fingers along her cheeks and jaw and eyes, convincing himself that she was all right.

"No. But they w-would have if y-you hadn't come."

"Dear God."

"I was s-so frightened. Oh, Nicholas. I was never so glad to s-see anyone in my life. I wanted you so badly, and then you were there."

"Pru."

He dipped his head and found her mouth with his. Her lips trembled slightly, but he did not care. She was frightened and he wanted to make her safe. He wanted to make her warm. He wanted . . . her.

She had waited all her life for this kiss. She ought to savor it. She out to pay close attention so that later, she could remember every detail. But she could think of nothing but that brute's hands on her, and all she wanted was to forget. She wanted to crawl right inside Nicholas, to bury herself in his warmth, to let him erase the memory of what had happened.

And so she pressed her mouth against his, and forgot everything.

His lips were soft and velvety and tasted slightly of ale. They moved against hers first this way, then that, forcing her lips to open. She made a little noise of surprise when he dipped his tongue inside her mouth. And then it touched hers, and began to circle and suck. Suddenly, everything else—the carriage, the street, the horses' hooves on the cobblestones, the memory of a dark alleyway—everything disappeared as her mind fell adrift on a tide of pure sensation.

He plundered her mouth with an urgency that sent the blood roaring in her head. He broke the kiss and arched her neck backward, trailing his lips to her throat and jaw, then to her eyes, and back to her mouth where it all began again.

She could not have said how long they kissed, but it seemed like a lifetime. And it was not long enough.

When it was over, he pressed her head to his shoulder once again and held her close. They did not speak. They did not move.

Pru snuggled against his poor, ruined neck-cloth, closed her eyes, and considered all that had happened. She did not want to think of Creed Lane and the two men who'd grabbed her. The big, slovenly one had tried to kiss her, but she'd wriggled away from his fleshy mouth and his foul breath. She was glad he had not kissed her. She would have felt violated, dirty, not worthy to have Nicholas's lips touch hers.

Somewhere in the recesses of her conscious-ness, there was a lingering terror over the assault. But it had been pushed aside by something more powerful. Something life-changing. Something she wanted to remember and savor forever.

Pru had read about kisses that ignited body and

soul. In truth, she had never been entirely certain such a thing was possible. She wasn't even sure what it meant, though she had fantasized about it, in the way young girls do. She'd thought perhaps it was a romantic ideal that didn't exist in the real world.

But now she knew. It was no fantasy. Body and soul could indeed be entirely overwhelmed by a kiss. It had been even more wonderful than she had imagined. She had not expected such a powerful physical response. No one ever told her that a person's body could feel like that, especially low in her belly, and lower still. She had not been prepared for it, but she knew she wanted more, even if she did not know quite what more there was.

If Nicholas was finally going to make her his wife in more than name, as she hoped, she was soon to discover what it was.

She had never been more ready. And she needed him. She needed his warmth.

The hackney pulled to a stop, and Pru stifled a groan. She did not want to move from Nicholas's lap.

"Are you all right?" he asked.

"Yes."

"Can you walk?"

"Of course."

And so he lifted her from his lap and placed her on the seat beside him. He opened the door and jumped down, paid off the jarvey, then reached in to hand her down. They walked in silence to the front steps.

Lucy opened the door and stepped aside to let them in. She looked a bit surprised to be handed Pru's bonnet along with Nicholas's hat, and her eyes grew saucerlike when she saw the blood on Nicholas's shirt.

"Sir? Are you all right?"

"Yes, thank you, Lucy," Nicholas said. "But will you be so good as to draw a bath for Mrs. Parrish? She has had a rather unsettling experience and will need to relax. And I think you'd better have a light supper sent up for her on a tray. Is that all right, Pru? You've been through a lot. I think it best if you went straight to bed."

She nodded her head. Her throat had closed up and she did not think she could speak without bursting into tears. He was sending her off to bed like a good little girl. After kissing her like that. After blistering her soul inside out. After setting her body on fire, he was *still* not going to make love to her.

How much more ready did he think she needed to be?

"Is my father at home?"

"No sir. He went out earlier. I believe he was going to the opera."

"He was going with Flora." She had lost her fire and found her voice, though even to her ear it sounded flat. She had no expression to give it. She had grown suddenly empty.

"With Flora?" Nicholas asked. "Did he tell you that?"

"No."

"Did Flora tell you?"

"No. But they were going together. I know."

Nicholas frowned and gave a little shrug. "Then I shall have my dinner in the back parlor, if you please, Lucy. Oh, and tell Mrs. Gibb we are sorry to be so late. It was all my fault. All my fault."

He turned to Pru and she was shocked at the look on his face. He appeared to be badly shaken. He was in the grip of some sort of powerful emotion, but she could not be sure what it was. Anger? Despair? Disappointment?

He took her hand in his. "I am so sorry, Pru. Dreadfully, dreadfully sorry. For everything."

Pru made her desultory way up the stairs and could feel his eyes staring after her as he stood below in the hall.

Had he really meant *everything*?

Chapter 14

Nick was not looking forward to this evening. He was in no mood for a ball, especially a grand aristocratic ball in a ducal mansion where he would have to smile a lot and pretend to be happy.

He was not happy.

The week had begun with an assault on his wife—or two assaults, if one counted his own—that had shaken him to his bootheels. Then had come the news that the *Ulysses* had been lost, taking with it a sizable investment of Nick's cash. And today, he'd learned the Culwyn canal project appeared close to failure.

And now, to top off the week, he had to dress up in his best coat and escort his wife to a ball given by the Duke and Duchess of Norwich. He would much prefer to sit home and get blindingly drunk. But he was not his own man anymore. He could not do everything he wanted.

"Stop pacing," his father said. "You'll wear a hole in the carpet."

"And God knows I cannot afford to replace it."

"Is it that bad?"

"It is not good. But I suppose in reality I am no worse off than I was last week. I simply have fewer prospects."

"Can I help you, son?"

Nick turned to his father, who was looking very distinguished in a dark blue jacket and silver knee breeches with paste buckles to match the buckles on his shoes. He had not seen him in such elegant attire in a dozen years or more.

"Thank you, Father, but you have done enough already. I have become impatient, that is all. I want to get started. But let's not talk about that tonight. I'm cross as a bear already. I need to put on a smile for Pru's family."

He walked to the sideboard and poured another glass of claret. What the devil was taking Pru so long?

"It was exceedingly kind of Prudence's father to arrange an invitation for me," his father said. "I met the duke once, you know. Your mother did some decorative work at Beaufoy years ago. A nice enough fellow, as I recall. A bit blustery."

"They're all blustery. You'll have to bellow to be heard above their voices."

"I can bellow with the best of them, my boy. And so can Flora. She is thrilled to be invited, by the way."

"Yes, I know. She has said so, quite often." Nick studied his father as he took another swallow of wine. "You know, Father, this whole business with Flora has taken me quite by surprise. Pru figured it out well before I did."

"Do you disapprove? Because of her past?"

"No."

"Because of your mother?"

"Good heavens, no. You've been alone far too long. It's just that I never would have imagined a woman like Flora would interest you."

"Why not? She reminds me of your mother."

"She does?"

"Not physically, of course. But she has that same way of grabbing on to life and enjoying every moment, of plunging headfirst into whatever takes her fancy, of never doing anything halfway."

"Hmm. I suppose you're right. Well, just remember Flora is a woman of the world."

"And I am not a complete fool, my boy. If I may give you a bit of fatherly advice: Mind your own business."

Nick grinned. "Point taken." He sat down in a chair opposite his father and placed his wineglass on the candlestand that stood beside it. The claret had soothed his nerves a bit, but he was still anxious to get on with the evening.

"Tell me, son, how is Prudence? Has she recovered, do you think, from that horrible incident the other evening?"

Nick shrugged. He wasn't sure which was the more horrible incident—being accosted by a pair of rowdies, or being taken advantage of by the man who had promised not to impose himself upon her. He hated what he had done, as much as he'd enjoyed it at the time. She'd been so small and sweet and vulnerable. And he'd been reeling from the strength of his reaction to finding her in danger. The sight of that brute's hands on her had made him see red. His blood was up, and he had not been able to stop himself.

Pru's response was as passionate as he could have hoped, but even in the moment, a part of him had been aware that she, too, was reacting to danger. She had needed comforting, and had taken it from him. When he realized he was about to fondle her breast, just as that savage in the alley had done, he had pulled away and wrapped her in his arms. Where he should have kept her the whole time. She had needed human warmth and comfort, not another assault on her person.

He'd been so ashamed, he had not been able to say a word. And even in the days since, nothing was said about it. But he'd thought about it constantly. About how much he wanted her. The depth of that desire quite startled him.

When this marriage had been forced upon them, Nick had never imagined anything more than a decorous coupling with Pru. He had been quite blind to the fire beneath the surface. There was no longer anything remotely decorous about his imaginings. He had tasted that fire, and he wanted more.

He was ashamed for thinking such thoughts when he knew full well Pru's passion had been born of terror. He was a cad for taking such despicable advantage of her.

"She seems to be all right," he said at last. "A bit quiet, but then she always was."

"Take care with her, my boy. She will be especially fragile for some time, I should think. I imagine it was a terrifying experience for her."

"Yes, it was, poor thing. And for me, too. I swear, Father, if she had not come running into my arms for safety, I think I might have killed the man. I don't know when I have ever felt such rage."

"You will feel the same if ever a child of yours is in danger," Bartholomew said. "When a loved one is threatened, I believe the rational brain ceases to function and pure animal instinct takes over. The instinct to protect and defend at any cost."

A loved one.

Before he could consider those words, the sound of voices announced the approach of Pru and Flora. At last. Flora had arrived a short while ago, and had disappeared upstairs to help Pru dress. She had managed, though, to whisper to Nick that he would see his wife in a whole new light tonight. He wasn't sure what that meant, but he was anxious to find out.

He and his father rose to their feet as the two ladies entered the drawing room. Nick's eyes found Pru, and the sight of her robbed him of breath. She seemed to float into the room in a cloud of some sort of soft lavender fabric that moved with her body in a disconcertingly sensual manner. But his eyes were drawn to her bosom, for he was seeing more of it tonight than he had ever seen, and it was a glorious revelation.

He realized he was staring when Flora began to laugh.

"I do believe I heard a gasp," she said. "Did you hear it, Pru?"

Nick walked toward his wife and offered his arm. He could not take his eyes from her. "You look magnificent, my dear."

Pru smiled, and only the slightest hint of a blush colored her cheeks. Her hair was again tortured into submission, gathered up with several gold combs in a classical style that suited her well, though he imagined a rebellious curl or two would spring loose before half an hour passed. That slender, bare neck, along with the additional expanse of bosom revealed by the deep neckline, was a feast of beautiful pale skin that simply cried out to be touched. And stroked. And kissed.

Flora was right. Nick was seeing his wife in a new light. And it was blinding.

"I will be the most envied gentleman at the ball, he said, "to have such a prize on my arm."

"What nonsense," she said, though her smile showed her pleasure at his words.

Hats and shawls were gathered up and the four

of them made their way downstairs. Flora had come in her own rather elegant carriage, and Bartholomew joined her there as her escort. Nick had rented a town carriage for the evening, knowing it was too grand an affair to arrive in a hackney coach. It was an expensive evening, and he still harbored a niggling aggravation over it, after a week when his meager capital had been seriously threatened. But every time he glanced down at his wife's bosom, he forgot to care.

He handed Pru up, and joined her inside. Lord, she even smelled good. It was getting very difficult to honor the promise he'd made to himself to keep his distance. For days he'd been feeling caddish for the way he had ravished her mouth after rescuing her from those two louts, knowing she'd been too vulnerable to reject him.

From the beginning of their marriage, he had promised her they would take it slow. And up to that point, he had done so. In the days since the assault, he'd sworn himself to backing off. Not all the way back. Though he had not touched her since then in any way that could be considered intimate, he'd hoped to persuade her into another kiss tonight. Something less explosive than the last one. But he had a feeling she would not entirely reject a gentle kiss. And then, one step at a time they could move toward complete intimacy.

He had been determined to stay that course because he knew, despite her active response to his kiss in the hackney, that she was still a bit skittish when it came to the sexual aspect of marriage. He must remember that before the assault, this had been a woman who trembled at his touch, blushed scarlet at the mention of marital intimacy, and gasped in shock at their first simple kiss.

Tonight, though, he would be hard-pressed to maintain his good intentions. She had a bosom, dammit. A very nice one, too. How the devil was he to keep his hands off her?

Sometimes it really was tiresome to be a gentleman of honor.

Pru had never been happier in all her life. Her husband thought she looked magnificent, and quite frankly, so did she. She hadn't been certain about the plunging neckline, but Nicholas had not been able to keep his eyes from it. And she was fairly certain he was not staring in disapproval. It was still a bit disconcerting to be so exposed, but Madame Lanchester had been right. She did feel more stylish, and her neckline was really no more daring than those of most of the women present.

She and Nicholas had danced the opening set, and to Pru's astonishment, several other gentleman had solicited her hand for a set. And not all of them cousins. For the first time in her life, she was promised for every single dance. She felt positively giddy.

"Every set, Pru? Nothing left for me?"

"I'm sorry, Nicholas."

"Not even the supper dance?"

"It is promised to my cousin Robert."

"Which one is he?"

"Tall, blond . . ."

Nicholas laughed. "Please. You will have to do better than that, my dear."

"He is the handsome one in the beautiful claret-colored waistcoat embroidered all over with golden dragonflies."

"Ah, yes." He scowled a bit, and Pru wondered why he would possibly object to Robert. Perhaps he thought the waistcoat too flashy.

"He is my uncle Frederick's youngest son," she said, "only a few years older than me, but I don't believe he has spoken three words to me since we were children. I cannot imagine why he invited me to join him for the supper dance. Or any of the others, either."

"Can you not?" His eyes drifted to her bosom and she blushed. "You look good enough to eat, Pru, and they all want a bite."

Pru stared at him and wondered if he had perhaps had too much to drink. He was acting strangely possessive. Almost . . . jealous.

But then she remembered that he always played the role of a lovestruck husband at family functions. It was all an act, of course.

"Prudence?" Her cousin Edgar had approached. "It is my set, I believe."

She danced set after set until her feet were sore and she welcomed the respite of supper. She sat with Robert Armitage at a small table near Bartholomew and Flora. And she was pleased to see Nick seated with Joanna Draycott. She hoped they would become friends, too.

"Marriage certainly agrees with you, Prudence," Robert said. "You are quite aglow, you know. You look wonderful."

"Thank you, Robert. You are very kind to say so, but I fear I am simply flushed from dancing."

"No, I think not. It is more than that." He leaned forward so that his face was inches from hers. "You are like a little butterfly just come out of its cocoon. It is your marriage, I think, that has made the difference. Are you in love, Prudence?" He flashed a suggestive smile.

"Perhaps," she said, then remembered the love match fiction. "Of course I am."

"It shows. I am pleased for you, cousin. I always thought you quite the little mouse, but I see now it just took the right man to unlock your secrets. Parrish is a very lucky fellow."

"Thank you, Robert." At first she thought he was teasing her, or even flirting with her, but she realized he was quite serious. She flashed him a warm smile. "And thank you for inviting me to dance and to supper. That was very kind of you, and quite unexpected."

"Because you are accustomed to being a wallflower?"

"Yes, I suppose so."

"I wanted to have supper with you so I could tell you how sorry I am about that. About letting you be a wallflower, I mean. We have all treated you shabbily over the years, and I regret that with all my heart. If I had known you would blossom so prettily, I would have paid more attention."

"You rogue, it is my dress and . . . my dress that makes you notice me, that is all."

He laughed. "It is a lovely dress, Prudence, and definitely shows you to advantage. And it is true that if you had worn such a dress long before now, you would never have been a wallflower. I would have danced with you, I promise."

"Are you flirting with me, Robert?"

"I don't dare. Your husband is glaring daggers at me."

She looked over to where Joanna and Nicholas sat, and he was indeed watching them. Pru smiled at him, but he only scowled and turned away. How very odd.

She settled in to eat the light supper, and she and Robert chatted and laughed over family gossip. In such a large family, there was never a shortage of news.

"The orchestra is starting," Robert said. "Are you ready to dance again?"

"I am always ready to dance. I have years of being a wallflower to make up for."

Robert laughed and took her arm. They came up beside Joanna and Nicholas as they made their way to the dance floor. Joanna touched her arm, leaned over, and whispered, "I believe your husband is jealous, my dear. That is a good sign, is it not?"

"I really think you might have saved me one more dance, Pru." Nick stood at the sideboard in their drawing room, poured himself another glass of wine, and took a swallow. He offered a glass to Pru, but she shook her head.

"I wish I had done so, but before I knew it, every set was taken. I'm sorry, Nicholas. I confess it surprised me no more than you. I've always hated going to balls because I never got to dance much, and my feet always itched to dance."

"You made up for it tonight."

"I did." She smiled. "And I had a wonderful time."

"I'll bet you did, with all those Vikings swarming upon you like bees to honey. You were quite the little honey pot tonight."

She shot him a quizzical look. "What do you mean?"

"Flirting with every blond buck and beau that solicited a dance."

"Flirting? Me?" She began to laugh.

He took another long swallow of wine, found the glass to be empty, and set it down on the sideboard. He walked toward her. "Yes, flirting. Smiling and beaming up into their eyes. You were flirting."

"Nicholas, I have only attempted to flirt with one person in my life, and it was a disaster. I assure you I was not flirting. If I was smiling, it was because I was enjoying myself."

He planted himself in front of her. "Because you know you look best when you smile, that your face lights up the room."

She blinked at him as though not comprehending. "My face lights up a room?"

"Of course it does, as you well know." He reached out a hand and gently stroked the back of a finger along her jaw. "You could have lit every chandelier tonight with your smiles."

An uncertain little half smile tugged at one corner of her mouth. "I could have?"

"And frankly, my dear, I did not appreciate watching you flirt over supper with that popinjay in the dragonfly waistcoat."

"My cousin Robert?"

He grasped her elbows and pulled her up against him. He ought not to have done that. He'd promised himself he'd be an honorable gentleman tonight. He'd also promised himself a kiss. Perhaps he wasn't going about it as gently as he'd planned, but his mind was too befuddled with drink to care. "You should not have flirted with him. We are supposed to be playacting a love match, you know."

She swallowed hard. "I know. I tried to play my part."

"Did you?" He wrapped his arms around her. She was too deliciously irresistible, damn it all, and he was tired of playing the gentleman. Tired of taking it slow. Tired of watching other man ogle her like animals when she belonged to him.

"Yes. R-Robert asked if I was in love with you. And I s-said I was."

"Good girl." He dipped his head and nibbled on the flesh beneath her ear. He'd been wanting to do that all night. There were a lot of things he'd been wanting to do all night. "It is not right, you know, to flirt with another man when you belong to someone else."

"Oh." Her breathing had become labored, and her beautifully exposed bosom swelled with every breath.

"You belong to me, Pru." He brought his mouth to hover over hers. "You're mine. Mine." He closed the space between their lips and crushed her mouth beneath his.

He had no patience for subtlety or finesse. No care for his promise to take it slow. The wine and champagne and brandy—and raw, unabashed jealousy—had destroyed all concern for that promise. He forced her lips open and thrust his tongue deep inside her mouth. She gave a little groan, and he pulled her closer against him so she would feel the strength of his desire.

Nick released her mouth and slid his lips to the sweet, white skin of her throat. "You belong to me," he murmured against her neck. "Say it, Pru. You belong to me. Say it."

"I b-belong to you. Oh!"

His lips had found the enticing swell of her breasts. Lord, they were soft. He wanted to see them. He wanted to see all of her.

She gave a startled cry when he swept her up into his arms. It almost unnerved him. But, God help him, he did not think he could stop now.

"I want to make you mine, Pru."

"Oh."

"Will you let me? You belong to me, Pru. I want to make you mine. Do you understand?"

"Yes."

"Will you let me?"

"Yes."

He bent down and kissed her. "Then come with me, wife."

Pru could hardly believe what was happening. She wanted to cry out with joy but was too scared and excited and nervous to do anything but hang on to his neck.

She so wanted to please him, but wasn't at all sure how. This was completely new territory, and she needed a guide. She wanted to tell him that she really did not know what to do, that he would have to show her. But her nervous tongue was tied in knots as usual—*more* than usual—and she could not have spoken if she tried. Which was just as well. She would be mortified for him to know how clumsy and stupid she felt.

When they reached his bedchamber—his, not hers; that surprised her—he deposited her on the floor and kissed her lingeringly and thoroughly. He tasted strongly of wine and smelled faintly of shaving soap. He stepped away to light a candle, then he shrugged out of his coat and waistcoat, and removed his neckcloth. Wearing only his shirt and breeches, he grabbed her for another kiss, then began to undress her. She was no doubt supposed to have done it herself, but she was shaking like a jelly, and her hands would have made a mess of it.

He managed to remove her beautiful tunic and bodice and underdress, and she stood in only her chemise and corset. His gaze raked her from head to toe as he surveyed her near nakedness. He stepped back and said, "Let your hair down, Pru."

She reached up to remove the combs, but her hands were shaking too much.

"Ah, Pru. You're trembling. Are you frightened?"

She shook her head.

"Nervous?"

She nodded vigorously.

"Ah, sweetheart." He folded her in his arms and held her close. In a moment, his hands were in her hair, removing combs, letting them drop on the floor. When the last comb was gone, her curly mass of hair spilled over her shoulders and down her back.

Nicholas released her and stood back a moment. "Magnificent," he said. "Glorious." He took her in his arms again and buried his face and his hands in her hair. He kissed her ear and it tickled, so that she gave a little squeak. He laughed and released her again.

He spun her around and went to work on her corset. He demonstrated a rather disturbing talent for unlacing stays and she did not care to consider where he had gained such deftness. It fell to the floor, and there was nothing left but her chemise and her stockings.

This would be the perfect time to snuff the candle, Pru thought. She did not think she could bear the next step in full light. But he did not move to do so, and she could not have formed the words in any case.

He stepped up behind her and brought his arms around to pull her close against him. He buried his nose in her hair and brought his hands up underneath her breasts. She sucked in a breath and held it while he gently moved his hands to cup them. When she was finally forced to breathe, it came out in a raspy moan.

"Oh, God, Pru."

He pressed against her, moving his hips, and she could feel . . . it. Dear God, she could feel his arousal through his breeches.

She sincerely hoped she would not swoon before they got to the most important part.

He abruptly let go of her, and she shyly turned to see what he did. And was suddenly glad the candle was still lit. He had removed his shirt. Oh, but he was beautiful. Having lived in a house with five brothers, Pru was not completely ignorant of the male form. She had never, however, seen it quite so thoroughly displayed, and was unprepared for the powerful effect the sight of all that gorgeous masculinity had on her. Her whole body tingled at the sight of him.

He was not bulky and broad like her brothers, but lean and firmly muscled, his upper chest and belly covered in soft, dark hair. He smiled to see her studying him, and her face flamed with embarrassment.

He reached out for the straps of her chemise. The moment of truth had come, and she did not know if she could stand it. She would die. Surely she would die.

She closed her eyes tight as he slipped the straps over her shoulders and let the chemise fall to the floor. Oh God oh God oh God. She was naked. And he was looking at her. Her eyes were closed, but she could feel his gaze upon her.

Now was the moment to die of embarrassment. If it was ever going to happen, now was the time.

Yes, she had wanted this. More than anything, she had wanted this. But somehow she had never thought of what it would feel like to stand naked before him. What it felt like was thoroughly, completely, excruciatingly embarrassing.

Her hands came up instinctively to cover her breasts. But Nicholas pulled them away and held them out to her sides. She must surely be scarlet all over. Every inch of her.

"Open your eyes, Pru."

She shook her head. She did not want to see him looking at her.

"Please. Open your eyes. Look at me."

She supposed she would have to do so, sooner or later. She took a deep breath and opened her eyes.

And he was looking at her. He studied her quite openly as he continued to hold her hands out to her sides. She wished he would not do that. He had obviously seen many women without clothes on, women a hundred times prettier and more shapely than she could ever be. And yet he stared at her with a look so heated, she thought it must surely be desire.

He dropped her hands and reached out and gently, ever so gently, touched her left breast. Her nipples immediately tightened into nubs, and again she thought it would be a good time to die.

But then he said, in a voice filled with wonder, "Look at you, Pru. Look at you."

She would rather not. And would just as soon he did not, either.

"You're perfect."

Her eyes widened. What?

"Just perfect. And all mine."

He drew her up against him and kissed her. This was much better. Kissing was better than looking. Oh, much better.

With her eyes closed and his mouth on hers, being naked was not so bad after all. She actually loved the feel of his bare chest against her naked breasts. The heat of his skin. The musky smell of it. The raw carnality of bare skin against bare skin. It was truly the most incredible sensation. She could not stop herself from rubbing up against him.

He groaned and broke the kiss, swept her up into his arms, and laid her on his bed. He removed her garters and stockings, leaving her completely exposed. She burrowed beneath the sheet while he removed his breeches, small clothes, and stockings.

She could not help staring when he stood beside the bed completely naked, completely aroused. She had never seen a fully naked man before, except in paintings and statues. And never fully aroused. It was fascinating, and a little terrifying. She knew what was going to happen, but she could not imagine how. Surely there would not be enough room. She was, after all, a small woman. How on earth were they ever to accomplish this consummation?

Nicholas pulled back the sheet and joined her on the bed, gathering her into his arms. It was then that all logical thought was ripped from her by an overwhelming of pure physical sensation, new and unfamiliar and exciting.

He kissed her all over. She had not expected that. When he took her breast into his mouth, she gave a little cry of pleasure. She ought to have been embarrassed at such a thing, but heavens, it was wonderful. It set up a tingling throughout her body, and she even arched up to him, silently asking for more. She could not seem to stop the little cries that escaped her lips again and again as his tongue circled her nipple and traced a path to the underside of each breast. There was a heat surging all through her body that seemed to collect in that most private part of her. It was startling and new and even a little frightening. But she did not want it to stop.

And his hands were everywhere. Touching, stroking, fondling. His hands were warm, almost hot, on her skin. Every place he touched felt singed. She was on fire. He even touched her *down there*, and oh, my God, she was wet. Surely she should be mortified, but she was beyond thinking. Her mind was not in control. Her body knew what it wanted and pressed up against his hand.

He came on top of her and spread her legs with his knees. She could feel his arousal where he'd touched her. He took her mouth in a succulent kiss and pressed himself against her. Her body was quivering, taut as a bow string with anticipation and need. Somehow, she knew she had to have him inside her to fulfill that craving, that need she could not articulate.

And then he *was* inside her. She cried out, but his mouth still covered hers, and he swallowed her cry. It hurt. Dear God, it hurt. But he kept pushing, slowly, deeper and deeper until there came a moment of searing pain, and then he was completely buried inside her.

Somehow, it had worked. But she felt stretched, even torn. She gave a little whimper against his lips, and he lifted his head. He stroked a hand across her forehead and around her cheek. "I'm sorry, sweetheart. But the worst is over. Try to relax."

Relax? Was he mad? How could she possibly relax?

Nicholas lifted himself onto his forearms and began to pull out of her. Or so she thought. It was not over. He moved in and out in a slow rhythm.

She had expected more pain, but it did not come. There was a lingering soreness, but as he moved, as each stoke came deeper, it began to feel . . . good. Oh yes, this was not bad at all. Soon, she realized her body was moving with his. Her hips seemed to move of their own accord, pressing upward to meet each thrust. Her fingers dug into the muscles of his shoulders, grasping for something she could not name. Her breathing became shallow. She was panting openmouthed. There was a roaring in her ears, and she felt as if the world were spinning.

"Oh, God, Pru!"

His rhythm increased to a crescendo, faster and faster, until he buried his face in her hair and gave an inarticulate cry. He stilled, let out a deep breath, and collapsed on top of her.

It was over.

She was finally a wife.

Chapter 15

Pru was oddly reluctant for it to be over. She could not explain it, but she felt as though there was something more. But apparently not, because Nicholas rolled off her and onto his back.

"Too much to drink," he muttered. "Sorry, Pru. Was it too terrible for you?"

She shook her head. Oh, no. Not terrible at all.

"Oh, bloody hell." His head fell to one side, and he was almost instantly asleep, snoring softly.

How could he sleep after all that?

Pru lay there slightly bemused, and smiled. She was his wife in truth now. A real wife. She was rather proud of herself. She had overcome all her maidenly fears and allowed him to see her naked, to kiss her and touch her in ways she had never imagined. And she had survived every embarrassing moment. She had not died. Instead, she felt more alive than ever.

Surely he would not have done all those things to her if he had not found her desirable. His passion had been undeniable. He'd called her "sweetheart" and said she was perfect. She would cherish those words forever. If he truly desired her, and she had to believe he did, then she had hopes that someday he would grow to love her as well.

For now, it was enough to have finally reached this point in their marriage. Pru was feeling prouder and braver than ever before in her life. She was ready and eager to enter into this new phase of their relationship. She could hardly wait for the next time, though she really would prefer to have the candles snuffed. She wasn't that brave yet.

It had all been rather amazing, and not at all what she'd expected. She supposed one could not really know what to expect when one had never done it before. But the physical sensations had been quite extraordinary. Stunning, in fact. She was a bit embarrassed at her own physical reactions, and how she'd been unable to control them.

Her body still tingled all over, more so in certain parts, and she could not shake the feeling that she had missed something, that there should have been more. Perhaps, in her ignorance, she had not done something she should have done to make the act complete.

Could that be why he groaned at the end, as though in pain? Or why he cursed when he rolled off her? Was he disappointed that she hadn't known what to do?

She would do better next time, she was sure. At least she would know what was going to happen and she would not be as nervous. There would not be so much pain again, either. A maidenhood could only be broken once, thank heaven, though she had to admit the pain had receded rather quickly and what happened afterward had been quite pleasant. More than pleasant. Much more.

There was still a bit of soreness, and that feeling of having been stretched. And something else.

She needed to use the chamber pot. Desperately. She wriggled slightly and had to clench her inner muscles when the need to relieve herself threatened to overtake her.

Dear God, what should she do?

The candle was still burning, and she allowed her eyes to take in the room. She'd been so nervous, she had never even looked around her to see what it was like. It was similar to her own, though somehow more masculine. There was a screen in the corner, and she knew there would be a chamber pot behind it, or in the cabinet beside the bed.

But she could never in a million years have used it. What if he woke later and needed to use it himself? Besides, she could not possibly use it while Nicholas was in the same room. Even if he was asleep. She turned on the pillow to look at him.

His head was tilted away from hers, and one

hand was curled up beneath his chin. But for the snoring, he looked quite boyish.

Her eyes darted again to the screen. She really had to go. Badly. But what if he woke up and heard what she was doing? She would die. She would really and truly die of humiliation.

There was only one solution. She had to return to her own room.

She inched to the edge of the bed, keeping her eyes on Nicholas the whole time. He did not stir. She slowly and quietly sat up, swung her legs over the side of the bed, and very carefully rose to her feet, trying her best not to disturb him.

She stood for a moment, closed her eyes, and simply basked in the wonder of it all—the changes in her body, the change in the way she felt about her body, the way he'd made her feel. "Perfect," he'd said. She hunched her shoulders and twisted her head a bit, sniffing the skin at her shoulder and all down her arm, at last bringing both hands to her face and breathing deeply. She wanted to inhale the essence of him that still clung to her body, to intensify the sensual memory of the touch and taste and smell of him.

She turned to make certain he had not woken, and gasped at what she saw. There was a very messy streak of red on the white sheets. Was it *her* blood? She looked down and saw similar streaks along the insides of her thighs. It *was* her blood, and oh, my God, she had ruined his sheets. She wanted to groan but was afraid of waking him.

What would he think of her? What would the servants think when they laundered the sheets?

How perfectly mortifying.

The only way she could think of to redeem the situation at all was to go to her room, clean herself up, then return to his bed and lie on top of the stains so he would not see them. She would put on her prettiest lace nightgown—the same one she'd worn in wretched solitude on her wedding night—and sleep beside him. If she could sleep.

Surely Nicholas would not blame her for ruining his sheets. He'd known she was a virgin. But she was a real wife now, and proud of it. To be sure, she had a lot more to learn, and she would do so, if he was willing to teach her. But at least, and at last, she had done this amazing thing, and would never be a pathetic spinster ever again.

In the meantime, she was desperate for the chamber pot. She gathered up her clothes from the floor, clutched them to her naked body, and hurried from the room.

She woke when sunlight from a gap in the curtains fell across her face. Her eyes flew open when a memory of last night burst vividly upon her mind. But something was wrong.

She was in her own bed in her own room.

Damn and blast.

Pru sat up, and as she came more fully awake she remembered what had happened. She had returned to her room, thanking heaven and all the saints that she had not run smack into Bartholomew in the corridor. After taking care of the most urgent business, she had cleaned herself and donned her best lace nightgown. But she had been a little sore, and she remembered sitting down on the bed for a moment. And then she had lain back and curled on her side, thinking she would lie still for a few moments, to compose herself and her tumultuous thoughts before returning to Nicholas.

She ought to have known she would fall asleep.

Stupid, stupid girl. Now he would wake to find her gone and with embarrassingly ruined sheets to remind him of what had happened. How would she ever be able to face him at breakfast? Especially if Bartholomew was there.

Heavens, why did it all have to be so mortifying? She was quite certain other wives did not behave so foolishly. Pru promised herself that she would work hard to overcome her embarrassment over the details of physical intimacy. It was to be a part of her life now, as a true wife to Nicholas, and she looked forward to it. But she must not face every night with such maidenly self-consciousness. Better to remember that he had called her "perfect" and go to him with unashamed desire.

If only he would snuff the candle next time.

She dressed and went downstairs for breakfast, which was routinely set out in the dining room, now that the Crimson Ladies had a work space in the new offices. Neither Nicholas nor Bartholomew was there. Her father-in-law was generally an early riser, but they had all been out late. In fact, she was fairly certain he had not yet returned home when she had dashed naked through the corridor last night.

Both men were no doubt sleeping late. She was almost glad not to have to face Nicholas just yet. But at the same time, she was anxious to have him take her in his arms again, to kiss her again, to make love to her again. Perhaps in the end, her desires would overcome her idiotic bashfulness and embarrassment.

She could not afford to wait for Nicholas to come downstairs, though, because she really had to get to the *Cabinet* offices. The new issue should have been distributed overnight, and she needed to make sure nothing had gone amiss. And the new engravings were due to arrive this morning, which meant the Crimson Ladies would be scheduled to work today. It was going to be a busy day.

She finished her breakfast and went into the hallway. She'd left her bonnet on the hall table, and watched in the mirror above as she put it on, adjusted it, and tied the ribbons beneath her chin. She took a moment to study her face. Did she look any different this morning? Would all the world be able to see that her life had changed drastically in one day, that she was no longer a maiden, that she was a wife in every sense of the word?

She looked just the same as always. But when a secret smile crept across her face, she could swear there was a new sparkle in her eyes.

* * *

Nick stared down at the rumpled sheets and the rather alarming red stain.

Good Lord, what had he done?

He'd slept like the dead—thanks to the drink—and had not thought it odd when he woke to find himself alone in his own bed. Until his muddled brain reminded him of what had happened. And now the results of last night's business stared him in the face.

He'd hurt her—ripped her to shreds, by the look of it—and she had fled.

Damnation.

He'd been angry about losing so much money, and had drunk too much wine and champagne and anything else that had come within his reach. And the drink had driven him to an irrational jealousy. More than all that, Pru had simply been irresistible. She had looked so beautiful, so captivating, he had not been able to keep his hands off her. And once he'd taken the first step, he hadn't been able to stop. He ought to have been able to resist the urge. He ought to have been able to keep his promise, to himself and to Pru. But the drink had pushed him over the edge. Instead of keeping to his plan to take things slowly, he had taken a great deal more. It had been an act of possession, marking her as his own. And he was profoundly ashamed for it.

He had caused her pain and frightened her away. He had tried to be gentle, but his desire for her—uninhibited by the drink—had taken away his control. He had botched it quite thoroughly.

He vaguely recalled asking her afterward if he'd hurt her badly. She had not responded, and that had been answer enough. He had hurt her. He stared down at the evidence of it.

A glimmer of gold caught his eye. One of Pru's combs lay on the floor beside the bed. He remembered removing them from her hair. When he'd watched all that glorious, wild hair tumbling over her shoulders and down her back and into his hands, he'd been a lost man.

Nick stooped to pick it up. There was nothing else of hers left behind. Except for the blood, of course. She had apparently collected her things and fled for her life.

He had moved too fast, wanting her for himself and not caring about her needs. But she had said yes when he asked if he could make her his own. He had pressured her, though, seduced her, and no doubt she knew he would not have easily accepted a rejection. And so Nick had taken what he wanted, and she silently had allowed him to do so.

Had he taken her against her will? Nick did not think so, even though she had been shaking like a leaf. She admitted to being nervous. Not with words. He could not recall that she had spoken a single word throughout. But she had not fought him, had not denied him, had in fact allowed him to arouse her. And she had responded.

Good Lord, she had looked so lovely, standing

there with her apricot curls floating about her and her perfect little body displayed to him for the first time. He had been reminded of all those scoundrels ogling her at the ball. But none of them would ever see her like this, he thought, and he had wanted to claim her as his own.

Had he been too rough? Is that why there was so much blood? He had been especially conscious of her virginity, though, and thought he had been as gentle as possible. He was fairly certain the drink hadn't clouded his mind on that point. He'd been very much aware of her, had tried to make her ready, and thought he had done so. Her pain, though, had been obvious. Perhaps it was because she was so small. In any case, he felt a great deal of shame and remorse for hurting her so badly.

Later on, when her body seemed to have recovered from the initial pain of entry and adjusted itself to his invasion, Pru had seemed to become aroused again. She moved with him, exciting him until he could bear it no more. He felt a bit guilty for not taking more time and allowing her to reach climax. But she had suffered such pain, it had seemed unlikely she would be able to attain full release this time. But next time . . .

Next time? Already he was thinking how he'd like to repeat the performance again tonight and every night thereafter. But he had been selfish enough already. He must think of Pru for once. He had not, after all, waited until she was ready. He had taken her too soon. He would give her time to heal, physically and emotionally, before imposing upon her again.

This time, Nick really would wait for her to be ready.

He washed and dressed quickly, hoping to catch Pru downstairs at breakfast, but found she had already left for the *Cabinet* offices. And so he poured himself a cup of coffee, picked up the morning newspaper, and sat down to enjoy a leisurely breakfast.

Sometime later, he heard the front door open. Nick rose from his chair and stepped into the hall, hoping Pru had come back for something. He really wanted to speak with her.

But it was Nick's father who stood in the hallway, removing his hat and gloves. He was still in evening dress.

"Hullo, Nick."

"Father? You are just now coming home? You have been out all night?"

Bartholomew's brows rose in question. "What? Are you going to scold me for coming home so late? Honestly, Nick, you are like an old woman sometimes. When did you become so conventional?"

Nick was startled into silence. His father had always been the conventional one. Nick's mother had been rather wild and unpredictable, with a passionate nature in keeping with her Italian blood and artistic temperament. She had led his father a merry dance. And sometimes not so merry. Bartholomew had always been steadfast and solid as a rock.

"You misunderstand me, Father. I am surprised, that's all. For most of my life you have been a quiet country gentleman. I am not used to this London gentleman yet. Come, have breakfast with me."

"I will have a cup of coffee, but no more. Frankly, I'd like to go upstairs and catch a few hours' sleep."

He left his hat and gloves on the hall table and followed Nick into the dining room. He sat down wearily and accepted the coffee Nick poured for him.

"Let me try to explain something to you," he said. "I have indeed been a quiet country gentleman these last fifteen years. But only because Helena was no longer there to bring a bit of noise into my life. A bit of laughter. A bit of fun. A great deal of passion. I have missed that, Nick."

"We have all missed Mother. But I always assumed your grief was so profound that you preferred to be alone with it. That is why, I thought, you never came to town."

"I have grown overly comfortable up in the Peak. I did remain there because of Helena. She died there, and I felt closer to her there. Even after the raw pain of losing her subsided, I grew lazy and set in my ways. I was perfectly content with my routine existence, with my books and my birds and the natural beauty of the Peak. At least,

I thought I was content. And then I came to Edwina's wedding."

"And met Flora."

"She took my breath away, Nick. And has brought me back to life."

"Then I shall always honor her for it. It is good to see you so happy again."

"I have not been unhappy, Nick. Please do not think so. I was just . . . settled. As one grows older, it is easier to simply keep things as they are. I daresay I needed someone to light a fire under me to make me change my ways."

"And Flora is that fire."

His father grinned, but did not comment, for which Nick was grateful. There were certain things about one's parents that were best kept private.

"Did she enjoy the ball?" Nick asked.

"Immensely. She was surreptitiously taking notes for some sort of article."

"One of her fashion reports, no doubt."

"She loves working on the magazine. Did you know? She thrives on it."

"I am glad to hear it. She has added a great deal to its success."

His father gave a huge, wide-mouthed yawn. "I am for bed, Nick. You will have to excuse me." He rose and walked to the door, then turned.

"By the way, Prudence was quite the belle of the ball last night, was she not?"

"Yes, she was."

"You must have been very proud. She looked quite beautiful."

He ought to have been proud, but he'd been stupidly jealous and possessive instead. "Yes, she was beautiful last night." An image came into his mind of her lying beneath him, her apricot curls in a wild disarray against the white linen of the pillow slip, her blue eyes dark and glassy with desire. "Very beautiful."

The *Cabinet* was bustling with activity. Pru had not had a moment's peace since arriving. The new engravings had been delivered, but they were short by several hundred copies. The binder stopped by to discuss more substantial wrappers, as the current stock was too flimsy to accommodate the recent increase in pages. Two booksellers had sent clerks to purchase additional copies of the new issue, and Pru had convinced them to increase their monthly orders. She received notes from several other booksellers requesting additional copies, and had to make arrangements with Imber for another short print run.

She had wondered what was causing the sudden surge of interest, until Flora strolled in, beaming with triumph.

"Have you heard? The day is barely half over and already all of London is abuzz with the news."

"What news?"

"*The Ladies' Fashionable Cabinet*'s first annual list

of the worst-dressed ladies in London, that's what."

"Oh! Should I be concerned, Flora, or pleased?"

"Very pleased, I should think. Everyone is talking about it. I would not be surprised if your subscription numbers increased."

Pru was fairly certain they already had done. "Well then, I shall elect to be pleased. Increased revenue is always a good thing."

"Miz Parrish?" Madge peeked her head in the office. "A Mr. Grossett to see you, ma'am. About 'is advertisements, 'e says."

"Oh, thank you, Madge. Please send him in. Flora, you had better check on the Ladies. The new engravings came in today."

Pru quickly completed her business with Mr. Grossett, who wanted to increase the advertisements for his hosiery emporium to a full column each month. A few minutes later, a stationer's representative came by to try to encourage her to upgrade the magazine stock. She was reviewing his samples and price list when Madge announced yet another caller. "A Lady Bertram, ma'am. She wouldn't tell me 'er business. Looks fit ter burstin', though."

Lady Bertram? Her name sounded familiar, but Pru could not place it. She was probably one of those women who thought she could write, and had brought along a story or poem to have printed in the *Cabinet*. Well, Pru did not have time for her today. She would take her pages, promise to look at them within the next month, and send her on her way.

"All right, Madge. Show her in."

Pru became distracted by the stock samples and did not hear the woman enter.

"Madam?"

Pru looked up at the sound of the chilly voice. A woman glared at her from the doorway. She was of average height and stocky build, and her brown hair was dressed in ringlets much too young for her face. They peeked out from beneath the brim of a Spanish cap with the most incongruously curled plume, reaching clear from the nape of her neck to dangle over her forehead.

Pru had a sudden premonition of why the woman was here.

"Yes? May I help you?"

"*I* am Lady Bertram."

"And I am Mrs. Parrish, acting editor of the *Cabinet*. What may I do for you, ma'am?"

"You may explain why you have sullied my reputation in your magazine?"

"Ah." Her suspicions were correct. Damnation. "Are you perhaps named in this month's special list?"

"You have branded me one of the worst-dressed woman in London. Can you deny writing such a lie?"

"I admit to publishing it. One of our staff members actually wrote the article."

"You are not Vestis Elegantis?"

"No, ma'am. But that person does work for me."

"Who is she? I will know her name at once."

"I am afraid I cannot tell you that, Lady Bertram. The identity of our writers and correspondents is strictly confidential."

"Then I shall hold *you* responsible. You may expect a visit from my solicitor. I plan a suit for libel."

Pru glanced down at stock samples and other work on her desk needing attention, and decided she simply did not have time for Lady Bertram's nonsense. She heaved a sigh and looked up at her. "That would be a very foolish thing to do, don't you think?"

The woman's face grew almost purple, and her eyes bulged wide. "How *dare* you speak to me like that. Do you know who I am?"

"You have said you are Lady Bertram. I see no reason to disbelieve you."

"Why, you brazen little trollop. We shall see how cool you will be when you are sued for every pathetic shilling in your coffers."

"Lady Bertram, if you sue the magazine I daresay you will find your sudden cachet as a list maker sink dramatically. The beau monde, you know, has no love for a person who makes a public fuss over nothing."

"And who are *you* to make judgments about your betters? A woman who works for a living in a business not fit for a lady. A woman who uses a rough-talking slattern as a gatekeeper. Who are *you* to pretend to know anything about the beau monde? A shopkeeper's daughter?" She gave an audible sniff.

Pru wasn't sure what came over her. Perhaps it was that sniff. She rose from her seat and glared at the woman. "Not that it is any of your business, Lady Bertram, but since you seem so keen to know, I will tell you. I am the granddaughter of the Duke of Norwich, niece of the current duke. My father is Lord Henry Armitage, and my mother was the daughter of Viscount St. Clair. I suspect, madam, that my blood is several shades bluer than yours."

The woman visibly flinched. "Oh." She had suddenly lost all the wind in her sails, and seemed not to know what to do.

"Lady Bertram, the list was a tongue-in-cheek bit of fun. I am sorry you were offended by it. But if you will accept a little advice, I would recommend that you take advantage of the temporary notoriety. You see, Lady Bertram's name will be on everyone's lips and everyone's invitation list. People will be paying attention to you and to what you wear. You will be flooded with invitations because everyone will want the notorious Lady Bertram at their social event. It is really quite the opportunity of a lifetime. I suggest you make the best of it, ma'am."

"Oh. I hadn't thought of it quite that way."

"I am sure if you put your mind to it, you will see I am right. Now, if you will excuse me, I have a great deal of work to do."

"Yes, ma'am. Thank you."

And she disappeared out the door.

"Brava, my dear."

"Nicholas!" Her cheeks flooded with heat. She

had not seen him since she'd left his bed last night. It was unsettling to find him standing there looking as superbly handsome as ever and with his usual friendly smile, and yet to remember his beautiful naked body and how he had used it. Her own body tingled at the memory. "I did not know you were here. Were you listening?"

"Flora and I were hovering in the shadows. You handled that shrew very well."

"Indeed you did," Flora said, peeking her head in the doorway. "I wish I could have seen her face when you told her who you are."

"What exactly did you write about her, Flora?" Nicholas asked.

"Just a description of the dress she wore to the opera. I believe I said she had been swathed in Venetian style drapery better suited to a drawing room window. That the color was unflattering and made her look overblown. Oh, and I might have mentioned something about the Easter altar lilies having apparently been transported to her head."

Nicholas threw back his head and laughed. "It is no great marvel she blew in with such a head of steam. I wonder if Pru can expect visits from the other nine ladies listed?"

"Good heavens, I hope not," Pru said. "I could not do that again. I still cannot believe I actually said those things to her. I have just been so busy that I was somewhat distracted. My mind was elsewhere. I daresay if I had been able to give her my full attention, I would have remembered to be nervous."

"You were brilliant," Flora said. "You must get distracted more often. And I shouldn't worry about the others. Lady Julia Howard, for example, is quite puffed up with her own consequence at being named to the list. It seems she is pleased with my 'fresh-from-the-tumbrel' description of her cropped hair and not at all offended to have her shocking dress referred to as a vulgar French affectation."

Nicholas laughed again. "Flora, I do believe you have a nasty streak."

"It will all balance out next month, when the best-dressed list is published. By the way, Pru, have you shown Nicholas the new engravings?"

"No."

"What engravings?" he asked.

"Next month's fashion prints," Flora said. "Come along and I'll show you. And you, too, Pru. I want you to see what the Ladies are doing."

Flora led the way to the workroom where the Crimson Ladies worked. Pru followed, and Nicholas touched the small of her back briefly, causing a tremor to dance up and down her spine. She could not help thinking of other ways he'd touched her.

The Ladies were hard at work, each one of them bent over a print, adding color. Flora stood over Polly and reached for a completed print. It was the one that showed Pru in her lavender tunic dress. Flora handed it to Nicholas, and his eyes widened.

"Pru? This is you? In the dress you wore last night?"

"Yes."

He stared long and hard at the print with an odd expression on his face that might have been wonder. "This is splendid." He looked up at her and smiled. "Truly splendid. And a smashing good likeness. You make a beautiful model, Pru. Especially in that dress."

"Doesn't she?" Flora said. "Polly, show Mrs. Parrish what you've done."

"I jus' mixed up a bit o' yeller and a bit o' pink to make the hair just your color, ma'am," Polly said. "Sort o' peachy, like. Oh, an' I been puttin' tiny dots o' blue on the eyes."

"And we're bein' exter careful wid the dress," Ginny said. "See this nice pale purply color Flora asked us ter use? Since it's a picher o' you, Miz Nick, we want to make it real nice."

Pru was so touched she wanted to cry. "Thank you, ladies. Thank you, all. I do appreciate your efforts."

"May I have a copy?" Nicholas asked, and Pru's heart swelled with pride.

" 'Course yer can, Mr. Nick," Ginny said. "Thought yer might be wantin' one. Here y'are. All nice and dry."

Pru watched Nicholas study the colored print and wondered what he was thinking. Was he remembering last night, when he'd removed that very dress and held her naked in his arms?

He looked at her and smiled. "I shall have this framed," he said. "It shall be a memento of the first ball at which you danced every single set."

It would be a memento for Pru of much, much more.

Chapter 16

Nick supposed it was never a good idea to tell a woman you wanted to have a talk with her. If he'd had any sense, he would have simply plunged ahead with what he had to say without giving her the time to fret over it.

For that was surely what Pru had done. She was perched on the edge of the settee, stiff-backed and tense, her hands clasped in her lap, and looked for all the world like a prisoner in the dock awaiting sentence.

As they had driven back to Golden Square from St. Paul's Churchyard, he had thought to offer his apology, but it simply had not seemed an appropriate setting for what was sure to be an awkward conversation. And so, like a dashed idiot, he had instead announced that he would like to have a talk with her when they returned home.

She had gone very quiet for a moment, then had said simply, "All right." She had not asked the purpose or subject of the talk. There was only one great issue hanging between them, so she undoubtedly guessed his intent. But the time spent driving home, washing up, and waiting for him to join her had allowed her to stew over it, and she was obviously strung tight with anxiety.

He sat down beside her, sitting almost sideways on the settee so he could face her. She did not look at him, but kept her eyes on the hands in her lap.

"I owe you an apology, Pru."

She closed her eyes briefly, and for an instant he thought she had winced. But it had been such a fleeting expression, he could not be sure. Her face went blank as an egg, and she stared straight ahead.

"I made a promise to you the day after our wedding, and twice now I have broken that promise, most shamefully last night." He tried to read her expression, to sense her feelings, but her face remained inscrutable. "I promised to give you time, to wait until you were ready before consummating our marriage. Instead, under the influence of anger and too much wine, I took advantage of you. I forced a sexual relationship on you before you wanted it. And I hurt you badly in the process."

Her eyes widened slightly and the color rose in her cheeks.

"I want you to know how sorry I am, Pru, and to assure you I will not behave so disgracefully again. If there is to be a physical relationship between us, and I hope there is, it shall be when you feel comfortable with it. When you are truly ready. Do you understand, Pru?"

She gave a stiff nod, but did not look at him.

He reached out and took her chin between his thumb and forefinger, and turned her face toward him. Her eyes were wide and bright with unshed tears. "Tell me, did I hurt you very badly? Physically, I mean."

She shook her head, and the color in her cheeks deepened. He wished he knew whether it was despair or embarrassment that made her so uncomfortable. He wished she would say something. He continued to hold her chin so he could at least look into her eyes and try to fathom her thoughts.

"I would never deliberately hurt you, Pru."

She swallowed. "I know." Her voice was barely a whisper. But it was something.

He stroked a thumb along her jaw, and willed her not to turn away again when he let go. And she did not.

"I want a real marriage with you," he said. "I want a physical relationship with you. I enjoyed what happened between us last night, even knowing the pain you suffered. At least you need not worry about that again. But I promise you, Pru, I will never force myself on you. When we make love again, it will be when you think it is right, when you feel comfortable about it."

"It was not force." She seemed to have found her voice, though it was still whispery soft.

"No, it wasn't. But it was coercion. When I pressed my attentions on you, I did not make it easy for you to object. And that was wrong. So I think we should start over. We must become accustomed to being private together, to being physical with each other, to touching, even kissing."

He cupped her face in his hand and brushed a soft kiss over her lips. She gave a little shudder, and he pulled away. "If I move too fast again, Pru, you must tell me. And I mean that. I cannot know what you want if you do not tell me. You are comfortable speaking to me of other things. Why not this, too?"

She turned slightly away from him and gave a little snort.

"Will you forgive my behavior last night?"

She looked at him again. "There is nothing to forgive."

He lifted her hand from her lap, took it to his lips, and kissed it. "Thank you, Pru."

"May I ask a question?"

"Of course."

"You said you were angry last night. Was it something I did? Was it because you thought I was flirting with my cousin?"

He stifled a groan. "No, my dear, I was not angry with you. I know you were not flirting. You were simply happy and enjoying yourself. It was churlish of me to suggest otherwise. It was the drink talking, and I apologize for that. No, I was angry about some bad news I'd had that morning."

"What news?"

"If I tell you, do you promise not to wag your finger and say, 'I told you so'?"

She cast him a quizzical look. "I promise."

"I learned that the Culwyn canal project is near failure. It seems an additional, and larger, engine is required for the pump if the water is ever to be drained. The company has run out of money. Rumor is they are going to put a halt to the project within the next week."

"And you are heavily invested?"

"Yes. And coming on the heels of the *Ulysses* loss, it was an especially unwelcome piece of news."

"I am sorry, Nicholas."

"So am I. But I still have a few irons in the fire, so to speak. One in particular that should net decent profits very soon."

"What is it? If you don't mind telling me."

"I have an sizable interest in a re-export scheme. We import sugar and coffee from the West Indies and America, then export it to Amsterdam."

She frowned. "It is still basically an investment in cargo shares, is it not?"

"Yes, but with greater potential for profit. I had a small share a while ago that paid enough to help me purchase the land in Derbyshire. I've sunk a larger amount this time, and the profits I anticipate will pay for much of the machinery and reconstruction costs."

"Do you not worry about losing another ship? It has been a terrible year for shipping."

"Most of the losses have been in the west, in

the Atlantic or the Irish Sea. This ship, the *Benjamin*, is in the North Sea, practically in Amsterdam already."

"I shall keep my fingers crossed, then."

"Thank you, my dear. You must know how badly I want to get started on the Derbyshire factory complex."

"Nicholas?" She tilted her head at a quizzical angle. "How did you become so passionate about factory reform?"

"You should know the answer to that, Pru. You know my political views. Heavens, you've edited enough of them over the years. Any progressive thinker would feel the same as I do."

"But I sense something more . . . personal at work. Was there something that set you on this course? Something specific?"

"You are sometimes very astute, Mrs. Parrish. Yes, there was something. A long time ago."

"What was it?"

Nick took a deep breath and blew it out his cheeks. It was a story that still pained him after all these years. And drove him.

"I had a playmate as a child," he began. "Alfie Blanden. He lived on a nearby tenant farm. Not one of ours, but close by. It was a very small farm, and not very productive. Alfie's family had been dirt poor, but it had never mattered to us as we romped about the countryside. The farm failed one too many years in a row, and his father moved the family up to Manchester where he took work in a textile factory. Alfie and his mother and all his siblings were going to work there as well."

Nick smiled wistfully at the memory of his little red-haired friend. "Poor old Alfie was beside himself with excitement. He felt very superior and very grown up to think that he would be working on some great huge machinery while I was still in the schoolroom. I didn't understand any of the implications of such a life and was seriously jealous. I couldn't stop thinking about Alfie and his grown-up factory job. About six months later, I actually ran away from home, picking up rides along the twenty or so miles to Manchester."

"How old were you?" Pru asked.

"Nine. Same as Alfie. I found the factory where he worked and figured he must live nearby, so I started asking around. I was finally able to locate the lodgings where his family lived. No one was there during the day, so I waited. I watched as one after another member of Alfie's family straggled home, looking exhausted and dirty. But not Alfie. He never came."

"Oh, no." A terrible sadness gathered in Pru's eyes. She would know what came next.

"I knocked on the door and was met by Alfie's mother, looking surly and tired. Behind the door was only a single room where the entire family lived. One small room for a family of seven. It was untidy and filthy, and smelled of human waste. I asked when Alfie would be back, and his mother told me he'd been killed in a machinery accident. Just like that. Very matter-of-fact. I'll never forget that moment. His mother hadn't even seemed to grieve for him. She had sounded as though such things were inevitable, and she'd call herself lucky if all she lost was one child."

Nick rubbed a hand across his forehead, massaging his temples. The day was still sharp in his memory, even twenty-three years later. "She did not invite me in, because there was no food to share. Why did you come, she asked me. To work alongside Alfie, I said. To have a job in a factory and my own money. She laughed out loud. Go home, she said. Go home to your soft bed and your safe life. There is nothing for you here. And she slammed the door in my face."

"Oh, Nicholas."

"Ever since that day, I have dreamed of helping to improve the life of factory workers. Without money, the best I can do is fight for parliamentary reform. But true reform—beyond whatever insignificant measures make it into law, real change that can only be implemented by progressive owners—takes money. The right owner with enough money can do it properly, can foster change and make a real difference in the lives of workers. And that is my dream, Pru. That is why I am forever trying to grow what little capital I have. To provide a safe workplace and decent living quarters for the families. To make sure that no more nine-year-old boys are forced to do a man's job and put their lives in danger."

"It's an excellent dream," Pru said. "I can see now why it is so important to you. And I promise to help, Nicholas, in any way you will allow."

* * *

Pru loved Nick more than life, but the man could be stubborn as a mule. He seemed to get certain ideas fixed in his head and there was no shaking them.

Like his crackbrained notion that she had allowed him to make love to her without her full consent. He said he'd had too much to drink. Was he so bosky he hadn't noticed she'd said yes when he asked? Hadn't noticed her embarrassingly complete cooperation? Hadn't noticed her idiotic grin of triumph afterward? No, probably not that, since he'd begun snoring the minute he rolled off her. But hadn't he paid any attention at all before falling asleep?

Pru was determined somehow to overcome her embarrassment and let him know she wanted to share his bed again. She wasn't sure how she would be able to say such a thing aloud, but she must try. She was tired, sick and tired, of his apologies. It broke her heart every time he told her he was sorry. She did not want his apologies. She wanted *him*. And she was resolved to let him know that. Somehow.

And then there was the factory project and his fixation on making money. It seemed to Pru that until Nicholas had enough capital to support his project, he would continue to be preoccupied with financial matters. Quite frankly, she would prefer him to be preoccupied with her, but that would not happen as long as he kept losing money. She hated to see him so on edge, so worried that his wonderful dream would never come true. He would never be truly happy until his financial future was settled. And because she loved him, she wanted him to be happy. But their lives would be a constant balancing act if he continued on his path of risky investments.

She adored Nicholas, loved his passion for social reform, his dedication to change. He was like Edwina in that respect, though with more zeal and less patience. She understood the drive that took him to France in support of the Revolution and now to a factory complex in Derbyshire. He wanted to be more than a man of words, writing speeches and political tracts and magazine articles. He wanted to be a man of action. He was filled with energy to *do* something.

And it was that aspect of his character she worried about when she thought of their financial future. He was too impulsive and too impatient—not a good combination for wise investment. He was going to lose his shirt if he was not careful.

All he needed was one good return, one large enough to put his project in action. Once he had done that, Pru was fairly confident she could convince him to let her advise him on the financial management of the business while he concentrated on the practical details of making it all work. He had already sheepishly admitted that he had taken her advice and invested in the Hull dock expansion project, so he obviously had some confidence in her opinion. Perhaps she could even convince him to let her manage that part of the business for him, because a man like Nicholas would never be happy with his head in an accounting ledger. Pru, on the other hand, rather enjoyed that sort of thing. She was methodical and cautious when it came to managing money, and that was exactly what a successful business required. She would have to give up the *Cabinet*, but she would happily do so if Nicholas needed her.

One good return. That was all it would take to make his dream come true.

And Pru was going to see that it happened.

With the help of her father's man of affairs, she tracked down Matthew Cracken, the agent for the Dutch export shipments, including those on the *Benjamin*. He confirmed her fears that the ship had not been sighted in days, and was already overdue at its destination. Mr. Cracken had all the records of Nick's share in the cargo, but was not confident in the expected returns.

"I would like to make a deal with you, Mr. Cracken."

"What sort of deal, ma'am?

"A very confidential deal. Between you and me alone."

The portly gentleman stared quizzically at her across his cluttered desk. "You intrigue me, Mrs. Parrish."

"Do I have your word that any transaction between us remains strictly confidential?"

"You have my word. But what are we talking about here? I gather you want to deceive your husband in some way?"

Pru winced at his words. She *would* be deceiving Nicholas, it was true. But not for something evil or sordid. For something good. For their future together. "It is a deception of sorts, yes," she said. "You see, I want him to make his profits on the *Benjamin's* cargo."

Cracken's bushy gray eyebrows shot up to his hairline. "And how do you expect me to do that when the cargo is still in question?"

"Because I am going to provide the profits."

He squinted and wrinkled up his nose. "How's that, again?"

Pru kept her gaze directly on his. She did not completely trust him, and she was certain he did not trust her. But she held on to her resolve and stood firm. It was amazing how her shyness or nervousness was seldom a problem with a business relationship, when she was confident of her position. It was only those pesky personal relationships that so often caused her embarrassment.

"Let me explain," she said. "I want you to inform Mr. Parrish that the cargo arrived safely in Amsterdam. And I want you to send him a bank draft for his share of the profits. I will, in turn, pay you the sum of the bank draft, plus a fee for keeping all this confidential."

"Well. It is certainly an interesting proposition."

"Will you do it?"

"It is highly irregular."

"Your fee will offset any irregularities."

"And how much would that fee be?"

Pru named a figure, a small percentage of the draft. He looked over his spectacles and boldly asked for more. They negotiated a fee somewhere in between, and she was satisfied.

"Do you have the draft with you?"

Pru was reluctant to admit she did. What if he had a gang of ruffians in hiding who were waiting to steal it from her? She had had enough of ruffians. She still had nightmares about the assault on Ludgate Hill.

"Mrs. Parrish, I am a businessman, not a thief. If you have the draft, turn it over to me, and I will take care of the rest."

"No," she said, "that is not how we will proceed. We will do it my way."

Her way was time-consuming and complicated, but it gave her more security. Pru accompanied Cracken to his own bank and asked for a copy of the receipt for the deposit of her draft. Back at his office, she stood by while he wrote the letter to Nicholas and made out the draft to him. She took both, and would see that Nicholas got them. And finally, she made Cracken sign a contract, in duplicate, that kept their transaction secret.

"You are a tough little customer, Mrs. Parrish. I send my compliments to Mr. Parrish on his choice of wife."

And so it was done. Very nearly every shilling of Aunt Elizabeth's legacy now belonged to Nicholas. Or soon would, once she made sure that he received Cracken's packet. She would keep it hidden for a few days, though, and not mention a word about finances in the meantime. She did not want him to suspect anything.

"I tell you, Simon, she is not the woman I married."

Nick's friend howled with laughter, and he immediately regretted confiding in him.

"She's grown beautiful, has she?"

"Well, yes. Sort of. Damn it all, Simon, stop laughing. Don't you remember what a dowdy little mouse we thought her?"

"*You* thought her."

"But just look at this." He pointed to the colored print of Pru he had slapped down on the card table. "Look at her, Simon. Is that the Pru you once knew? Look at her! How the devil am I supposed to keep my hands off her?"

"Who says you have to? She's your wife, for God's sake. What is this, anyway? A print for the *Cabinet*?"

"Yes. Flora apparently got her to pose for it. Can you imagine? Shy little Pru posing for a fashion print? I tell you, Simon, the woman is full of surprises. I'm on my way to have it framed."

"Are you?" Simon leaned back in his chair and grinned. "Well, well. It appears I was right after all."

"About what?"

"About how this marriage would turn out. You're in love with her."

Nick rolled his eyes to the heavens. "Don't be

ridiculous. God, you are such a romantic, Simon. Not everyone is as dreamy-eyed as you are. We cannot all have the sort of love match you have with Eleanor. In love with Pru? How absurd. I will admit to a certain amount of unexpected lust. But you should see her, man. She is a perfect little Venus."

"Don't tell me I should see her, old boy. If I did, I suspect I would soon be looking down the barrel of your gun."

"And so you would."

"Why is it so hard for you to admit you're in love with your own wife?"

"Dash it all, I am *not* in love with her."

"Then you're either blind or stupid. Or both. Listen to yourself, Nick. You have just spent the last half hour telling me about her music. About how she plays like an angel. About how she has this fantastic plan for a music school that you secretly admire even if you won't admit it. About how shockingly knowledgeable she is regarding financial investment. About how brilliantly she is handling the *Cabinet* while Edwina is away. About how angry you have been to see how her relatives ignore her. About how you wanted to kill that brute who'd dared to touch her. And then there is all that talk about her hair and her eyes and her skin and her . . . other assets. I don't know. Perhaps I *am* a romantic fool, but all that sounds like a man in love to me."

Nick blinked. "Did I really say all that?"

"And more."

"Well." Nick was quite frankly abashed. As he listened to his friend repeat back his own words about Pru, it occurred to him that he really had grown to admire her and respect her. His affection for her had grown as well. Not to mention his desire. He certainly felt protective of her, sometimes even possessive. Could there be some truth in Simon's words? Was he, after all, in love with his wife? "I will, um, consider what you have said."

Two days later, he was still considering it when he accompanied Pru to her aunt Sarah's garden party in Richmond. It was a beautiful day, and Pru was as radiant as the sunshine in a pale green dress and matching bonnet. They strolled into the breeze, and the soft muslin of her skirts clung to her in the most enticing manner, revealing with each step the shape of her slender legs and the curve of her hips.

Nick was proud to have her on his arm as they walked through the gardens, greeting and chatting with one Armitage after another. Their hosts, Lord and Lady George, had even made a little fuss about what a happy couple they were. Nick realized the pretense of a love match had become second nature to him. In fact, it no longer felt in the least like pretense. It felt right to act as though he loved her. It felt real.

Well, he thought, how about that?

"Did you and Lord Caldecott have a good talk?" Pru asked.

"We did indeed. I thank you for arranging the meeting, my dear. He was very interested in my views on the factory bill. He will be a solid advocate in Lords. I was pleasantly surprised. He seems a right-thinking fellow, Pru."

"For an earl?"

He smiled down at her. "For a man. If I have learned one thing from you, Mrs. Parrish, it is not to judge a man by his rank. No matter how high it is." He stopped walking and looked down at her. "I have actually learned a great deal from you, Pru. I wish I'd known you better all these years. You're a remarkable woman, you know."

He took her arm and pulled her behind a large tree. She giggled as he leaned against the trunk and swung her into his arms. He dipped his head and kissed her.

It was too public a place, with too many Armitages about, to get overly passionate. So he kept it simple and slow and closemouthed. When he broke away, he smiled at her and said, "I'm sorry, Pru. I keep promising to take it slow, and I keep breaking my promise. But you are looking quite irresistible this afternoon, my dear, and I simply could not help myself."

"Please don't apologize again, Nicholas."

"No?"

"No. I hate apologies. Just shut up and kiss me."

And he did. This time her lips parted, inviting him in, and her tongue met his with an eagerness that set his blood racing. After a long moment, he pulled back, afraid if they kissed any longer he would be raising her skirts and taking her against the tree trunk.

He turned his head at the sound of soft footsteps on the grass, and saw Joanna Draycott walking away. She stopped and turned to look over her shoulder, caught his eye, and winked.

It was like the night of the Norwich ball. Pru was feeling blissfully and completely happy as they drove back from Richmond. She could not stop smiling. Except when Nicholas kissed her. Which was often.

Once she managed to convey to him that she actually *wanted* him to kiss her—heavens, had she really told him to shut up?—he had hardly stopped doing so. And it was a very, very long drive back to Golden Square.

When they arrived home, Pru spied the packet on the hall table, and she drew in a sharp breath. She'd been so wrapped up in her own happiness, she'd forgotten all about it. But now a flutter of anticipation gripped her stomach.

She walked around Nick, trying her best to be nonchalant, and headed up the stairs. There were lights in the drawing room, so she stepped inside. Bartholomew sat in front of the fireplace—where no fire burned since it was a warm afternoon— reading a book. He looked up and saw her.

"Hullo, Prudence." He rose to his feet, smiling, and crossed the room. "How was the party?"

"It was lovely, sir, thank you. We—"

"Pru! Father!" Nicholas came bounding into the room, grinning from ear to ear. "You'll never guess what's happened."

"Then you had better tell us," Bartholomew said with an answering grin.

Nicholas looked at Pru, eyes flashing, excitement fairly shimmering all about him. "The first Amsterdam shipment paid off. And at a much larger profit than I'd expected. I have the bank draft right here. Pru, do you know what this means?"

She beamed a smile at him. "Yes. Yes, I do. Oh, Nicholas!"

"Ha ha!" He lifted her by the waist and swung her around and around, laughing and whooping, until she cried out to be put down. He had to steady her when he did for she was bobbling with dizziness. He pulled her into his arms and held her tight. "Finally. Finally, Pru, I have enough to get started. After so many disasters, I can hardly believe it."

"Well done, my boy. Well done."

Nicholas released her and took his father in a great bear hug. "Father! Isn't it marvelous?"

"Please don't swing me around, Nick. I'm much too old for that sort of thing."

"We must celebrate." Nicholas, so filled with energy he seemed ready to explode, dashed to the doorway and shouted for Lucy. He turned back to Pru. "We must have champagne. Lots of champagne. We shall drink and get giddy and celebrate all night."

"But Nicholas, we are supposed to attend the theater tonight with Margaret and Arabella."

His face fell, and he looked like a child whose favorite toy had been taken away. "Must we?"

She could not deny him. Not tonight. "I suppose I can send a note with our excuses, if you prefer."

He grinned. "I do prefer. Let us have a private celebration right here. I will send out for champagne and ask Mrs. Gibb to prepare a fine supper. And we'll invite Simon and Eleanor."

Pru looked at Bartholomew. "And Flora."

"Definitely," Nicholas said. "We cannot have a party without Flora."

He grabbed Pru again and crushed her in his embrace. "Ah, Mrs. Parrish. What a day this has been."

And he kissed her, then and there, with his father looking on.

Chapter 17

It was a boisterous evening, and the champagne flowed freely. Bartholomew had sent out for several bottles, then both Simon and Flora arrived with more. Over dinner they had joked and laughed and told stories. And now they were gathered around the pianoforte singing "Lavender's Blue" to Pru's accompaniment.

She learned something new about her husband tonight. He could not carry a tune.

Nicholas sat beside her on the bench and sang loudly in her ear. But she didn't care since his knee was rubbing up against hers in a very suggestive manner. Pru could not recall when she had been so happy. She felt she might actually burst with joy and had every expectation that the evening would end with her in Nicholas's bed. In truth, she would be utterly devastated if she spent another night alone, staring at the closed door of her bedchamber.

But she was determined that would not happen. If she had been able to muster enough courage to tell the man to shut up and kiss her, surely she could manage to ask him to make love to her. Couldn't she?

Pru forced her concentration on the music.

Verse after verse was sung of the old song, with several new ones made up on the spot. Simon was quick to spin sweet, sentimental rhymes directed to his wife. Flora added several bawdy verses that had them all howling.

Finally, Eleanor fell to laughing and shrieked, "Enough! I can't bear another 'diddle diddle.' Pru, play something we cannot possibly sing."

"Oh, yes," Nicholas said, vacating the bench and leaving her knee bereft and lonesome. "You must hear at least one serious piece. Pru is the most splendid talent, you know."

And so she played part of an Eckard sonata that was an easy piece for her, one she could play almost without thought. Cheers and applause followed, and she beamed with appreciation, though the entire company—with the exception of Eleanor, who was increasing—was a bit the worse for champagne and not a proper audience.

"Pru, you are a marvel," Eleanor said, "but we should not wear you out. Let me take your place for a while. I'm not as skilled, but this lot won't notice."

Pru stood and stretched out her fingers. She'd been playing longer than she realized. She wondered how late it was.

Eleanor pulled the bench back to make room for her expanding waistline, and began to play "Barbara Allen." Her husband took Pru's arm and led her to the other side of the room where empty champagne bottles littered the sideboard.

"I haven't had a chance," Simon said as he poured them each another glass, "to tell you how pleased I am that your marriage has worked out so well. It is almost difficult to recall how miserable the two of you were at the wedding ceremony. You seem so happy now."

"I am happy, Simon."

"It shows. You are quite radiant tonight."

"The glow of too much champagne, I daresay."

"No, it is much more than that and you know it. You are very much in love with him, aren't you?"

Pru smiled and gave a little shrug. "You, sir, are an incurable romantic."

He grinned. "Guilty as charged. And I shan't pry any further, I promise. But I can see you are both happy and I cannot tell you how much that pleases me. I have long hoped that Nick would find the same happiness I have with Eleanor. I told him before your wedding that this marriage would be the best thing that ever happened to him."

"You did?"

"Yes. And I believe he has come to learn I was right."

"He has?"

"It certainly looks that way. But I really should keep my tongue between my teeth. Whatever Nick feels is for you to discover." He flashed a grin. "But I am, after all, the Busybody, and forever poking my nose into other people's affairs."

"Simon, old boy," Bartholomew shouted across the room, "bring that bottle and refill all our glasses. I have an announcement."

Pru's eyes found her husband's and they each lifted their brows in question. She went to his side and took his arm.

"Have a seat, everyone," Bartholomew said. "I believe I am going to make a little speech."

Nicholas led her to the settee and they sat close together. Flora and Eleanor took the two armchairs, and Simon stood behind his wife, resting his hands on her shoulders.

Bartholomew stood facing them and cleared his throat. His eyes were a trifle glassy from the champagne. "As you know," he said, with only the merest hint of a slur, "I came to London to become acquainted with my new daughter-in-law. And I can say now, with all honesty, that I could not have asked for a better wife for my son."

Nicholas put his arm around Pru and gave a squeeze.

"Prudence," Bartholomew said, "I am honored to welcome you to our family. Paltry as it is, compared to your own. Did you know," he said, speaking directly to Eleanor, "that she has fifty-two first cousins?"

Eleanor's mouth fell open and she stared at Pru, who smiled at her and nodded.

"And so," Bartholomew said, "I would like to offer a toast to Prudence, my second daughter." He raised his glass and waited until the others had done the same.

"To Prudence," Simon said, and the rest echoed the toast.

Pru was glad Nicholas kept his arm around her. She felt like crying. "Thank you," she whispered. "Thank you Bartholomew."

"And it occurred to me," Bartholomew continued, "that since my son has got himself such an excellent wife, he should have a house of his own to share with her. And so, Nick, I have decided this house, which Prudence has already made into such a comfortable home, should belong to you." He reached into his pocket and pulled out a folded parchment. "Here is the deed, my boy. I have signed it over to you."

"Good Lord." Nicholas rose from the settee and took the document from his father. He looked down at it for a moment and shook his head in disbelief. "I don't know what to say. Thank you." His voice was heavy with emotion. He took Bartholomew's hand and shook it firmly. "Thank you, Father. Thank you."

Pru batted back tears. What a wonderful thing for Bartholomew to do. Did he realize how much it meant? That they would always have the security of a house, no matter what happened with Nicholas's factory?

She stood and went to her father-in-law, raised up on her toes, and kissed him on the cheek. "Thank you, sir. It is an extremely kind and generous thing to do."

Bartholomew waved away her words. "It is nothing. Nick has spent more years here than I ever did. It is more his home than mine. This just makes it official."

"Well done, sir," Simon said. "Another toast is in order, I think."

And they all raised their glasses to Bartholomew.

Nicholas and Pru returned to the settee, and he took her hand in his.

"One more thing," Bartholomew said, still standing. "Now that the house belongs to you, Nick, I think it is high time I let you and Prudence have it all to yourselves. A newly married couple should not have to contend with a resident father-in-law, and I am sorry I have imposed so long. I plan to remove myself within the next day or so."

"Are your returning to Derbyshire?" Pru asked, darting a glance to Flora, who was smiling. She did not believe Flora was a countryside sort of person. The former courtesan was very much a Town lady.

"No, not just yet," Bartholomew said. "I have kept myself away from London too long, and I have discovered that I rather enjoy life in Town." He glanced at Flora. "More than I ever thought possible. Indeed, I have decided I would like to spend a great deal more time here. I have found a charming little house on Conduit Street. It's a bit smaller than this, and without the garden in back, but I quite like it. In fact, I have taken a long lease on it."

"Father! Another house in Town? After giving this one up, you find another?"

"I believe he wants some privacy, Nicholas," Pru said, smiling at her father-in-law.

"Well, you could have kept this one, you know," Nicholas said. "Pru and I could have taken the smaller house."

"No, you need more space, my boy. Especially when the children come along."

Pru felt her color rise. At least this time she was blushing because it actually *might* happen, not because it couldn't possibly.

"Won't you be lonely," Eleanor asked, "all alone in the house?"

"I am accustomed to being alone," Bartholomew said. "I have spent the last fifteen years alone. And quite frankly, I am tired of it. But I have hope that I shall not be alone forever." He looked longingly at Flora, who smiled at him.

He said no more, and no one asked what he meant. The look he gave Flora was perfectly clear. Pru hoped she would make the poor besotted man happy. Her smile suggested she just might.

Imagine that. Pru might have Flora as a mother-in-law. She giggled at the idea, and realized the champagne had gone to her head.

* * *

Nick stood with Pru in the entry hall, having just ushered out their guests. His father had escorted Flora home, and Nick suspected he would not return.

"What a night it has been," he said, taking Pru's arm and leading her to the stairs. "My head is spinning, and not just because of the champagne. First the *Benjamin* profits. Then the deed to this house. Do you believe it, Pru? This is *our* house now. Really ours. You could have knocked me over with a feather when Father made that announcement."

"It was exceedingly kind of him," she said. "A lovely gesture."

"And this business with Flora." He laughed. "She could become my stepmother, Pru. The notorious Mrs. Gallager. He's top over tail in love with her, you know. I wonder if she will marry him?"

"I have wondered that, too. I hope she doesn't break his heart. She has never seemed the marrying type, what with her history and all."

"And yet there must have been a Mr. Gallagher at some point."

Pru stopped on the landing and stared at him. "Good heavens, you're right. Funny, I never even thought of that."

"I'd be willing to guess it was a youthful folly of some kind. Before her first protector took her out of St. Giles. Oh, my God. You don't think she is still married to him, do you? And that is why she can't marry Father?"

"Oh Nicholas, I hope not."

"Well, I am sure they will work things out. She does seem fond of him, does she not?"

"Yes, I think so."

Nick stepped into the drawing room and snuffed all the candles. When he turned toward the door, it was so dark he could not see Pru. Dear God, she hadn't bolted upstairs alone, had she? Not tonight. Please, not tonight. "Pru?"

"I'm here."

He reached out and found her hand, then pulled her to him and wrapped his arms around her. "I thought you'd run away."

"Never."

"Ah, Pru." He kissed her.

He coaxed her lips apart and slid his tongue deep inside, stroking her tongue and the warm flesh of her mouth. Her arms crept up and around his shoulders, and he pulled her closer, pressing his hips against her belly. The undulation of her hips, a maddening combination of innocence and desire, sent a great, hot wave of desire rolling through him.

He pulled back and rested his forehead against hers. "It has been a night for celebrating."

"Yes."

"I would like the celebration to continue, Pru. I'd like to make love to you. But only if you want it."

He could feel her smile. "I want it."

"You do?"

"Yes."

"You're sure?"

"Nicholas, shut up and—"

He kissed her. And then took her by the hand and led her upstairs.

He pulled her into his bedchamber and kissed her again. When he moved to light a candle, she said, "No, please."

"You prefer the dark."

"Yes."

"Because you get embarrassed?"

"Yes."

"It shall be as you wish, my dear. But you have nothing to be ashamed of, you know. You're a beautiful, desirable woman."

She made a little snorting sound that might have been laughter.

"You don't believe me? Pru, you have played the quiet, shy little mouse for too long. But I have discovered your secret self. You're a lovely, passionate, exceedingly desirable woman. You can't hide that from me anymore. Even in the dark."

They undressed each other, and he took her soft, naked body against his and kissed her, hungrily, and she eagerly responded. He set up a rhythmic thrusting and sucking of her tongue that she instantly understood to be a prelude of what was to come. Following his lead, she tentatively sucked his tongue, and he felt his temperature rise.

He was ready to explode, to take her quickly to quell his raging hunger. But this time, it would be for her. He wanted to make it good for her, especially after the pain of the first time. He would not rush things. He wanted Pru to experience the full pleasure of lovemaking.

He laid her on the bed and set about loving her with his hands and lips and tongue, using every bit of sexual expertise he'd developed over the years to arouse her. The darkness emboldened her, and she tentatively explored him with her fingers, taking him to the edge of madness.

When he could bear no more, he positioned himself above her and between her thighs. "Ah, my love." He put his hands beneath her sweet little bottom and lifted her slightly, then, taking it as slowly as he was able, he eased himself inside. With no barrier this time, she was slick and tight and welcoming.

He held her as he set up a slow rhythm, moving her with him, showing her with his hands how to rotate her hips in counter rhythm to each thrust and withdrawal. Her breathing became ragged and she clutched at his shoulders. He could feel her muscles tense and she began to moan softly. He knew she was close to climax, but not how close, so he held himself back by a supreme effort of willpower and determination.

Her body suddenly went still, every muscle tensed. "Please," she whispered. "Please, Nicholas."

He increased the rhythm, moving inside her faster, faster. He wrapped his arms around her and held her close.

"Nicholas! Oh, my God, Nicholas! Oh. OH!"

He held her tight as her body jerked and

bucked against him, and finally shuddered into stillness. It was only then that he let himself go, pumping hard toward his own release.

They lay together, damp and panting, Nick's face buried in the soft curls at her neck. He lifted his head, and even in the dark could see the look of pure wonder on her face. She had never looked more beautiful.

And in the darkness, a flash of blinding clarity exploded in his brain.

He loved her.

Nicholas rolled to his side, taking Pru with him, their arms still wrapped around each other. He looked into her eyes and smiled. She had never loved him more than she did at that moment. She was so filled with joy, she almost felt like crying. For this was quite literally her dream come true. But she did not dare cry. He might misunderstand and apologize again, and she could not have borne it.

He reached down and pulled the covers over them. He kissed her softly and lingeringly, then rolled to his back and tucked her up against him. Her head fit quite nicely in the curve of his shoulder. She wrapped a leg over his and rested a hand on his chest. In a matter of a moment, she could tell he'd fallen asleep.

How did he *do* that? How anyone could fall asleep after such a momentous experience was beyond her understanding. Especially now that she knew why she had instinctively wanted more last time.

There had been more. And it had been spectacular, and so totally unexpected, it had been almost terrifying. She had been in the grip of such a powerful tension it had felt as if she were going to shatter into a thousand tiny pieces. And so she had. She had come all undone, then had floated back to earth to reassemble again in his arms.

Pru lay there beside him, wide awake, and thought that she felt truly married now. Curled up with Nicholas like a single entity, a partnership of bodies and souls. It was surely the happiest moment of her life.

He had called her "my love."

Two days later, she was feeling a bit aggravated with herself for orchestrating his financial windfall. Nicholas had been so busy arranging for the empty warehouse in Derbyshire to be refitted as a factory that she hardly saw him. Except at night, when he made glorious love to her. And now, even that was to be sacrificed.

"I have to go, Pru," he said when he'd come to fetch her at the *Cabinet* that evening. "I have to be there to make sure the plans are drawn up properly to accommodate the equipment. And I need to visit the manufacturer in Manchester to examine the machinery and arrange for its purchase. I am sorry, but I really do have to go."

"How long will you be gone?" she asked.

"No more than a fortnight, this time. But I fear it will be only the first of many such trips, my love."

Two weeks? How was she to bear it? After only a few nights of sharing a bed with him, she was already accustomed to falling asleep while curled up against his warmth. As much as she adored his lovemaking, Pru sometimes foolishly thought it was the aftermath of loving that was the best part of all, when she felt the closest bond to Nicholas. She loved it when he pulled her against him, her back to his front, and nestled their bodies together like spoons. With his arm wrapped around her and his breath against her neck, Pru was as contented as a kitten. She always thought she would not be able to fall asleep, she was so acutely conscious of his presence. But she did sleep, and often woke to the soft touch of his lips on hers.

To sleep alone again would be painful to endure.

"Perhaps when Edwina returns," she said, "I can take some time away from the *Cabinet* and join you on one of your trips."

"I would like that, Pru."

He left the next day, giving her a farewell kiss that was soul-searing in its intensity. She waited until he was gone before she cried.

She kept herself busy at the *Cabinet* so that she would not have to think so much about missing Nicholas. It was easy enough to keep distracted during the day. The nights, though, were miserably lonely. She did not even have Bartholomew to keep her company anymore. He had moved to the little house on Conduit Street and seemed perfectly happy there.

Nicholas had been gone a little over a week when something happened to take away a bit of her loneliness. Edwina returned.

Pru was never more surprised in her life to look up from her desk one morning to find her friend standing in the doorway. She shrieked with delight and practically leaped from her chair to grab Edwina, her new sister, in a warm embrace.

Edwina was the most beautiful woman Pru had ever known, and she looked prettier than ever in a very stylish, very French-looking robe with full sleeves

"Pru! When did all *this* happen?" She made a sweeping gesture to indicate the offices. "I went straight to Golden Square this morning, hoping to catch up on what the *Cabinet* team has accomplished in my absence. Imagine my surprise to learn you had moved to real offices! Pru, this is fantastic! Show me everything. Do the Crimson Ladies work here, too?"

Pru spent most of an hour showing Edwina about and explaining her reasoning behind certain of the arrangements. Edwina had a few minor suggestions to improve efficiency, but on the whole was thrilled and excited to have so much space.

"And this was all Father's doing?" she asked.

"It was his doing but Flora's idea. She apparently talked him into it."

"Flora?"

Pru grinned. "There is great deal of news to catch up on."

Her eyebrows lifted. "Indeed. Then we had better get started. I want to know everything."

They settled in Pru's office, and Madge brought them a pot of tea. As Pru might have guessed, her friend first wanted to know about her marriage to Nicholas. And so Pru told her everything. Or almost. She explained how it had come about, in much more detail than she had done in her letters. She told her how kind Nicholas had been in the way he handled Pru's family, and how he began the pretense of a love match.

"He has shown such concern for my reputation," she said, "and my family's reaction to the marriage. He really has been quite wonderful. Despite finding himself aligned to a more aristocratic family than he would have liked."

"I could shake you for that, Pru. Why did you never mention it? In all these years? I thought we were friends."

"It had nothing to do with our friendship. It simply never mattered. And . . ."

"And you were afraid that such steadfast republicans would scorn you because of it."

Pru shrugged. "I suppose that had something to do with it. But only a very small part. Mostly, I just did not think it was important. It did not matter."

"We would never have scorned you, Pru. You must know that. Your ideals have always been true. And you are a separate person from your heritage. You are a unique individual, not defined by your birth. If you want my opinion, Nickie is lucky to have you."

"I am the lucky one," Pru said, and blushed.

"You are happy together, then?"

"Oh, yes."

Edwina heaved a great sigh. "I am so relieved. I told him I would have his head on a platter if he dared to break your heart."

They chatted more about the magazine, and Pru told her about Flora and her father, which thoroughly delighted her. Unlike her brother, Edwina seemed to sense at once what a perfect match they were.

When Flora happened to come in, Edwina took her in a warm embrace and beamed with delight.

Before Nicholas left, he had arranged for his father to fetch Pru each evening. But when Edwina announced she was off to visit her father in his new London home, Pru decided to take advantage of the situation and save Bartholomew the trip. She had been working so hard the last week, she was more than caught up. She could afford to leave a bit earlier than usual.

Edwina dropped her at Golden Square, and told Pru to expect her back at the office in the morning. "I am itching to get back to work," she said. "I have missed it."

When Pru entered the house, she stopped at the hall table and checked for mail. She removed her bonnet and climbed the stairs. When she reached the landing outside the drawing room, she was startled by a familiar voice.

"What the bloody hell have you done, Pru?"

Chapter 18

Nick had never been so angry in all his life. He had been within hours—mere hours—of signing the purchase contract for the first delivery of machinery when he had discovered he'd been duped.

He wanted to take her by the shoulders and shake her until her teeth rattled, but he kept his distance, standing across the room in front of the fireplace, while she remained in the drawing room doorway, her eyes wide with anxiety.

"Did you think I would not find out? Did you think me that stupid?"

"What d-do you mean?"

"Come on, Pru, don't play innocent with me. I know what you've done. You defied me."

She said nothing, but her silence spoke volumes. She knew exactly what he was talking about.

She stepped slowly into the room, her arms hanging stiffly at her sides. "Please, Nicholas, tell m-me what has happened."

"I discovered your ruse, that's what. Surely you must have known that I check the shipping news religiously each day. Did you think I would not notice the report that the *Benjamin* had been lost?"

"Oh, God."

"There were no profits. No windfall. How could there have been? Everything was lost, Pru. Everything. And yet somehow I managed to make a great deal of money on that lost cargo."

He moved to stand in front of her, making an effort not to reach out and throttle her. "Why did you do it, Pru? Why? You must have gone to a great deal of trouble to put your little deception into action. Why? After I refused over and over to take your money."

She chewed on her lower lip, and her eyes had grown large and bright. But she kept her gaze on his, unwavering. "I wanted you to have it," she said in a soft voice.

"Even though you *knew* I did not want it?"

"You needed it. And so I made certain you should have it. Is that so wrong?"

"Wrong?" His voice had risen almost to a shout and he flung his hands out in a gesture of frustration. "My God, Pru, you went behind my back. You made some sort of private deal with the shipping agent to make it look like the money came from him. You do not think that is wrong?"

"I hoped you would not find out." Her voice was so soft, he had to strain to hear. "I am very sorry, Nicholas. I swear to you, I meant well."

Nick snorted in disgust. "You went against my wishes, you defied me, but you meant well so that should make it all right?"

"I'm sorry, Nicholas. Truly I am." She reached out, as though to touch him, but apparently thought better of it and lowered her hand. "But your story about Alfie moved me, you see, and made me better understand how important the Derby project is to you. I wanted to help you to help other children like Alfie. I only wanted you to have the capital you needed for the factory."

"I will make my own capital, madam. I do not need yours."

Her chin lifted a notch. "Yes, you do. I knew if you were to continue investing in these risky ventures, you would never reach your goal. You are more likely to lose everything."

"How *dare* you, Pru!" His voice rose in anger, and it was all he could do not to shake her silly. "How dare you try to manipulate me like that. I tell you, I won't stand for it. I won't stand for it."

A powerful emotion he could not identify gathered in her eyes, and tears threatened to spill down her cheeks. Even so, she did not drop her gaze. She did not look away. "Nicholas," she said softly, "I did it so you could have your dream. I did it because I care for you."

He gave a sputtering little grunt of derision. "How can you say you care for me when you defy my express wishes? It is not caring. It is outright deception and manipulation. And it makes me so angry I could wring your interfering little neck."

Pru suddenly felt something inside her snap. She'd done it for him and he did not care at all. He did not care.

Four years of loving him blindly seemed to crumble into dust. All those annoying little things about him that she had ignored or explained away or made excuses for were suddenly standing out there big and bright as the aggravations they really were.

She was tired of making excuses, tired of ignoring every fault and weakness. She was tired of his temper and his impatience and his stubbornness. As much as she loved him, she really did not know if she wanted to live with all that anymore.

Her hands balled up into fists, and all at once the frustration and disappointment could no longer be contained. The words spilled out from somewhere deep inside her, and she could not stop them.

"I have lived with your stubborn male pride for some time now," she said in a soft voice, enunciating each word slowly and deliberately. "And I have never complained. I allowed my deep affection for you—my love for you—to blind me to your weaknesses. I had always thought you so wonderful, so perfect, and I wanted so much for you to feel something of that for me, too. But I am tired of trying to make you care. I am tired of doing everything your way. I am tired of having my own feelings ignored. I am just . . . tired."

She paused to let the lump in her throat settle. She did not care about the tears in her eyes. She would not be embarrassed for them. But she wanted her words to be absolutely clear.

"I am tired of trying so hard to make you want me, to make you love me, by capitulating to your every wish. I have learned, to my regret, that you are a very selfish man, Nicholas, with no consideration for what others may want. I wanted us to have a home of our own, but you would not allow me to buy one because you were so worried someone would think you a fortune hunter. It is only through your father's generosity that we now have our own home."

"I never—"

She held up her hand. "Please. Let me finish. I know I am supposed to be the quiet one, but I would like to be allowed to speak."

"Go on, then." His mouth was set in a tight line.

"You have never cared for my feelings, Nicholas. I know you did not want to marry me, but it has pleased you to play the gentleman, the martyr, to have done the honorable thing. But you have not been a true gentleman, because you have never cared for my feelings at all."

"Pru, that is not—"

"I wanted to buy us a house because I felt so terribly awkward here with your father. Not because of anything he has done, of course. He is a kind and thoughtful man. But to have him in our house—which was not really our house—so soon after being married was horribly awkward for me. You never cared about how uncomfortable it has been, with his bedroom on the other side of the wall from my own. To see his questioning look each day as he wondered how our marriage was progressing. To know he was well aware that we did not share a bed. To worry that he was listening each night to see if we finally did. But you never cared about how I felt. You would rather hold on to your foolish pride than to allow me to buy us a bit of privacy."

"It is no longer an issue," he said, and glared at her through narrowed eyes. "The house is ours. You should have no complaints, madam. You got what you wanted, did you not?"

"No, I did not. I wanted a true partnership with you, Nicholas, but you barred me from the most important part of your life. You always talk about your fine republican principles, but if you truly believed them, you would have welcomed my offer to share resources. Had you been a true republican, you would have been happy to use the money I offered so that you could finance your grand utopian dream. Money I had planned to use for a dream of my own, but was more than willing to give to you. But no. You are too self-absorbed to be a true republican. Too full of pride."

"Dammit, Pru, that is a lie."

"Is it? You are more concerned with your own heroic role in social reform than for the people who will be helped by that reform. If you cared about them, you would have taken my money. Or if you had cared about me."

Her face was wet with tears and she reached up to wipe them away. "I am tired of your stubborn pride, Nicholas. I don't think I can live with it anymore. I do not think I want to live any longer with someone who is incapable of accepting a gift given in love."

She spun on her heels and left the room. She blindly dashed up the stairs to her bedroom, slammed the door shut, and threw herself on her bed. She sobbed and sobbed. For her lost dream of love, the dream she had thought, by some miracle of miracles, was so close to coming true. For being foolish enough ever to have believed that. For realizing at last that he would never love her enough to share his dreams with her. For the heartache that threatened to overwhelm her with despair.

When she was drained, when there were no more tears left in her, she got up, packed a small bandbox, and left the house.

Nick was still sitting in the drawing room when he heard her come down the stairs. She did not stop on the landing but continued to the ground floor, and when he heard the front door open and close, he got up and looked out the window.

Pru was walking across the square carrying a

bandbox. He watched as she flagged down a hackney and stepped inside.

She had left him.

He was almost glad for it, because he had no idea how he was ever to face her again, or even if he wanted to. How dare she say such things to him? First she had defied him and deceived him, and then she had railed at him like some harpy. She was like a stranger to him. What had become of his quiet, shy, sweet little wife? The one he'd fallen in love with?

He still loved her, despite his anger. God knew he still wanted her. But he had come charging home to make sure she understood that he wanted her on his own terms. Not her reinterpretation of those terms. He had been ready to shake her silly for defying him, but once she understood she had done wrong, he would have taken her to bed and demonstrated who was in charge. She would admit she was wrong, and things would eventually go back to the way they'd been before he left for Derbyshire.

But she had not cowered in the face of his anger. She had stood as straight and tall as was possible for such a small woman, and accused *him* of being the one at fault. Then she had thrown lies in his face and stormed out of his life. She'd ruined everything.

Damn her!

He slammed his fist down hard on the tea table, jarring the top loose from its lock so that it tilted upward so fast it nearly knocked him flat. The tea service slid to the floor with a resounding crash, sending a thousand porcelain shards skittering across the floor, and the broken tea table tottered and finally fell over, its top slapping the parquet floor with a sharp crack.

Damn her!

The sound of footsteps charging up the stairs was followed by the entrance of Lucy, who stood openmouthed and pale in the doorway, her wide-eyed gaze taking in the wreck of the drawing room.

"Sir? Are you all right?"

"Yes, yes. Do your best to clean this mess up, will you?"

Nick trudged up the stairs, taking two at a time in his fury. He quickly changed his coat and boots, grabbed a hat, and made his way from the house. He was going to find a good bottle of brandy and make his way to the bottom, then start on another.

Damn her.

Pru dragged herself to the *Cabinet* early the next morning, arriving well before anyone else. She hadn't slept, even though her comfortable old bed in her father's house was very soft and welcoming and familiar. No one had been home when she'd arrived the afternoon before, and the housekeeper had been very happy to make up Pru's bedchamber for her and send up a pot of tea and a piece of cold meat pie. But Pru had not been hungry, and besides, she was so dried up inside, she could not have choked down a single bite. She had simply curled up in the old window seat where she had spent a lifetime spinning girlish fantasies and dreaming dreams of love.

But her dreams were lost, and instead she pondered how she was to go on, how she was to bear life without Nicholas.

Her brothers had sense enough to leave her alone when they arrived home that evening. Only her father had come by to see how she was. He said very little, but surprised her by taking her in his arms and letting her cry. He had not held her like that since she'd been a little girl.

"Shall I kill him, Prudie?" he asked, using the old nickname only William ever used anymore. "Shall I at least break both his legs? His arms? His thick skull, perhaps?"

"No," she had said, smiling as he had meant for her to do. "I love him, Papa."

"Ah. Then what will you do?"

"I don't know. Hope and pray, I suppose."

"For what? That will he come to get you?"

"That he will come to his senses. That he will realize all that stubborn male pride is just . . . stupid. That he will realize how much I love him and not hate me for what I did and what I said. And that maybe, someday, he will want me back."

"And in the meantime?"

"I'll wait."

Pru did not know how long she would have to wait. She knew Nicholas was angry, and so was she, though most of her anger had dissipated with her tears. More than anything, she was astounded that she had said such hateful things to him, even if they were true. She did not know where she had found the courage, or the stupidity, to reproach him like that. In all her life, she'd never spoken so harshly to anyone.

She supposed that's what happened when one's heart was involved. Love and hurt overcame reason and logic. She had loved him so much and for so long that when he'd raged at her and had not for even an instant appreciated the motive behind her deception, disappointment had cut deep. And from that wound, her words had poured forth, unchecked.

If she ever saw him again, she did not know how she was to face him. She supposed she ought to apologize, but only for having spoken aloud what she felt, not for feeling it. She still believed everything she had said to him was true. He was all those things she'd accused him of, and, God help her, she still loved him. She no longer cared that he wasn't perfect. She just wanted him to think about her now and then instead of only himself. She wanted to share everything with him, including his dreams. She wanted to be allowed to be a partner to him. Was that so much to ask?

Pru tried to put him out of her mind and went to work on the latest page proofs. Edwina came bouncing into the office later that morning.

"Here I am," she announced as she stood in the doorway to Pru's office, "itching to get back to work. Where shall I—Pru! Dear God, you look terrible. What on earth has happened?"

Pru took one look at Edwina, who looked so much like her brother, and burst into tears.

Nick paced the drawing room floor, trying to ignore the pounding in his head. He'd had much too much brandy the night before, and it had done nothing at all to dull the pain in his heart. In fact, the more he'd drunk, the more maudlin and sentimental he'd become.

He'd wanted to be angry, dammit. He'd wanted to wallow in his anger, to wrap himself up in its righteous warmth and enjoy it. But he had not enjoyed it. Instead he'd been miserable with it, especially when he'd turned it on himself. He discovered, to his dismay, that he wanted to take back much of what he'd said. Because one thing above all else mattered.

She'd left him. And he was not sure if he could bear it.

That morning—or was it afternoon already?—the heartache was much worse, for he'd slept alone in his bed last night, in the bed where he'd found such passion and joy with Pru.

She had good cause to leave, he supposed, considering all he'd said to her. But he'd been in the right, blast it all. He'd been the one to be deceived. He had not deserved her harsh judgment.

Yet it was her words that rang in his head as he paced. Her words that stung him like a thousand lashes. Selfish. Stubborn. Inconsiderate. Prideful. No true gentleman. A sham republican.

One thing she'd said, though, more than anything else, ripped at his heart and tore it into shreds.

She had done it because she loved him.

And, fool that he was, he had thrown that love back in her face.

But he had not known. He had not known she loved him. After all, she had been forced into the marriage against her will, just as he was. Until recently, Nick had thought she found the notion of marriage to him somewhat less than appealing. But knowing she loved him—or had once loved him—shook him to the core of his soul.

How could two people who loved each other have so thoroughly bungled a marriage?

He paced back and forth, back and forth, considering everything that had been said between them. In one moment, he convinced himself that he was in the right and she was overreacting. In the next moment, he knew her to be absolutely right and himself a cad.

And he wondered where she had gone.

He was not sure how long he'd been pacing the drawing room floor when he heard the front door open. His head jerked up. Was she back?

He heard Lucy's voice and another female. Pru? He stood still and waited. He did not know what he would say. A part of him just wanted to take her in his arms and forget all that had happened. If nothing else, they would talk through this, try to repair the rent in their relationship. At least she'd come back home. She had not left him for good. He followed the sound of her footsteps on the stairs, waited for her to reach the landing. His heart pounded. She was almost there.

"Nickie!"

He gave a groan of frustration and his shoulders slumped as anxiety fizzled into disappointment.

"Well, that is not quite the welcome I'd anticipated."

Edwina stepped into the room. He stared at her for a moment, trying to clear his muddled brain. It was not Pru. But how could it be Edwina, who was still in France? He had not seen her in over five months.

But it really was his sister, and he walked across the room and gathered her in his arms. "Ed, I'm so sorry for the beastly welcome. I was expecting . . . someone else." He pulled out of the embrace and looked at her. She was as beautiful as ever. "When did you return?"

"The day before yesterday." She stepped back and frowned. "My God, Nickie, you look terrible. So does Pru, by the way."

"You've seen her?"

"She's at the *Cabinet*."

"Do you know where she stayed last night?" he asked, suddenly anxious to know that Pru was safe. "Did she come to you, Ed?"

"No, she is back at her father's house."

"Oh, God." He raked his fingers through his hair. "I have made such a mess of everything, Ed."

"Come and sit down, Nickie, and tell me what happened. I just saw her yesterday, you know. She was fine. She was radiant with happiness, in fact. And today she is miserable. She will not tell me what happened. What the devil did you do?"

And he told her. Every cruel thing he'd said to Pru, and every accusation she'd flung back at him.

"Was she right, Ed? I think she must have been. She would not have left otherwise. But was she right about me? Am I so self-absorbed? Am I so thoughtless?"

Edwina sighed. "You will remember that I experienced a similar confrontation with Anthony."

Nick sighed. "Yes, and that was all my fault, too. I am good at mucking things up, am I not?"

She reached out and patted his hand. "No, it was not your fault. But Anthony did throw the same kinds of accusations at me. Remember when I told you?"

"Yes, that was when you decided to resign from the *Cabinet*."

"He said I was arrogant for thinking I knew what the poor needed. He said I was a woman of privilege playing at reform, in order to feel virtuous and self-important. He said I talked a good line but I never took real action. And I convinced myself he was right. That was when I began my work in St. Giles and Seven Dials. Facing those wretched women each day brought all my lofty ideals down to earth."

"And so you think he and Pru are right? That we are sham republicans, all ideals and no follow-through? No action? But I am *trying* to take action, to make a real impact. I am trying. It is not sham idealism simply because I have not yet succeeded. Is it?"

"You must take what Pru said to you and examine it with your heart, Nickie. You must decide for yourself if she spoke the truth. But know this. Your ideals are real and true and heartfelt. You must hold on to them if you ever hope to see a better world. And continue to act on them when you can."

"Act on them." He shook his head. "I am in a quandary about that, Ed. I didn't go through with the purchase in Manchester once I discovered Pru's deception. I still have her money. What is the right thing to do? Should I keep it and go through with my plans after all? Would that be what Pru would want?"

"Is that what *you* want?"

"I don't know, Ed." His voice had risen in frustration, and he made an effort to compose himself. "This has all happened so fast, I haven't had time to figure out what I want. And to tell you the truth, I can't even think about the damned factory. All I can think of is how she said she did it for love. And God damn me, I threw that love back in her face. A love I had not expected. A love I certainly do not deserve. A love that I now find I want most desperately."

"You've fallen in love with her, Nickie?"

He gave a mirthless chuckle. "Isn't that a joke? I woman I never wanted to marry. A woman I barely even noticed. A woman from a class I have always scorned. And I love her."

"Oh, Nickie." She touched his arm lightly.

"And I don't want to live without her, Ed."

"Then why not just march up to her father's house and tell her so?"

Nick shook his head. "I don't think that would be enough. It's too easy. Hell, I doubt she'd believe me, after all the hateful things I said to her."

"Then you must prove it to her. Prove to her that you love her."

"How?"

Edwina smiled. "You'll think of something."

Chapter 19

Two days later, he still had not thought of anything. When one of Lord Henry's footmen arrived with a housemaid to collect more of Pru's things, Nick had sunk deeper into despair and confusion. He had finally decided, though, that the time apart was probably good for both him and Pru just now. They each had lashed out in anger, and they each needed to cool down. A few days to himself had given Nick a fresh perspective. He had concluded that a great deal of what Pru had said was right, especially in regard to his lack of consideration for her. And he was desperately ashamed for it.

He had not yet, however, come to any conclusion about the money. He was willing to accept Pru's claim that if he really cared about the project and the people it could help, he would take it. But for the life of him, he could not quite shake off his pride enough to do so. He supposed it was the biggest of all his deadly sins, for it was the one he could not seem to overcome.

He'd spent the evening with Simon, commiserating over the mess he'd made of his marriage and stoically submitting to his friend's scolding. Ever the romantic, Simon could not fathom how Nick could have refused Pru's fortune when it was offered outright, much less after she'd gone to such lengths to ensure he got it anyway.

"It was a selfless act of love," he'd said, shaking his head in disgust. "You must have hurt her deeply by so thoroughly rejecting it. I really do not know how you could have been so cruel. You ought to be ashamed."

When Nick had looked up to find Eleanor standing in the doorway scowling at him, he'd had enough and left. He did not need to hear any more. He understood. He was an arrogant, selfish bully. All right, he admitted it. But how was he to make things right? Pru deserved more than a simple apology.

After leaving Simon's town house, he'd gone to a tavern with one of his colleagues from the Scottish Martyrs Club and proceeded to get seriously drunk. Again.

He returned to Golden Square at some ungodly hour and stumbled into the hallway feeling maudlin and morose. The emptiness of the house echoed the emptiness within him. She had been there only two months, and yet it seemed somehow incomplete without her. He missed her. He missed her quiet presence, her music, her soft voice, her blushes, her sweet little body curled up against his at night. Her face. Strange, but in such a short time she had somehow become very precious and dear to him. He hadn't realized how dear until she was gone.

Perhaps it was time to go knock on Lord Henry's door after all, and ask her to come back. To come home.

With some difficulty, Nick managed to light the taper on the hall table. It was then that he saw the packet. His breath caught in his throat. It was the same type of packet he'd received earlier from Cracken, the one with the bank draft for the bogus profits.

He scrunched up his face and shook his head to clear it. When he opened his eyes, the packet was still there. For a moment, he thought it was the same one Pru had somehow manipulated Cracken into sending. But his slow-working brain finally came to realize that it could not be the same packet. He still had that one up in his bedchamber, waiting for him to decide what to do with it.

His fingers shook as he broke the seal, and he gasped aloud when a bank draft fell out and onto the table. He carefully picked it up. It was for an amount half again as much as Pru's draft. A staggering amount. He pulled out the accompanying document, and saw it was a receipt for his share of the cargoes delivered to Amsterdam on the *Reso-*

lution, the second ship he'd invested in through Cracken.

Could it be another deception by Pru? One she had set in action before leaving? Could she possibly have enough cash to fund two spurious investment returns? His mind was too muddled with drink to make any sense of it right now. He needed a clear head. He would not decide what to do until he'd met with Cracken, first thing tomorrow.

And as it happened, Nick came to discover that the profits were perfectly legitimate. The *Resolution* had delivered a cargo of sugar that had reaped unexpectedly high profits due to the loss of the same commodity on the *Benjamin*. Pru had had nothing to do with it.

She hadn't needed to sacrifice her own money after all. Nick now had more than enough cash to begin his project. He ought to have been ecstatic, but it was a bittersweet victory. His first thought was to return to Derbyshire at once and settle the purchase of the machinery and refitting. He could resume plans for the factory without further delay. But then he recalled Edwina's words.

You must prove to her that you love her.

Nick did not return to Derbyshire, but set out to put another plan into action instead.

"You look exhausted, Pru. You should go home."

Home. She wasn't sure where that was anymore. She did not feel at all at home in her father's house, despite having lived there for twenty-seven years and three months. It was strange, but she still thought of the house in Golden Square as home, after only two months.

Because she had found her dream there.

"I still have a few pages to proof, Edwina. And the subscription lists to update."

"I am worried about you, Pru." Edwina stood in the doorway of Pru's office and leaned against the jamb. Her look of concern had not faltered for a week and made Pru exceedingly self-conscious. "You look so tired."

Pru was very much aware of her haggard appearance, thank you very much. She did look into a mirror now and then. "I have been having trouble sleeping."

"I don't doubt it. But he will come back to you. I am quite sure of it."

She looked up sharply. "Has he said something to you?"

"No, nothing specific. I know he wanted time apart to get over his anger. And he is over it, Pru. He is more miserable than angry."

Then why hadn't he come to her? She'd been praying Nicholas would come to her father's house and ask her to come back home. But he had not done so. She had been away for over a week, and he had not contacted her. Because she had said such hateful things to him. Perhaps he never wanted to see her again.

"I ought to have remained the quiet little mouse and never told him what I thought," she said. "I don't know what came over me."

"You needed to tell him how you felt, Pru. If you had not done so, you would have continued to harbor resentment, and it would have grown and grown until you despised him. And more than that, Nickie needed to hear those words. He needed to see himself through your eyes."

"I did not enjoy saying those words any more than he enjoyed hearing them. It drove us apart, just when—"

"You may take comfort in knowing he feels the same way."

"Then why—"

"Why hasn't he come to see you? I don't know, Pru. Do you *want* him back?"

Of course she did. She loved him. But she had gone a little mad when he'd been so angry with her. The first night back at her father's house, she knew she couldn't bear to live without him. She'd loved him for too long to really think badly of him. But she had discovered that loving an imperfect, all-too-human man was a far more profound experience than loving a perfect idol. In fact, she had learned that love could be a terrible thing indeed.

But love him she did, and she had pushed him away, pushed so hard, it looked as if he would never come back to her. Stubborn pride and all, he was still her dream of happiness. And having once tasted of that dream, she knew she would give anything to have it back again.

"Pru?"

"Yes. Yes, I do want him back. Should I . . . Do you think I should stop waiting for him to come for me, and go back to him instead?" She wasn't even certain she would have the courage to do it, if it came down to that. But Nicholas's pride ran deep, and he was unlikely to make the first move. So it might be up to Pru to do what must be done to save their marriage. "Should I go to him?"

"That is up to you, Pru."

"I think I should. Devil take it, I am being as stubborn as he is. I am going to go back to him."

"Are you?"

"Yes." Now that she'd decided, she did not want to wait another moment. She'd wasted a week already. "Right now. This very moment." She rose from her desk.

Edwina turned at the sound of the front door opening, then looked back at Pru and smiled. "I don't think that will be necessary." And she left.

A moment later, Nicholas stood in the same spot, looking as handsome as ever, save for the frown that creased his brow. Her heart did a little flip-flop in her chest.

"Hullo, Pru."

"Nicholas."

"You are well?"

"Yes, thank you. And . . . and you?" How foolish they sounded, so stiff and formal.

"I am well," he said, and then paused, looking slightly flustered, before speaking again. "I wonder if I might have a moment of your time? A few moments. A half hour, perhaps."

"Of course." Since he had finally come to see her,

she would not perhaps mention that she had just decided to go back to him. "Come in and sit down."

"No, I need you to come with me."

Pru's pulse was racing so hard, she could hear the blood rushing in her ears. Did he want her to come home? "Come with you where?"

"I have a carriage waiting outside. I want to show you something. It won't take long."

She hesitated, only because she was so nervous and agitated, but he misunderstood her lack of response.

"Please, Pru. Please."

"All right. Let me just find my bonnet."

They spoke very little in the carriage. He asked about her family. She asked about Lucy and Mrs. Gibb. He had not touched her, except to hand her inside.

Pru had been so tense and anxious, she had not paid any attention to the journey. When the carriage came to a stop, she had no idea where they were. Nicholas leaped down and held out his hand for her. She took it and stepped onto the pavement in front of the familiar brick building in Clerkenwell.

Her school building.

She turned to Nicholas, who still held her hand, and raised her brows in question.

"Come," he said.

He kept her hand and led her up the short path to the front door with its beautiful tracery fan-light. To the left of the entrance was a shiny brass sign.

The Prudence Armitage Parrish School of Music.
She gave a little squeal of surprise and brought
a hand to cover her mouth. Was it true? She tried
to quell the fluttering of hope in her breast. She
turned to him. "Nicholas?" Her voice came in a
strangled whisper. "What is this?"

He took her other hand so that he held them
both. "You gave up your dream for me," he said,
"and that was not right. Your dreams are as important as mine. More important, because you are
more important to me."

"Oh." She could barely speak for holding her
breath.

"You are precious to me, Pru. And I have hurt
you in more ways than I can count. But I hope you
will give me another chance. Everything you said
was true, but I love you enough to try to change."

"You love me?" Her voice came out in a high
squeak.

"With all my heart. I hope you will accept the
school as my gift of love to you, Pru. And will not
fling it back in my face as I did your gift."

Pru choked back a sob and threw her arms
around his neck. He loved her! "Oh, Nicholas."

He chuckled and held her close. "Does that
mean yes? You will accept the school?"

"Yes. Oh, yes."

"And will you forgive me? Will you give me a
second chance? Will you come home, my love?"

"Yes and yes and yes!"

She rained kisses over his face, heedless of the

people walking past them or the open carriages driving by, not caring who saw, feeling not a hint of embarrassment. Not even when he took her mouth in a long, passionate kiss.

When he pulled away and smiled down at her, she said, "But how were you able to buy the school, Nicholas? Did you use the money I gave you?"

"That would not be much of a gift, would it?"

"Then how?"

He smiled. "My other ship came in."

"Your other ship?"

"I had made two investments in Amsterdam cargo. The *Benjamin* was lost. But the *Resolution* was not, and its cargo turned a much higher profit than I could ever have imagined. *We*, dear wife and partner, made a tidy windfall. And I decided to put *our* money to good use."

"But what about the Derby project?"

"I have enough for a good start with the money you gave me and a bit from the *Resolution*."

She stared up at him, wide-eyed. "Nicholas? You are going to use my money?"

"I have had a great deal of time to think during this past week, and one thing has become very clear to me, Pru. If you love me enough to offer your money, then I certainly love you enough to accept it."

"Oh, Nicholas." She buried her face in his neck-cloth, overcome with emotion.

"You said I had not allowed you to be a true partner to me," Nicholas said, "and you were right. But I *do* want you for my partner, Pru. In everything. In every way."

She lifted her head and gazed up at him. "Even though I am not the woman you would have chosen for your wife?"

He closed his eyes briefly, and a pained expression clouded his brow. "You are right," he said at last, clutching the hand that she rested on his chest. "I would not have chosen you for my wife. But fortune has shined upon me, undeserving though I am, and given me a wife more precious, more perfect than any I might have found had I searched the world over."

"Oh, Nicholas." She blinked back tears and hoped to heaven she would not dissolve into a puddle of joy at his feet. Thank God he gathered her in his arms and held her close.

"I wish," he said, "that I could take back all the horrid things I said to you. I wish we could wipe the slate clean and forget all that has happened."

She tilted her head to look up at him. "No, I don't think we should forget. We have both learned a great deal about each other and about ourselves, and each of us is, I think, the better for it. Our marriage, our partnership, will be the better for it, for it has been tested and survived."

"Because we love each other."

"Yes."

He held her tight once again, then released her. "But there is one more thing. Something I did with *my* money before I made it *our* money." He took her hand, removed the kid glove, and slipped off her finger the ribbon-wrapped signet ring she had continued to wear, even after she'd left him. He then reached into his pocket and pulled out a new ring. A beautiful sapphire set in gold.

"Our marriage had a rather inauspicious beginning," he said, "but I am hoping we can make a fresh start. And this ring will be the symbol of a new love and life together."

He slid the ring onto her finger and lifted her hand to his lips. "A real ring this time. And a real love match, too. I love you, Mrs. Parrish."

"And I love you, Mr. Parrish."

Pedestrians clucked and tsked, or smiled indulgently as they were forced to walk around the shameless young couple making such a spectacle of themselves on a public street in broad daylight.